BOR
BRED

*The slums are full of girls like Lee Sissle—
fiery, troublesome girls who want more out
of life than they are getting—but who go
about it the wrong way… When the girls at
the stocking factory showed Lee how to pick
up extra money by stealing nylons, she
caught on fast—but then she was caught
and fired. Her landlady promptly threw her
out, but Lee was not deserted by the
landlady's son, Goosey Mullins, who drove a
truck for Ricco the racketeer. Goosey took
the homeless girl to the Vagabond Club
where she lived as a member of the gang.
This, then, was the beginning of the criminal
career of this beautiful girl. It took Lee only
a short time to discover that a cellar club
existence was not for her. Playing both
ends against the middle, taking men for all
they were worth, stirring up desire and
trouble wherever she went, Lee continued
her reckless existence as a gang moll until
fate in the form of an avenging racketeer
inevitably caught up with her.*

FOR A COMPLETE SECOND NOVEL TURN TO PAGE 147

POLICE LINEUP:

LEE SISSLE

She was jail-bait with a snug hipline, sexy curves, and firm breasts that softly resolved into molded, flaunting contours of trouble!

RICCO

Just a typical, slimy racketeer, but he had a certain smoothness about him that covered up the glitter of his depravity.

GOOSEY

Goosey was a big-hearted lunk who fell in with the wrong crowd—but especially with the wrong woman.

JULIA BRINK

On the surface she seemed like a sweet old lady that loved cats and enjoyed helping people in need—on the surface.

LEFTY

He was the big cheese for a local gang of hooligans, and he always seemed to get what he wanted…usually with his fists!

SONNY PIERSON

The fact that he always seemed to have a lot of dough made it obvious that he was more than just a simple bellhop.

MADGE

She had a hard smile and a devious mind—and wasn't afraid to use a sharpened knitting needle if she had to!

TOM SISSLE

With a penchant for hard booze and loose women, fatherhood wasn't exactly something he was good at.

GANG MOLL

By
ALBERT L. QUANDT

ARMCHAIR FICTION
PO Box 4369, Medford, Oregon 97504

CHAPTER ONE

LEE DIDN'T know it then, but it was the last time she would see her father. He was in bed when she came in, with the overripe waitress from the Clover Cafe standing in front of the dresser fixing her hair.

She halted at the door, taking in the scene with expressionless eyes. It was nothing new to her. Her father had always carried on with some woman or other, even during the years of an apparently happy marriage. Mary Sissle's death didn't alter his mode of living. He went right on drinking and having affairs, as if he hadn't a responsibility in the world.

The waitress knew why Lee had come. But all she did was cast a glance at the recumbent form on the bed and continue pinning up the thick peroxided strands. She was conscious of the girl's revulsion but chose to ignore it. Her dressing gown was openly revealing but she made no move to close it, smiling at the exposed reflection with haunting satisfaction.

"You better come back later," she said to Lee. "Your old man isn't in any shape to talk to you, like you can see. I'll tell him you were here." She turned slowly, smirking, adjusting the cartridge of cheap lipstick between plump fingers. "You should of known better than to come so early in the morning. He's going to be awful sore when he finds out you saw me. A kid your age has no right learning about life so fast. It might give you bad ideas."

The girl with the dark, gleaming hair and intense, pretty face folded her arms under the bold thrust of her sweater and leaned against the panels. "If you think this would make me want to be like you, you're crazy. I know what the score is. Is this what you call living? Or him there, on the bed?" She tossed her head, scornfully. "I'm learning, all right. More than they could ever teach me in a month full of Sundays. Maybe my old man doesn't know it, but he's done me more good than any preacher that ever lived. Look at you—the two of you. Do I have to explain any further?"

5

The heavy-lipped smile faded. "You're a pretty snotty kid, talking like that to me! If I didn't feel sorry for you, I'd kick you the hell out and tell him not to give you a cent! If it wasn't for me, you'd be starving now, walking the streets!" The red tip of the lipstick jabbed in the direction of the sleeping man. "He hasn't worked in weeks, do you know that? The money you been getting for your board was my money, the nickels, dimes, and quarters I wore my feet out to earn! And you got the nerve to come around, after I been so nice to you, and insult me!"

"I don't care where he gets the money, or who gives it to him. The law says he's got to look after me until I'm twenty-one. You're not the only woman he's suckered. My old lady worked for him most of her life, just like you're doing now, and some of the others before you. He never fooled me, like he did the rest of you. I was on to him the minute I got to see what was going on." She glared at the handsome, fleshy man sprawled in desiccated sleep. "Sure, it would of just suited him fine for me to get a job, to hand over my pay like a dutiful daughter. So he could spend it on whiskey and cheap trollops. But that ain't the way it's going to be! He's going to take care of me, or else find himself explaining why not to the judge!"

The man on the bed turned restlessly, making little sounds as he showed them the broad of his back. The plump waitress hurried over, covering him solicitously.

Lee didn't move. She stood there, arms folded, looking on contemptuously. "I'm not leaving until I get the board money to pay Mrs. Mullins," she said. "I'm sick and tired of making excuses. You better get it up if you don't want me to start trouble."

"Come back later. You can't expect me to have dough so early in the morning."

"You were working last night. What happened? Did he drink it all up on you?"

The buxom blonde bounced across the room, fiercely. "Keep your mouth shut and get out of here! I'll have the money for you—tonight! If you were any kind of a daughter you'd get a job and stop hounding your father! You ain't any better than me, for all your snotty talk! If I had my way—"

"But you haven't got your way. And he hasn't either." Lee lowered her arms stiffly. "I lied to the court last time just to keep him out of trouble, but I'll be damned if I'll ever do it again! I said he had a job when he didn't, when all the time he was living off you! You wanted it that way, and now you got it!" She put out her hand. "Mrs. Mullins is waiting for the board money, and I want it—now!"

"But I tell you I haven't got it, you little fool! Why should I lie to you?"

The girl laughed—nastily. "Because you lied to me before—and I believed you. The time the rent was three weeks behind and I had to borrow the money from Goosey. Maybe you thought it was easy for me to be nice to him, as easy as it is for you to date a flush customer."

It happened so quickly that Lee didn't have a chance to get out of the way. The plump hand slapped her squarely across the cheek, knocking her against the door.

"You little tramp! Take it back! Take it back, do you hear? If you ever speak that way to me again, I'll kill you!"

Before the livid welts had a chance to appear Lee found herself staggering from the second blow. She cried out, squirming away from the raging grasp, and lurched against the table, upsetting the empty liquor bottle. It seemed to spin in the air, crazily, landing against the rim of the sink with a shattering crash.

The man on the bed rolled over on his back and sat up, supporting himself on his elbows. "What the hell's going on here?" he cried. "Why are you making so much noise?"

The two women froze into silence, their eyes fastened on the handsome, ravaged face.

He caught sight of Lee and the expletive died on his lips. He dragged himself erect slowly, his expression at once puzzled and grim. "What are you doing here, Lee? I thought I told you never to stick your nose where it didn't belong?"

"I'll tell you why she came!" the blonde cried. "She came to make trouble! She called me a bum to my face and said if we didn't fork over on time she'd haul you before the judge again! That's your sweet little daughter for you, the one you keep weeping in your beer about!"

The bloodshot eyes looked up at the woman standing over him, compelling despite their lusterless mark of dissipation. "You'll answer me when I speak to you! Shut up and let me settle this with Lee."

He pushed her to one side, swinging his legs over the edge of the bed, his once fine torso fatty and gone to seed. He combed his thick black hair, so much like Lee's, with open fingers, and rose to his feet. His huge body seemed to fill the room.

He pointed to the floor in front of him, and said, "Come here."

Lee didn't move. She stared back defiantly, her pretty face tense with fear.

"I said come here!"

She started toward him, changed her mind. She waited sullenly at his shuffling approach. As he reached out, she knocked his hand away. "Don't touch me! If you want to go on living like a kept man, don't touch me!"

He gaped, taken aback at her brutal effrontery.

"You got an obligation to meet," Lee went on. "Momma let you get away with it because she was blind for the love of you. But I'm not blind. You owe me support. And I'm going to see that I get it." She didn't raise her voice. The words came out sharply, like bullets from a leveled gun.

The big man swayed before her unsteadily, unable to credit his senses. He drew his lips against his teeth then, and said, "I ought to beat the hell out of you for speaking to me like that! And I got a right to! The court don't say nothing about forcing me to hold back on my duty! And if anybody ever needed a beating, you do."

Lee was frightened but she didn't give an inch. "Lay a hand on me and it will be the sorriest day of your life. I won't lie for you this time. The judge will hear all about how you're living, and who's paying for my support."

The blonde plumped herself down and laughed. "Listen to her!" she cried, "Your loving daughter! When are you going to get wise to yourself and listen to me? You don't have to take this! All we have to do is—"

"Shut up!" He swung toward her, helplessly raging. "I told you to keep out of this! Another word out of you, and I'll—"

"Sure! Take it out on me! Wallop me instead of the one who deserves it! Maybe if you taught her a lesson she wouldn't come around here talking like she owned us!"

He raised his hand but Lee was at his side, her fingers digging into his wrist. "This won't get you anywhere," she said. "Pull yourself together. If there's any kind of trouble they'll put you on probation and you know what that means."

The blonde laughed again, scornfully. "Yeah, he knows what it means. Look at him! What's the matter, did you change your mind? Ain't you going to hit me? But then if the court found out they'd make you get a job and report to the station every month. They'd keep hounding you more than Lee here, and we all know you're too sick to work!"

Tom Sissle turned away savagely, padding toward the window in his bare feet, pinching his fingers to his eyes. He looked at the shattered bottle in the sink and ran his tongue over his lips.

The waitress got up and put her hand on Lee's shoulder. "He's going to get rough any minute now," she warned. "I know that look already. We pushed him a little too far. You better beat it."

Lee felt her heart skip a beat. "The money—" she began.

"I told you I'd have it for you tonight. Meet me at the cafe around ten and I'll give it to you." She prodded Lee towards the door. As she saw the girl hesitate, she went on quickly, "Don't worry about me. I'll be able to handle him if we're alone. Please go now!"

They jumped as he picked up the neck of the bottle and smashed it back into the sink. "I need a drink!" he cried. "You got to get me a drink!"

Lee was at the door, ready to go out. He lunged at her, grabbing her arm. "And just where do you think you're going? I'm not finished with you yet, you little—"

The blonde intervened. "Let her go, Tom! We'll settle everything later. Lee promised she'd wait."

"Now ain't that generous of her!"

"Forget what she said, will you? She didn't mean it anyway."

"Oh no? How many times does this have to happen before she really gets me down before the judge? I'm going to put an end to her threats once and for all! I'll show her that she can't blackmail her own father!"

He struck out at Lee but his fist never reached her face. Instead, it caught the blonde head that suddenly leaped between them, and her heavy weight sagged against him, sending him back on his heels.

He was helping her up from the floor when he heard the door slam, and he knew that Lee had gone.

The blonde was on her feet now, hanging on to his shoulders, muttering angrily under her breath. He shoved her towards the bed and she fell on it, lying prone. He started to dress but she sat up and snatched the garment from his hand, panting dizzily.

"You crazy loon! Where do you think you're going? Let her be, will you? When the hell are you going to get some brains? I told you what we should do! We can be out of this whole mess inside of a few hours!"

He tried to get his trousers from her but she threw them behind the bed. When he reached to get them she put her arms around him and pulled him down.

"Be sensible, won't you, Tom? All I have to do is wire Chi and the job is mine. You won't have to worry about a thing, I promise you."

"No."

She looked up into the handsome, dissolute face pleadingly. Their lips were almost touching. "Lee don't mean that much to you. She never did. She'll get along without your help. She's a smart kid. Tom—"

"She's still my flesh and blood, I can't forget that. Even though there are times I could just—"

"Tom. It's the only way out. Believe me. She wouldn't live with us even if we asked her to. This way—we'll both be free—to live the way we want—just the two of us. Tom—" She took his hand and held it to her.

"I'm—crazy about you, Tom. We—can have a wonderful life together. I'll do anything to keep you. You know that. Just be sensible and forget about Lee."

"But I just can't run away, and—"

"Yes you can, Tom. I'll make you forget her once we're away. We're not happy here, shelling out for her. That money could be ours. You would have a lot more to drink, and me—I would have you all to myself then. Tom—" She pressed her lips to his, drawing the breath out of him.

"It ain't right," he muttered, but she cut him off with another kiss, and a sound escaped his throat at the pressing boldness of her.

"Tom," she whispered. "We can forget everything—but this. No matter how they look, they'll never find us."

There was anger in his voice when he spoke, and weakness. "I can't! What are you trying to make of me? I feel like scum already! How low can a father get? How can you ask me to leave her, to practically throw her into the gutter—"

"It's her or me, Tom. And right now you got me. See, Tom? You got me. Like—this— But her—she hates you. All she wants is your money. While I—all I want is to give…"

He wanted to rise and break away, but the spell was upon him, the inevitable weakness.

"We'll have a drink on it—later," she said. "Later. Tom, you're listening? You're—"

"No. Let me up. You can't make me. I won't listen." But he didn't get up, he didn't break away.

"A drink," she breathed in his ear. "Later."

"Later," she said again, and sank back, trembling with breathlessness.

"Later…" he echoed, "later…"

CHAPTER TWO

"THAT'S ALL I can tell you," the manager said. "She said she was quitting so I paid her off and she left."

Lee rose numbly from the chair. "She didn't say—"

"I didn't ask any questions. It's her life. It's none of my business where she goes or what she does." He got up from behind the desk and went to the door. "I'm a busy man," he said. "Excuse me."

Lee thanked him and left the Clover Cafe, her mind filled with bitter conjectures. She hurried to the rooming house but when she got there the landlady gave her the same story.

"They left like the place was on fire," she said. "They piled all their personal junk into a taxi and rode off." She stabbed her knuckles into her hips viciously. "You'd think they'd have the decency to give a few days notice, at least! After all I did for them, too! Those two gave me more trouble than anybody I ever had! You got no idea—"

"They didn't leave a forwarding address?"

"No."

"Will you let me know if you get any mail from them? I'll come around from time to time, and—"

"Why?" The unsympathetic eyes grew wary. "You lookin' to make trouble for them? If you are, I don't want any part of it. I got enough troubles of my own without—"

Lee turned away. "Thank you," she said, and walked off.

She started back for Mrs. Mullins' but the thought of facing her without the board money checked her steps. What was she going to do? How could she possibly explain? If Goosey's mother found out that there wouldn't be another dime coming in, that Tom Sissle had disappeared—

Lee's lovely lips twisted into a bitter oath. So it had finally happened! All these years, through the never-ending nightmare of successive mistresses, she had fearfully awaited the officious knock on the door, the humiliating, heartbreaking ride to the home for unwanted children. She had grown old beyond her time, waiting. Old and shrewd and hard. It made a difference, not being like other kids, not having a home, never for one moment certain of the next day.

Sure, Mrs. Mullins had been kind to her. She grew up with Goosey like they were brother and sister. But just let the board money be skipped a week or two, and all the surface affection went out the window. "We got to buy food! We got to pay rent!" she could hear Mrs. Mullins shouting. "I got my own family to look after!"

It got worse as the years went on, as Tom got more careless about paying. Lee got used to the abuse after a while, but not wholly. The impervious shell of resistance was not quite as thick as Mrs. Mullins believed. There were many nights when Lee in childish desperation thought of ending it all, nights when she couldn't sleep for weeping.

She made no friends because she was ashamed. It made her spiteful and domineering. She refused to study, refused to adapt herself. Now she was eighteen. She had a seductive body and was always conscious of it. She grew up knowing it. The boys of the neighborhood didn't give her a chance to forget. Goosey was crazy about her. After all, he knew her more intimately than the rest. They had grown up together in the same apartment, shared the same bed as kids, were carelessly informal in each other's presence—up to the time Goosey's curiosity developed into something disturbingly pointed and uncontrolled...

When he was sixteen he asked her to run away with him and get married. He was almost twenty now and still felt the same way about her. She didn't mind when Goosey kissed her. It was like a brother kissing her. Even when he fooled around and got fresh she didn't mind. It made her feel good to brush him off, to see the anguish in his eyes. Once in a while she got excited too. But it was safe to get excited with Goosey.

Lee's decision came quickly.

He was the only one she had now, the only one she could turn to. He would give her the money out of his savings, just as he had done several times before, without his mother's knowledge. But this time there would be no paying him back. And after Mrs. Mullins found out what had been going on behind her back, when the time came for the truth to be told—

She shrugged off the unpleasant thought and headed in the direction of the *New York Press*. Goosey would be there, loading Ricco's truck with the early-morning edition. He would have a few dollars in his pocket. Enough to placate Mrs. Mullins until she could get the rest of it.

Lee looked at her cheap wristwatch and saw that she would have to rush to catch him before the truck left on its rounds. Hoyt Street was a long way off and she would never make it on foot. She fretted on the street-corner waiting for the crosstown bus, thinking of red-faced Mrs. Mullins stewing in the apartment, counting the money even before she had it.

Minutes went by with no sign of a bus, coming or going. A cabbie pulled up hopefully, spotting her white beret and tight sweater, looking her over as she stood impatiently under the spray of yellow lamplight.

"A buck for wherever you want to go," he said, "flat rate. I'll keep my flag up. Is it a deal?"

Lee didn't send him on his way. She sauntered over. "I haven't got a buck," she said. "But I got to get to Hoyt Street, in a hurry. If I catch the right guy there, you'll get paid. And if I don't—"

"No dice, sister. I can't eat promises."

Lee opened the back door and got in. The cabbie jerked around and stared at her. "Hey! You heard what I said! Are you deaf, or something?"

She sat back in the darkness, crossing her legs, and took out a cigarette. "Get me to the *New York Press*," she said. "You won't regret it. Ricco doesn't forget favors. I'll take down your name and number—"

The hackie stuck his head over the partition. "Are you kiddin'? If you knew Ricco you'd be able to buy this heap! What are you tryin' to give me?"

The match flared and its dancing light glowed against the youthful, attractive lines of her face. She drew on the cigarette, leaning forward, and said, "I was just introduced to him—over the telephone. There might be more than a buck in it for you if you get me there on time."

He pushed back his cap and scratched his head. "It sounds phony to me," he began. "You don't look like the type."

Lee put on a show of impatience. "Never mind what I look like." She reached for the door. "Are you willing to take a chance or aren't you?"

He laughed. "I've heard a lot of good ones in my time, but this sure does take the cake! It's almost worth it to take the chance and call your bluff."

"Then what are you waiting for?"

He laughed again, appreciatively. "Sister, I'm makin' a bet with myself. That I won't see the buck and I won't see Ricco. But what the hell—the entertainment alone'll be worth it." He turned back to the wheel and stepped on the gas.

Lee sat back in the dark, smiling grimly. Why worry? She would catch Goosey before he left and the hackie would be paid and that would be that. She shouldn't have mentioned not having the buck when he made the deal. But it was a natural mistake. Next time she'd know better. Live and learn. If she could only find a simple way like this in dealing with Goosey's mother... She vowed to learn quickly.

There was hardly any traffic at all, but while cutting through Howard Street they were stopped by a long trailer truck that had jack-knifed backing against the curb. Precious time was wasted as the hackie maneuvered the cab between parked cars in order to pass the jam over the sidewalk. Finally they were on their way, but Lee was taut, hoping against hope that they could make it.

When they reached the rear of the *New York Press* building she saw with relief that a large number of Ricco's trucks were still loading. She told the hackie to wait and got out, taking the few steps up to the loading platform and entering the glass-enclosed office without hesitation.

The dispatcher took his eyes from the sheet when she came in, flipping back his green eyeshade and giving her a wolfish grin. "Hello, Dreamboat," he said. "What can I do for you?"

Lee didn't waste any words. "I got to see Goosey Mullins. Where is he?"

The dispatcher was annoyingly deliberate. He scratched his head with the end of the pencil, and said, "I think he's on truck twenty-two." Lee started out. "But truck twenty-two just left, Dreamboat. How about waitin' around till he comes back?"

She stopped as if a hand had been laid on her shoulder. The thin man drew himself up in the manner of an English butler, and mocked, "Whom shall I say called, modom?"

She gave him a dirty look and closed the glass door behind her. The hackie was on the platform, waiting for her.

"Well?" he asked.

"I have to look for him," Lee said. "He's on the platform somewhere."

"Why look? If he's here, let him come to us." He cupped his hands to his lips before she could stop him, and bellowed, "Ricco! Ricco! Where are you?"

Everything seemed to come to a sudden halt. The busy sounds of working died abruptly, like a radio being turned off.

The thin dispatcher darted out of the office and grabbed the hackie by the arm, "What's the idea? Are you a wise guy or something?"

The hackie shook him off. "My fare's got to see Ricco, urgent. And me too. About gettin' paid off."

"Ricco?" The green eyeshade bobbed up and down cynically. "What's the idea, Dreamboat? You told me—"

Lee started away. "Never mind, I guess he's not here."

"Hey!" The hackie ran after her. But Lee stopped.

A thick-set figure appeared from nowhere and stepped in front of her. "What's all the noise about, sister? Your friend lookin' for a hole in the head?"

The driver was trying to explain when the sound of leather heels tapping along the concrete platform caused his questioner to cut him off and turn respectfully to greet the approaching figure.

A strong, hard face regarded them from under the snap-brim fedora, cut across by deceptive shadows, broad shoulders tautly poised like an athlete waiting for the starting gun.

"This dame claims she knows you," the thick-set man said. "She owes the hackie a bill and said you would pay off."

Lee's mouth ran dry. She looked up into Ricco's face boldly, but her knees were trembling under her.

Ricco smiled. It seemed that way at least, from the moving shadows on his face. "Sure," he said. "I know her." His voice was surprisingly soft. "What's the charge, hackie?"

"A buck, Mr. Ricco. But—"

"Here's five. Beat it."

"Sure thing, Mr. Ricco. Thanks." He scurried away.

Ricco slipped his arm through Lee's. "You're a nervy kid," he said. "What's your name?"

She told him, and started to apologize.

"Save it for later. Get into my car and wait there. I want to talk to you. Joe, take her to the car." He turned his back and walked down the length of the busy platform.

Lee didn't know what to do.

"Come on," Joe said. "Follow me." He imitated Ricco's swagger and Lee followed him.

He sat her next to the driving wheel of the big convertible and stood guard by the door, resting his elbow on the metal frame. He cracked Indian nuts between his teeth and spit out the shells without putting his fingers to his mouth.

Lee waited, not daring to speak, feeling as if someone had punched her in the stomach. She had done a crazy thing, telling the hackie about Ricco. If Goosey lost his job on account of it—

"All right," Ricco's voice said, and the thick-set man moved away.

Ricco got behind the wheel and started the motor. "You were lucky," he said to Lee. "I'm usually not around. My office is in Radio City. But there was a little trouble tonight."

He backed the car out from under the delivery shed and drove toward Flatbush Avenue. "We'll have a little drink," he said, "and then you'll tell me what it's all about."

She started to say something but he turned on the radio. The news commentator was giving the highlights of the crime investigation and Ricco listened intently. He shut it off after they gave the weather report and drove along with peculiar concentration. Lee, sitting as far as she could from him, kept her eyes on his strong profile, afraid, yet filled with speculation. She had heard a lot about Ricco. From Goosey. He was hardly mentioned in the papers, but somehow the public got to know about him. Goosey thought the sun rose and set on him. But big as he was, he was only a man. Lee smoothed the provocative curve of her sweater and continued to speculate.

"Here we are," Ricco said, and parked in a space marked *No Parking*. He helped her out of the car and tipped the doorman as they entered the gaudy bar and grill.

Lee saw herself reflected many times in the flesh-tinted mirrors, catching Ricco's glance of interest as the headwaiter seated them in the choice booth.

"A double Scotch for me and a champagne cocktail for the lady," Ricco said, and the waiter went away. He folded well-groomed hands on the tabletop and fastened his eyes on Lee's face. "All right," he said. "Let's have it. Without the soft music."

Lee leaned back and stretched, nonchalantly. Her heart was pounding but she didn't want the advantage to be his. She saw his eyes follow the upward curve of her breasts and smiled inwardly. He wasn't any different than the rest. Why should she be afraid?

"Now that you got me looking," Ricco said, "what about answering my questions?"

Ricco was slightly bald, and when he caught her glance his finger went to his hair instinctively. "Well?" he said again.

Lee told him. About not having money. About wanting to get it from Goosey.

"Tell me all of it," Ricco said. "You're leaving something out."

She didn't want him to know how young she was but he would only find out from Goosey, so she told him. She told him about her father and the blonde waitress and what had happened.

The drinks came and Ricco drank his without touching glasses and sat back and studied her. "You got a lot of nerve but you're stupid," he said. "Why are you wasting yourself on a guy like Goosey?"

Lee pretended to laugh. "Maybe you know of someone better who would be willing to pay my board?"

He looked her right in the eye and said, "I don't. But he shouldn't be too hard to find. For me, personally, you're too young. Jail bait. I got too much to lose. But I can see where you could make any other well-fixed guy forget the risk."

"Thanks. But I'm not up for sale."

He smiled then, and it did something to his face. The hard look vanished. "Maybe I should tell you to hang on to Goosey. He'll never amount to much but he's a good kid. You're pretty and well-stacked, but so are thousands of other dames. Dames who make a little because they're young but end up going from bar to bar. That shouldn't be for you. A couple of kids and a clean little flat with a guy like Goosey taking care of you should bring you all the happiness you need. Take it from me. I've been around."

"You talk as if I had an idea of making you."

"Maybe you didn't start out with that idea, but you got it riding along with me in the car."

Lee sipped her cocktail, smiling at him over the rim and feeling headily sophisticated. "I like you," she said. "You're trying to insult me but I don't mind. You think I'm only a kid and you're trying to talk yourself out of it. Am I right?"

Ricco laughed. Heartily. "You're damn well right. But I'm not going to change my mind. Here..." He reached into his pocket and came out with some folded bills. "How much is your board?"

"Fifteen dollars a week."

He gave her three fives and two singles. "The rest is for cab fare home," he said. "Now finish your drink and beat it."

Lee took the money without thanking him and stuffed it into her little purse. "I'd like to see you again, Mr. Ricco. Would you let me?"

"No." He got up and walked around the table and took her arm. "Maybe you better go home now."

She leaned forward, edging out between the seat and the table and brushed against him. He smiled at her but didn't move his arm.

"Thanks," he said. "But it won't change my mind."

Lee flushed and walked to the door in silence.

"Give my love to Goosey," Ricco said. He tipped the doorman again but didn't go out.

She knew he was watching her as she walked to the curb, watching and thinking about her as all men think about a seductive woman.

But then she heard him laugh, and hurried across the street against the lights, making up her mind that he hadn't seen the last of her. Ricco had money. And he was interested. Maybe she was wrong but she had to concentrate on seeing him again, and it had to be soon.

She thought of her father and what he was and the spring went out of her gait. She wasn't any different. She was just like him.

She took the bus home, feeling everyone's eyes on her, filled with guilt and shame.

But that's the way she was. She had to live with herself. She had to make the best of it.

Before she went to bed she looked at herself and felt that if Ricco could see her the way she was he would forget that she was jail bait and go overboard. She kept looking at herself for a long time and got so excited thinking of it that when she finally got to bed she couldn't sleep.

Mrs. Mullins found it easy to sleep. Because the board had been paid and the coming week could be gotten through without too much penny-pinching. All she had to worry about was the following week, and the months after that, and the years…

CHAPTER THREE

LEE DIDN'T tell Goosey about Ricco but he found out when his pay envelope came through fifteen dollars short. He waited until after his mother went to visit an ailing neighbor and then got Lee alone in her room.

Goosey was big and lumbering and good-natured but Lee had gone too far. "I almost got fired on account of you!" he cried. "I thought they were pullin' a fast one! 'Loan deduction,' they write on the slip, with me not knowin' anything about it! Nobody knew what it meant until Ricco told me himself!"

Goosey jammed his fists into the pockets of his windbreaker and glared at Lee. "You been takin' me for a sucker for a long time, Lee, but this puts the lid on it! How much do you think I can take?"

She looked at him calmly, sure of her attraction, sure of her hold over him. She slipped her hands to his shoulders and pouted repentantly. "I'm sorry, Goosey. I meant to tell you. But I've been so upset about my old man leaving me high and dry that I forgot all about it. Besides, I didn't think Ricco would be so cheap. I thought, well, that it was sort of a present."

"Sure," Goosey sneered, "catch Ricco givin' you something for nothin'!"

"I thought you liked him, that you were great friends."

"Yeah, great friends! Him with an office in Radio City, and me a helper on one of his trucks! He's a big deal, that's all, and I look up to him—but as for that friend stuff—"

"Maybe he'll be your friend now that he's seen me."

Goosey stared. "Are you kiddin'? What has that got to do with it?"

Lee smiled. "You *are* dumb, aren't you, Goosey? But never mind. Don't be surprised if pretty soon he'll be making you a driver—and maybe a collector."

He forgot that he was mad at her, and laughed. "What you been smokin' lately, baby? Gimme a drag on the pipe before you throw it away!"

Lee laughed with him. She leaned close and pecked his cheek. "I guess you think I'm wacky, huh?"

"Only slightly." And his arms crept around her. He kissed her ear and said, "You shouldn't of done it, Lee. Not like that, anyway. You should of asked me first. You know I would of given it to you."

"I know. But I got panicky, finding my father gone, and thinking of your old lady, sitting here waiting with her hand open. You know how she is. I don't have to tell you."

"Yeah, I know, Lee."

She gave a funny little laugh and said, "I could see myself walking out with my bag and wondering where I was going to spend the night."

His arms tightened about her. "That'll never happen while I'm around. You know that. You should never even think that way."

Her cheek was against his shoulder, her lustrous hair soft against his face. "I know, Goosey, but I still can't help feeling that way. The last time your mother had to wait for the board she got so excited that she got sick. Suppose something did happen to her heart on account of me? You'd hate me for it. You'd never want to see me again."

"No. It ain't true. I wouldn't let you go no matter what happened, no matter what anybody said. I'm crazy about you, Lee."

She nestled close. "Crazy enough to keep paying my board?"

"For as long as you live."

His hands moved and she waited for his intimate caress. Goosey was like that. He couldn't help himself when he was near her. His hand stopped and she let him hold her. She was hardly excited at all.

"When are you goin' to marry me, Lee?"

"It'll be the death of your mother, Goosey."

"Stop kiddin'. She'll get used to the idea. There are a lot of things we don't like that we got to get used to."

"I'm afraid to take the chance, Goosey."

"You mean you don't want to marry me?"

Lee drew away, reluctantly. "Maybe that's it, Goosey. I just can't make up my mind about you."

His face was flushed with emotion. "You don't have to make up your mind about takin' my money, though!"

Her hands flew to her face. "Goosey!"

He turned away but she took his arm and forced him around. "I'll pay you back," she said, "every cent of it! Now you better get out. I'm tired and I got a lot to think about."

"Lee, I didn't mean—"

"Maybe you didn't, but you said it. I'm not in the mood to take it." She went to the door and held it open. "I'll find some way to pay my board. Maybe I'll get a job and move somewhere else."

"Now, Lee—"

"Don't talk to me! I'm sick and tired of listening to your mother's complaints, and of feeling your hands on me every time you do me a favor!"

Goosey looked as if she had stabbed him through the heart. He brushed back his limp, reddish hair and stood by the door, pleading silently with his eyes.

"This has been going on for a long time, Goosey. Too long to suit me. I'm getting fed up with the whole thing."

He shifted from one foot to the other, blinking his eyes, so much in love with her that he couldn't think straight.

"Forget about the money," he began. "You don't have to pay me back. You don't—"

"But I am going to pay you back. And I'm going to speak to your mother tonight. I'm going to tell her about my old man and ask her to wait until I can find something to do. If she turns me down, I'll pack right up and get out tomorrow morning!"

"You don't mean it, Lee…"

"You'll find out if I mean it or not. I can't force my old man to pay but I'll soon know how I stand around here."

Something clicked in Goosey's mind. "You're bluffin'," he said. "You don't want to work. You wouldn't take a job even if it was given to you. My old lady plenty of times got offers for you. But you wouldn't lift a finger."

Lee was filled with a cold rage. "You know damn well why I wouldn't work! But now I got to."

"Yeah, now you got to. But you don't want to. You'd let me go on payin' your board and takin' it easy if I didn't want you should marry me." The faint spark of anger died out of his eyes and he shook his head, sighing. "It's crazy," he said. "The whole thing. What you're sayin', and what I'm sayin'. All on account of a lousy fifteen bucks. We shouldn't be fightin' like this, Lee. It don't make sense, the two of us fightin'. Not the way we feel about each other. After all we been through together we should know better." He forced a smile to his lips. "I think I'll go down for a beer. Want to come along?"

"No. I'm going to wait for your mother."

He edged back into the room and took her hand. "Think careful about it, won't you, Lee? No use flyin' off the handle and bein' sorry about it after. We'll work it out some way. We always have. What do you say, Lee? No hard feelings?"

She looked at him with her dark, shouldering eyes, and said finally, smiling, "No hard feelings. I guess we'll be together long enough to have a lot more fights like these."

He put his arm around her waist. "Then let's make up and have a couple of seidels. Mom'll be here when we get back. She won't run away."

Lee shrugged, patting his cheek. "Okay. I'll do it just to keep peace in the family. Wait until I make myself pretty."

Mom was there when they got back. She was waiting for them.

The news of Tom Sissle's sudden departure had reached the neighborhood and the sick friend told Mrs. Mullins all about it, with a few embroidered details.

The wiry, red-faced woman let Lee have it as soon as she stepped through the door. "I heard about your father," she said. "Why didn't you tell me what happened? You knew about it a week ago!"

"Now, Mom—" Goosey began, but she shut him up with a gesture.

"Well, Toledo, what are you goin' to do about it? Where are you goin' to get the money to pay your board?"

Goosey's mother had her shoes off because they always hurt, and it gave her the appearance of a belligerent bantam, red face thrust upward at the two unhappy kids. "Well, you heard what I said! Where are you goin' to get the money, now that your father left you to starve?"

Lee started to answer back angrily, but Goosey pressed her hand and she checked herself. "He didn't leave without my knowing it," she lied. "He was getting a better job and promised to send along the money as soon as he was sure of keeping it."

Mrs. Mullins blinked. "A likely story! And how long do you think it'll be before he sends anything?"

"That—I don't know."

The congested face grew darker. "Well, I do. Never! He's gone and that's the end of it! You can't fool me, Lee. He got sick of supportin' you, that's what, a big strong girl like you. Not that he still isn't a tramp in my eyes, but I'm not takin' any chances. Tomorrow mornin' you're gettin' out early to look for a job. And if you don't find one in a couple of weeks—"

"Mom—"

"Shut up, Goosey! What do you think we are anyway? Rich millionaires? I'd be out workin' myself if I didn't have such a bad heart. Now I don't want to hear another word out of either of you! I been sweatin' and strugglin' my whole life to bring, up a stranger's brat, and what thanks will I get for it in the end? A spit in the eye, that's what, the same as all mothers get after the brats are big enough to talk back. And that goes for you too, Goosey!" She pressed her hand to her heart—and groped behind her for a chair. Goosey leaped as if at an unspoken command. He had the chair under her in a second, pasty-faced and shaking with anxiety.

"Mom! Are you all right? Do you need anything? Should I call a doctor?"

Mrs. Mullins sank back, gasping loudly. She rolled her eyes but didn't look any sicker than before. "A doctor! How can poor people like us afford a doctor? Just—get me some water, Goosey—there's the good boy."

As Goosey hurried into the kitchen the old lady sat up and glared at Lee. "I know what you're thinkin'!" she cried. "You hope I die, don't you, so that you can marry Goosey and have an easy life with my insurance! But I ain't goin' to die, see! And you ain't goin' to marry my boy. If you try to take him away from me I'll put the mother's curse on you! I'll—"

"Save your curses for someone else. And if I ever do marry Goosey, it'll be because you don t want me to. Just to spite you for treating me like a dog all these years!"

"Goosey! Goosey!" Mrs. Mullins shrieked. "Bring me the water! Bring me the water!"

"Comin' Ma! Comin'!" But half the water was out of the glass by the time he held it out to her, and she sent him back for more.

"Remember my words!" Mrs. Mullins cried, shaking a bony finger at Lee. "You led me a hard life with all the bad things you did, and I gave you more than a mother's devotion. If you turn Goosey against me now, showin' yourself off in front of him and lettin' him see what he shouldn't, my curse'll follow you till the day you die!"

Lee didn't wait to hear anymore. She hurried to her room, the shrill voice bounding after her, digging into her mind like a festering splinter.

The next morning she left without having breakfast and waited for Ricco in front of his office. She gave him a big smile when he showed up but he looked at her coldly and asked what she was doing there.

"I'm looking for a job, Mr. Ricco," she said. "I thought maybe you could help me." She was wearing a tight satin dress with hardly anything underneath and Ricco knew the reason.

"You come to the wrong place," he said. "With that dress you got on you ought to be making the rounds near Shubert Alley."

"Please, Mr. Ricco—"

He looked at her again, his eyes clinging to her figure as he pushed back the door and nodded for her to go in.

His office was disappointingly small. And plain. A lone girl sat in a small cubicle before a partition that screened off Ricco's desk. "In there," Ricco said, and collected his mail as he followed her.

He waved her to a plain hard chair and sat down behind the desk, throwing the letters unopened into the wastebasket. He watched Lee as she crossed her legs carelessly, a thin smile on his lips. "Are you looking for trouble or do you really want a job, Beautiful?"

Her eyes held his coolly. "I thought if you became interested, you'd find me something decent. I don't know much about anything. I never had a job before."

He bit off the end of a cigar and leaned back on the swivel. "Look," he said. "I don't care if you never get a job. And I don't care if I ever see you again. I tried to make that plain when I deducted the fifteen bucks from Goosey's salary. Now I'm going to give you an address and when you walk out of this door I want it to be for the last time. Do you understand?"

Lee's eyes flashed. But she checked her temper and nodded stiffly. "All right. But some day I'm going to make you eat those words, Mr. Ricco. I won't always be jail bait, like you say. Time has a way of changing things."

He laughed. "Maybe I'll be glad to have you around a couple of years from now. Who knows? But right now you're pure poison to me."

He wrote something on the back of his business card and gave it to her. "Sam is an old friend of mine. Maybe he'll have something for you. Good luck."

Lee put it in her pocketbook without looking at it.

Ricco stared. Then he said, waving his cigar at her, "Beat it. And remember what I told you."

She got up and walked around to where he was sitting, standing quite close to him. She was wearing perfume and the cheap scent was like a brazen invitation.

"You're afraid of me, aren't you, Mr. Ricco? You know that if you lay your hands on me you'll never let go. That I'll ask for anything I want and you'll give it to me."

Ricco turned in the swivel and their knees touched. He didn't say a word. He put down the cigar and embraced her without getting up, curving his fingers in a savage caress. Then he drew himself up and choked back her breath with his bruising lips.

Lee staggered back against the desk and he shoved her away, laughing. "All right, Cleopatra," he said. "Does that satisfy you?"

He wiped off her lipstick with his 'kerchief and retrieved the cigar. "Maybe you'll have better luck with Sam," he said. "He's not as careful as I am." He pressed the buzzer and the girl came in and he told her that Miss Sissle was leaving. "Don't ever let her get into this office again, do you understand?"

Lee slapped him. Hard. And walked out.

Ricco didn't get mad. He just laughed. His cheek was stinging but it was all part of the way he felt. The way the palms of his hands were stinging, and the deep trembling of his flesh at the remembered contact.

He tried to dismiss her from his mind but when he settled down to business all he could think of was the exciting firmness of her, the invitation of her body as he bent her over the desk.

CHAPTER FOUR

IT WASN'T MUCH OF A JOB, but it would keep her going for a while, until she found something better.

Sam Mangum, the owner of the Mercury Hosiery Company, offered Lee the job somewhat apologetically. He kept turning Ricco's card in his hands, alternately smiling and frowning, a frightened man if there ever was one. He was small and dapper and distinctly the ladies' man, but his manner with Lee was both deferential and frankly curious.

"Always glad to do a favor for Mr. Ricco," he said, "but I'm afraid I haven't got many good openings at the moment. If you'd care to wait a few weeks, Miss Sissle—"

"I need a job now. It doesn't have to be anything fancy. As long as it pays well."

Mangum fumbled with the card and it slipped from his fingers and fluttered to the blotter. He smiled at Lee, reached for the phone, hesitated, and said, "I gather you've just met Mr. Ricco? Your relationship with him is still—is still in its early stages?"

"Will that make a difference about the kind of job I get?"

"That's—hard to say, Miss Sissle. Maybe if I called him—"

"Don't bother. Just give me the job. What do I do?"

Mangum paused. "So that's the way it is," he murmured, and a look of relief came to his face. "Very well, Miss Sissle. Please follow me."

Lee didn't like the job at all. It was kid stuff, folding nylons into flat, oblong boxes by size. You had to pack a certain amount per day. Young boys kept you supplied with boxes and the forelady saw to it that the stockings reached you in a steady stream.

Most of the girls in the department were barely literate, and not too clean. The place was like a morgue, except for the occasional chatter of the girls.

Mangum studied her face, anxiously. "This kind of work doesn't appeal to you, does it? Maybe Mr. Ricco would rather have you doing something else?"

"How much does it pay?"

"Twenty-eight dollars a week."

Lee remained silent.

"If you only had some sort of training," Mangum began.

"It isn't your fault that I don't know anything. I'll be glad to take the job—temporarily. If it's all right with you."

"It's entirely up to you, my dear. But something else might pop up. You never know."

Lee saw herself getting up at seven in the morning, wolfing a breakfast and rushing to the subway; eating lunch out of a bag, trying to make friends with the girls working at her table—and then back to the subway crush after five o'clock; and to the moody supper table and the endless evenings of hanging around chafing with frustration. Her purse had been empty before, but at least her time was her own, and she could sleep, and keep herself fresh and ready for the kind of break she was looking for. But now there would be no chance of meeting anyone else but Goosey or the boys of the neighborhood; and she had outgrown them long ago…

"You may start any time you wish," Mr. Mangum said. "Shall we say tomorrow at nine?"

"Tomorrow—at nine."

Goosey was apprehensive when she told him about the job. "With the tax deductions and everything," he said, "you won't have much left for yourself. Not enough, that is, for you to live alone and eat out all the time—"

"That's just what I was thinking when I took the job. I'll just have to put up with your mother until I figure out another angle."

Goosey's face lit up. "Then you ain't—"

"No. I won't be moving. Not right away."

He shook his head like a swimmer emerging from a dive. "Whew! For a minute I thought I lost you! Let's—go upstairs and tell Ma. She—"

"There's time enough for that. I don't want to go upstairs. I feel like going out and having a good time. I—just—got to do something—"

"Sure! I feel like celebratin' too! Where do you want to go—to a movie, or dancin'?"

"No. Nothing like that. Something better. Something more glamorous. Like listening to music—and having a few drinks."

"We can always pick up a bottle and go to the Vagabond Club—"

Lee gestured impatiently. "I'm not talking about kid stuff now! You and your Vagabonds! Who wants to sit in a stinking cellar all night—"

"Cripes, it was only a suggestion! You don't have to jump down my throat like that."

"All right. But get it through your head that I don't go for that rough club stuff. I don't trust any of that mob. My old man's reputation hurt me bad enough without me getting a worse name hanging around those hoodlums."

Goosey looked aggrieved. "Hoodlums! They ain't hoodlums. They're all the kids we know, the kids we grew up with."

"Look, I'm not going to argue with you all night. Do you want to take me where I want to go, or don't you?"

Goosey shuffled sullenly. "You ain't told me where you want to go."

Lee told him. "There's a place on Flatbush Avenue. A nice place, with lights and music, where people with money go. It's called the *Golden Rooster*. That's where I want you to take me."

Goosey wasn't impressed. "It sounds just like another ginmill to me."

29

"It is. But it's high-class." Excitement crept into her voice, and anticipation. "Come on, Goosey. I won't let you spend too much. And if you do—well, now that I got a job—"

He brushed his knuckles against her chin, playfully. "You're still only a kid," he smiled. "You want to be a glamour dame but for me you'll always be just a wonderful sweet girl—lookin' to wear the moon for a pearl earring."

"It's good to be crazy like that, Goosey. At least I won't get my fingers dirty digging in the gutter. There's the difference."

He grinned, taking her arm. "As long as you say so, Lee."

She patted his hand. "That's my nice doggie." And they were on their way.

As soon as they walked into the place she looked to see if Ricco was there. He was but she pretended not to see him and slid into the booth next to Goosey, an obscure location reserved for transient customers. Ricco was at the bar, talking to someone who had the face and posture of a gorilla. It was obvious to Lee, as it had been from the beginning, that the *Golden Rooster* was Ricco's secret headquarters.

She ordered a champagne cocktail and Goosey's eyes opened wide. He ran his finger down the price list and pursed his lips in a silent whistle. "Hey, what kind of a job did you say you got?"

She gave him a full-lipped smile. "Relax, Goosey. You want to make me happy, don't you?"

"Me," Goosey said. "I'm havin' a beer. Just in case we don't want to walk home."

The waiter put the drinks before them after depositing a bowl of tidbits and popcorn on the table, and Goosey took a handful of both, feeding himself like a seal as Lee watched, laughing at his antics.

She raised her glass and said, "Let's drink to something."

"I don't need any excuses," Goosey said, still kidding, and put the stein to his lips.

It was then that Lee pretended to see Ricco for the first time. "Goosey!" she cried. "You'll never guess who's here…"

He almost choked on his beer. His fleshy face got white, and he whispered, "Who? Not my old lady…?"

"No, screwball! Ricco. There he is. At the bar in the back." Goosey craned his neck. "Jeez! It is Ricco. Let's go over and say hello."

"No. You can if you want to, but I won't. It don't look nice."

"Should I bring him to the table?"

"If you want to. Then I can thank him for the job he sent me after."

"Sure." Goosey got up, all excited, and walked down the length of the mellow-lighted room. Lee waited, conscious of the heavy pulsing in her throat.

Ricco came back with Goosey. There was a smile on his face but it wasn't very pleasant.

He sat down across the table from Lee and ignored her extended hand. "Goosey told me about your job," he said. "I'm glad Sam was able to take care of you. But let me put you wise to something. I want you to hear this too, Goosey. Stop following me around! Stop making a pest of yourself. And don't ever come looking for me here again. If you do I'll fire Goosey and see that he never gets another job!" He slapped his fingers on the flat of the table so hard that the glasses jumped.

Goosey's mouth flew open. He drew back, gaping.

Lee sat as if turned to stone. "They got names for guys like you, Mr. Ricco."

"I could think of a few names that would fit you too, you little pest! What's the matter? Isn't Goosey here good enough for you? Isn't he man enough to take care of you?"

Lee's hand shot out but Ricco grabbed it, knocking over Goosey's stein of beer. The beer splashed on the table and ran down on Goosey's pants but the two antagonists had eyes only for each other.

Ricco flung her hand from him and got up. "Get out," he said. "Settle your bill and don't ever come back again. And don't forget what I told you, Goosey." He stalked back towards the bar.

Goosey was as white as a sheet. He said to Lee, mopping his pants with the napkin, "What the matter with him? Is he nuts or something?"

"I know what's the matter with him," Lee said. Her eyes were hard-bright, burning with resentment. "He tried to put the make on me this morning. In his office. I wouldn't let him."

"But—"

"Just because I went there asking for a job. He held me against the desk but I slapped his face and got away."

Goosey blinked like a punch-drunk fighter. "But I don't get it. If all that happened why did you want me to bring him to the table?"

"What's the matter? Can't you use your brains? I wanted to show him that I was a good sport, that I didn't hold nothing against him."

Goosey groped in his pocket for money. "We better get out of here," he said. "I don't want to lose my job."

"Go ahead, if you want to, but I'm staying."

"Lee—take it easy. Don't go lookin' for trouble. Ricco is no guy to fool around with."

"To hell with him! He don't own the world! I'm staying right here. And drinking."

"Lee—"

"Go on, put your tail between your legs and run! I can see how much I mean to you now. When it comes to a showdown—"

"It ain't that, Lee. Honest, it ain't."

"I'm not asking you to bust him one. Just to stick with me. You fool, don't you think he'll come over after you leave?"

"Then let's—"

The waiter came over with a fresh tablecloth and they remained silent until he left. She called him back as Goosey got to his feet and ordered another champagne cocktail. Goosey sat down again, looking green around the gills, and nodded loosely as the waiter asked if he wanted another beer.

Ricco stopped by the table on his way out, just as Lee was downing her third cocktail. He looked at her and said, "Crazy kid! Get wise to yourself!"

Goosey cringed back, waiting to be bawled out, but Ricco didn't give him as much as a glance.

"So long, Big Shot," Lee sneered, and hiccupped into her glass. The big man with the broad shoulders and hard, handsome face made a gesture of disgust and walked away, shaking his head.

Goosey wanted to leave right away but Lee insisted on having one more drink. "Just to show him," she said thickly, "and you, too, that I'm as good as anybody—anywhere, anytime! I should of known," she went on, "that I'd get my fingers dirty, digging in the gutter!"

Goosey looked unhappy. He had a problem on his hands. Lee was drunk now. He watched her as she weaved unsteadily towards the ladies' room, thinking of his mother and what she would say if she saw him bringing Lee home drunk.

He asked the doorman to call a taxi, and when Lee came back to the table she found it cleared, with Goosey waiting for her with his hat on. "Ricco told them not to give us any more," he lied, and Lee said, "Then to hell with them. We'll go someplace else."

But she fell asleep in the taxi, with her head resting on Goosey's shoulder, and he held her close, thinking of how much he loved her, and how crazy she was to let Ricco upset her.

He thought of how Ricco tried to put the make on her and anger rose within him. He kissed her just to show himself that she belonged to him, he put his hands on her just to show that every part of her belonged to him, every firm, sweet part, and he got to hating everything that stood between them, especially his mother.

Lee didn't even know what he was doing. She just slept through it all, hiccupping gently now and then as Goosey intensified his caresses.

Finally he gave the driver the Vagabond Club address, and they reached the old brownstone house fifteen minutes later, with the hackie looking on as Goosey unlocked the door with one hand while supporting Lee with the other.

Goosey was sweating, and as he carried her through the dark, narrow room towards the couch in the back he kept trying to think up excuses to tell his mother.

He didn't put on the light but just laid her on the couch, wondering whether he had the nerve, staring down at her seductive outline in the gloom, breathing like he had run a hundred miles.

He slid to the floor beside her and trembled at the warmth of her, the smooth, silken warmth of her surged through his fingertips, as the angry, yet delicate search set his eardrums singing.

It would be all right. Because he wanted to marry her. Lee knew that he wanted to marry her. He didn't mean any harm. He just loved her, that's all. All these years he loved her, all through the painful years when she used to tease and taunt him, sending him scurrying to his room, excited beyond measure, laughing when he locked the door, as he hid in the farthest corner, gripped with bruising shame.

It was different now. The thought of her wouldn't send him to a corner because she was right here, under his hands. Oh, how he loved her! If he could only be sure that she wouldn't hate him for it later, that she would believe him when he explained that it was love that made him do it, and nothing else!

But he was afraid. It would be too terrible never to see her again, never to listen to her taunts, never to hold her like she let him do at times. She'd marry him. He just had to wait. He just had to grit his teeth and wait until she let him come to her of her own free will. It would be beautiful then, and not like this, like a crazy animal in the dark, forgetting everything but the fiery urge of the moment…

Goosey dragged himself to his feet and went into the little room a few feet away and closed the door.

When he came out he had a glass of water in his hands and seemed strangely calm. He switched on the light and covered Lee's knees with her skirt and sprinkled water on her upturned face.

She stirred, drawing up her legs and letting them down again, her lips parted in a long drawn sigh.

"Lee, are you all right? It's me, Goosey. How do you feel?"

The eyelids fluttered open and she looked at him. "I feel sick, Goosey. Lousy sick."

He helped her sit up and after she got over the dizziness he stood with her in the little room, both his arms around her waist, and, waited as she cleared her stomach.

He wondered as he helped her back to the couch if she knew what he had been doing, what he had been thinking, as she lay helpless under his hands.

Lee answered him as if she had read his mind. "You had yourself a good time, didn't you?" Her smile took the sting out of her words. "I wasn't out cold, Goosey. Not all the way. I know what you were doing."

Goosey started to stammer. "Lee, I—"

"Forget it. Maybe I don't deserve better."

"No! It ain't true! Not about you, Lee! You never let anybody—"

"Maybe I would have let you," she said slyly, "if you would have kept trying. You missed your chance, Goosey."

"Lee, don't talk like that! You know you don't mean it. You're teasin' me again, like you always did. Please, Lee, don't say no more!"

She laughed. It was only a whisper, but it frightened him. "Let's stay a while, Goosey. Kiss me."

"No! I'm takin' you right home! This minute!"

Lee wasn't thinking of Goosey. She was thinking of Ricco. She knew now why she had kept after him, why she wanted to see him. It was crazy. Somewhere she had read that it happened to many people. She hadn't believed it then, but now she did.

Ricco.

All the while Goosey was doing things to her she was pretending it was Ricco. It was easy, lying there in the dark, making out Goosey was Ricco, burning up inside as she waited, burning up and knowing all the time that it wasn't the same as if Ricco was with her. Because Ricco was a man, because there was something about him that Goosey didn't have. Someday she would get to Ricco, and make him get on his knees to her. Someday—

"Come on, Lee. We better be gettin' home."

She let Goosey take her out again and after a long wait they got another cab.

They thought they were in luck when they let themselves into the flat. The place was dark and silent, but when she went to her room Mrs. Mullins was there, waiting for her and Goosey.

After the wild scene that followed she made up her mind that she had had enough. She had to figure out a way to get more money, or a better job. She couldn't take it anymore. Besides, she was getting too careless with Goosey. Suppose she would have let him? Then what?

She fell asleep towards morning and dreamt that Ricco showered her with jewels, that she let him see her and he went mad with desire, taking her on a bed of pearls and diamonds, with Goosey standing by talking about the moon she was wearing for an earring and how dirty her hands were from digging in the gutter.

CHAPTER FIVE

SHE OPENED her first pay envelope in the comfort room and counted the soiled bills and the handful of change with a disgust that was there for everyone to see. Her back ached from the long hours on her feet and her fingers had taken on a funny color from handling the nylon. Lee muttered under her breath and spilled the money back into the envelope. "Peanuts!" she said. "Six days a week on my feet for this!"

The girl leaning on the wall nearby took the cigarette from between carmined lips and laughed. "The first hundred years are the hardest. You'll get used to it."

"Like hell I will! I'm going in to see Mangum now, and ask for more…"

"Don't be a dope."

Lee glared at the small girl in the loose, shapeless dress but didn't bother to answer.

"You look wonderful in that tight sweater," the girl said. "I like for the boys to whistle after me too, but not at the expense of my bank account." She laughed. "Look, I'm pretty well-built too, for a half-pint." She pulled the dress tight against her bosom. "See? But there's a time and a place for everything."

The sullen look remained on Lee's face. "You been talking crazy all week. Why don't you come out and say what you mean? Maybe I'll ask to be put at another table, just to get away from your senseless jabbering."

The cigarette hung down from her lower lip unsupported, as the girl studied Lee, squinting through the coiling smoke. "I been tryin' to make sense, but you're too stuck-up to listen. You don't like none of us and we don't like you, so the feelin' is mutual.

Maybe if you were nicer to me you wouldn't have to worry about workin' for peanuts, but I ain't runnin' after nobody to make friends." She turned away and flipped her cigarette into the washbasin.

Lee didn't move.

The girl faced her again, smiling. "I see you're interested."

"Who isn't interested in making an extra buck?"

The short girl darted a glance at the door and stepped close. "I wouldn't say nothin', only I hate that Mangum's guts so much! He suspects what I'm doin', but he can't touch me. He knows if he opens his yap I'll start talkin' about the night I stayed over in his office." The knowing eyes took in Lee's figure, slowly. "I don't know why he hasn't tried it with you yet, with what you got."

"He knows better than to start up with me."

The small girl shrugged. "He'll get to the point soon enough." The direction of her glance set Lee's ears burning. "But now you're gettin' mad and I don't want you to get mad—not at me, anyway. Look," she said, "let me show you something." And she stepped back and lifted her dress. Beyond her knees, and higher.

"All you need is a little cellophane tape to fasten them to your skin," the girl said. "I carry a hand roll in the pocket of my dress. I got a guy who'll buy as many as I can get. I'll send you to him if you want."

Lee stared at the nylons neatly dangling from the rounded thighs.

"I got more around my waist," the girl said. "That's why I don't wear skin-tight sweaters on the job. Understand?" The dress fell back into place. "Still interested?"

"Sure. But how—"

"I'll learn you how. Only we got to make a deal. I get part of what you sell. Now, don't start complainin' already! You'll drag enough out of this place to almost double your salary. Ain't that fair enough?"

"I—don't know. I never stole before. I—"

"You'll get used to the idea. And like it. Especially when you see your pocketbook bulgin' with the green stuff."

The two girls at the far end of the room who had been silently watching sauntered over and joined in the discussion. Lee edged away warily.

"This is big-time stuff," one of them said, "a real organization. You don't have to be afraid. You'll get protection."

"I don't like the idea of stealing."

The small girl grinned. "Who does? But you got to make a decent livin' some way."

Lee took in the three watchful faces and said nothing.

The third girl spoke with an accent like the rest of them in the shop, with the exception of the two standing near her. She pointed at the small one and said, "With her it is more personal. Mangum made a promise and didn't pay off. But with the rest it is pure business—like it can be with you. Once in a while the little pig calls us in and makes us lift our dresses, but we get to know pretty good when he has something like that on his mind, so we are careful. But with you it would be different. He would be afraid to put the make on you, and you could take out a lot every day. Then we would all get a bigger cut."

"I don't like the sound of it. If I work, I work alone, for myself."

"Not in this place, you don't."

Lee shrugged. "Then maybe we all ought to forget it."

The third girl stepped close. "If you go to the little pig with this—"

"I'm not a fool. Let go of my arm."

The others moved in threateningly. The small girl whom Lee knew only as Madge came up with a sharpened knitting needle. "Think it over. Real careful. We been waitin' for someone like you to come along. Someone sent straight from the top. Mangum won't even fire us like he used to. He'll be too scared."

And then it dawned on Lee, as she stood there, reading the hard faces, that she was on to something big, something terribly important. *Someone sent straight from the top.* Could it be what she thought it meant? Could it—

"You can give us your answer Monday," Madge said. "No hurry. Only the answer got to be right."

Lee made up her mind then and there but she didn't let on to it. She spent the weekend by herself, thinking of Ricco and hating him for having such a low opinion of her. He knew her better than she knew herself, and that's why it hurt. It was as if he had turned her inside out and knew every little thing about her, the things she would do and the things she wouldn't. He was so sure of what she was like that he hadn't even bothered to tell her why he had sent her to Mangum. He thought of her as being a susceptible, greedy girl who could be lured or pushed into doing anything he wanted.

But now that she knew about him, the shoe was on the other foot. She'd show him. She'd make trouble. She'd go to him after she joined up and lift her dress right in front of him and show him the nylons fastened to her skin with cellophane tape. And then she'd tell him what she found out and force him to cut her in.

He would respect her then, and not take her for a hotheaded little fool anymore. Maybe he wouldn't be so hard to convince when he saw that she had a brain of her own, and could use it. Maybe it would be different between them, and he would treat her like she wanted him to, not like jail-bait, but as a woman who knew what she wanted.

She told the girls of her decision during the Monday lunch hour, and before the day was over she was learning how to shuffle the full boxes with the empties and mark them with her fingernails. Then there was the switching of the damaged singles and the trip to the stockroom with the pile of discards and the taping of the odds to her legs, always making certain of the replacements so that the stock count came out right, that the empty boxes now holding the discards could be counted over and over again without detection.

They agreed on a place to meet and Madge took the nylons from her and brought in the money the next day. "All of the dough is yours for the first couple of weeks just to show that we ain't pigs," she said. "After you get to know the racket better and can be trusted you'll take your regular turn at deliverin' the stuff and collectin', but right now you're on probation."

Lee was anxious to find out who the go-between was but she kept her mouth shut and played along with the gang. For the first few nights she couldn't sleep, worrying about the risk, but after the third week, with Mangum acting as if she didn't exist, she fell into the routine and thought nothing of it.

She soon found out that Madge was playing a double game, selling on the side to a private dealer, the man she had inadvertently mentioned to Lee the first day she had put the question to her. It was just the information Lee was looking for, and she used it to force Madge to turn over the next delivery and collection to her.

If she could connect this man with Ricco—if she could learn enough about the operation so she could back up her words with evidence, then—

"You ask too many questions," the bald man said, sorting the nylons into sizes.

It was quiet in the warehouse, except for the lapping of the river close by. Lee studied him intently. He had a bony face that looked as if it never got washed and his eyes were big and sunk deep in his skull. They had the dull opaque look of the dead and remained unnervingly still.

"I was just curious," Lee said, forcing a smile. "I was just thinking that maybe someday I'll be buying a pair of these over the counter somewhere, paying good money for—"

"You won't buy these in this town, sister. Does that satisfy you? Or would you like to know more?"

He put through a phone call after she left and the man at the other end just laughed and said that he would take care of it.

Four days later, the night she was going to tell Goosey's mother that she was leaving, Mangum called her into his office and asked her to lift her dress.

Lee refused. She went cold with fright but put up a bold front, pretending to be shocked at his suggestion.

"You can do it before witnesses, or just for me," the small man said. "How would you rather have it?"

Her lips were like a burning scar across the white of her face. "And if I refuse to do it at all?"

He leaned on the desktop with his knuckles, and said, "Then I'll have to call the police and have you searched."

Lee didn't say anything. Her stomach had turned upside-down and the pain made her knees tremble. What now? What was she going to do now?

Mangum walked around to the front of the desk and sat against it, his little eyes at once mocking and determined. He rubbed his palms together, and said, "If you like the job well enough to stay on, I won't fire you. I know you're not the only girl who steals from me. I could ask you to name them but I won't. I'm insured against theft and the insurance company's been pretty agreeable about my claims." His thin lips quivered strangely. "Maybe the time has come for me to give you a better paying job. Would you like that, Lee?"

"You're—you're trying to blackmail me."

"Yes, in a way I am."

"What do you want me to do?"

He looked at her legs and said, "I want you to be willing."

"I'd rather go to jail!"

He smiled. "I don't think so, Lee. Am I really so repulsive to you?"

Instinctively she took a backward step. Mangum held up his hand. "Don't try to run away. You'll get caught and then everybody will know about it. Think of the disgrace."

"Somebody tipped you off!" she cried. "Somebody—"

"You gave yourself away," he said quietly. "You shouldn't have stopped wearing those nice, tight sweaters." He moved forward.

"If you touch me," she cried desperately, "I'll—I'll go to Ricco, I'll—"

"He won't do anything to help you. He doesn't care what happens to you. That's why he sent you to work for me. Because you were a nuisance to him."

Fear gave way to rage. An ugly word exploded past her lips.

"That's just the way I feel about him too," Mangum confessed. "But let's not lose sight of your reason for being here. I have an alternate proposition to make. Do you care to listen?"

"What else can I do?"

"Of course." He rubbed his palms together again. "I have a small dressing room behind my office," he said. "You may go back there and get rid of the evidence if you want. When you come back here I'll tell you the rest of it."

"Tell me the rest of it now."

"I suppose it would simplify matters." He paused. "I am a collector of photographs, Lee. Since you are unwilling—to be willing, so to speak—all you have to do to walk out of this office a free woman, is to—"

Lee shouted. "No! You filthy little swine! Don't you dare say another word!"

He regarded her calmly. "You're very hard to please, aren't you? I'm afraid I'll have to call the police after all."

Lee intercepted his hand as he reached for the buzzer.

He was surprisingly strong for his size and twisted her arm behind her, forcing her against the desk. "Don't be a little fool!" he grated. "Be reasonable and you won't get hurt..."

But the pain was too much and she cried out.

He stopped the sound with a kiss, digging his bony frame to hers.

She felt the tape pull off her leg as his hand moved, and the sound of his laughter rasped against her ear. "The evidence, Lee!" he said, and laughed again.

He kissed her only once. He asked if she would like to change her mind and when she said yes, he let her go. But it was a mistake; because Lee shoved him with all the strength she had in her, and he seemed to cartwheel over the chair and crash to the floor, his head making a dull sound on the rug as it struck.

He made no attempt to get up and Lee ran out and hurried to the flat for Goosey's help.

Mrs. Mullins was out shopping and Goosey was in the tub reading a comic book when she got there, and she got him to rush out, dripping wet, and sobbingly told him about Mangum and the stolen nylons.

Goosey groaned. His robe was soaked through and stuck to his skin like cold glue, but all he was conscious of was Lee shivering in his arms, pleading with him to understand, to help her.

"Cripes!" he cried, "but this washes us up for sure! If Mom ever finds out what you done—"

"You got to stick by me, Goosey! I just won't go back anymore. Mangum can't prove anything now. If I run away now it'll look real bad."

"Yeah," Goosey said. "Yeah." He couldn't think of anything else to say.

"If anyone comes around to ask questions you'll tell them I quit because I got sick. No matter what Mangum says, he's got no proof—"

"Yeah, yeah. He got no proof." And then the painful words came out of him, twisting from his lips as if it burned his tongue to say them. "But—why did you have to steal, Lee? What made you want to steal?"

"It's your mother's fault," she cried. "It's all your mother's fault! She drove me crazy with her nagging, and I needed money to move away. That's why I did it, Goosey. That's why I did it!"

"Jeez! But to get into trouble over something like that. You should of asked me first, Lee. What's the good of gettin' into trouble for something so unimportant? I just don't know what to say to you, Lee." He put his cheek to her hair and held her close. "You can't be sure that Mangum won't send the cops anyway. We can't afford to take that chance. How—much dough did you save out of it, from the sales?"

"Everything I had is in my locker—in Mangum's place."

Goosey groaned again. "You'll never explain how you got all that money. Just when you need it now, too! Maybe we should ask Ricco what to do. He knows all the angles. Maybe—"

"No! To hell with him! Leave Ricco out of this, Goosey. I wouldn't go to him now if the cops were beating down the door this minute!"

Goosey got mad, and shook her. "But what are you goin' to do for, dough? How the hell are you goin' to get another job? I ain't got enough to help you, not that much—"

She broke away, full of scorn and full of anger. "I should of known better than to depend on you! All the time I knew what you were like! But I just kept kidding myself—"

"No, Lee! Don't say that! I'll help you! You know I'll help you!"

"Then think of something, and just don't stand there shaking, your head!"

The seconds passed as Goosey tried to think. As Lee was about to speak, he said, "I got it! The Vagabond Club! You can stay there, Lee, until we figure out a way— There's absolutely nothing else you can do."

"No."

"You got to, Lee! Nobody'll think of lookin' for you there! You'll be safe. I promise. I'll sneak your stuff back to you little by little—"

"It's crazy! I don't like it at all!"

Someone knocked on the door and they both jumped. Lee fled into the bedroom.

Goosey walked across the floor slowly, wondering what he was going to say if the caller turned out to be a policeman. He stopped, took a deep breath, and reached for the knob.

The little man on the other side looked up at Goosey and said, "I'd like to speak to Lee Sissle. I believe she lives here."

"You believe wrong, mister. Nobody by that name lives here."

"But—"

"You heard what I said, mister. Beat it!"

Goosey slammed the door shut.

Lee came out of the bedroom, her face paler than before.

"It was Mangum, wasn't it?" Goosey asked, and Lee said, "Yes."

"You better do like I said then, Lee. Go to the club and I'll meet you there later. He might come back with a cop the next time."

All her courage seemed to dribble away as she stood there, nodding dully. "All right, Goosey," she said. "I'll—go."

CHAPTER SIX

THE ROOM with the couch in it had a lock on the door and for that Lee was thankful. She felt terribly alone after Goosey left, sitting in the semi-gloom wondering where it was all going to end. Maybe they should have gone to Ricco, like he suggested, but when she thought of the way he had used her, anger flared and she vowed never to beg him, no matter what. She would rather die than to have him lord it over her, to sneer and treat her like she belonged in an institution.

She got up, feeling beaten and tired, and peered through the unwashed windows facing the littered backyard. It was just getting dark and the little bit of green that showed in a square patch surrounding the leafless tree fought off the encroaching gloom with a brightness that was not lost upon her. It seemed such a hopeless struggle, fighting the cement and the grime and the uncaring neglect, but the will to go on remained, and the scrubby patch refused to admit defeat.

"Just like me," Lee thought, and smiled wanly at the comparison.

From somewhere close by came the mewing of a cat, and Lee turned to see two gleaming eyes watching her from the doorway.

"Now how did you get in here?" she asked aloud, but the cat just mewed again and padded toward her, friendly and trustful.

It wasn't an ordinary cat, Lee saw as it sat at her feet, looking up. It had a long, gleaming coat and a thick, fluffy tail, its neck encircled with a neat leather collar.

Lee frowned. She could have sworn that the cat hadn't been around at the time of their arrival. She had gone through every room with Goosey. There hadn't been the slightest sign of life. And now, here was the cat, coming out of nowhere.

Lee stepped through the door and the cat followed her, still mewing. She turned on the light in the long, narrow clubroom and walked to the front windows to see if they were closed. They were. The front door was closed, too.

The ventilator high in the wall of the unused kitchen was shut tight. And so was the barred window of the bathroom.

"Hello," a voice said. "You're new here, aren't you?"

Lee's heart jumped to her throat. She swung around, frightened stiff.

A little old lady, dressed in flowing muslin, was smiling at her not more than a foot away. She had the cat in her arms, and was stroking it gently.

"I was upstairs at my window and I saw Goosey bring you in," she said. "You're not a bad girl, are you? Not the kind who stays with boys?" The china-blue eyes, young eyes in a parchment-old face, stabbed at Lee with piercing intelligence. "You don't mind my asking? I really must know these things. You see, I own this old house. My name is Julia Brink."

Lee stared, confused beyond thinking.

"I'm afraid I've frightened you, haven't I, dear?" And the thin, pale lips turned upward in an apologetic smile.

"How did you get in here?" Lee asked.

The bright eyes twinkled. "But that's my little secret. Won't you make yourself more comfortable? Let's sit down, shall we?" And she walked out, quite sure that Lee would follow.

She found a chair by the wall of the clubroom and sat in it. "You're a very pretty girl," the old lady said. "Where do you live?"

Lee finally found voice. "Here," she said, "temporarily."

The thin, translucent hand toyed with the locket suspended from a velvet ribbon. "You're in trouble, aren't you?"

Lee didn't answer.

"Please don't be afraid to tell me. I'll help you if I can."

"It's not what you think," Lee said.

Julia Brink sat back, stroking the cat. She looked relieved. "Then it must have something to do with stealing."

"It has. But I don't see why I have to tell you!" Lee was herself again, hard and suspicious.

"I really don't want to know anymore. I was just thinking of the effect you'd have on the boys. You'll try to behave, won't you?"

Lee entwined her fingers painfully, and said, "You better stop talking like that!"

The little old lady got up, smoothing the black muslin with her free hand. The faint smile remained on her lips, secretive, infuriating. "You must come up and visit me sometime," she said. "Whenever you can spare a few minutes. I promise not to get nosey." She laughed. It had a pleasant, tinkling sound. "Not too nosey, that is."

She started away, her feet barely visible under the long folds of the dress. She seemed to glide along, noiselessly, like an automaton on a wire.

She turned before going through the door and gave the bewildered girl a bright, friendly smile. "Goodnight, dear," she said, and went out.

Lee decided to follow. When she ran into the hall Julia Brink no longer was visible. Lee ran up the stairs leading from the entrance to the ground floor. The door was locked. And in the faint glimmer of light seeping upward from the clubroom she saw the large nail-heads that fastened the frame to the jamb.

In the musty darkness under the staircase she found another door, letting down into the cellar. It was open.

She stared into the pitch-black well, listening.

Nothing. Not a sound emanated from the darkness below.

She closed the door and returned to the friendly brightness of the clubroom, wondering why Goosey hadn't told her about the old lady. But to hell with it. She had other problems to solve. There was no sense in letting it bother her.

She was on her way back to the room Goosey said would be hers, when she heard the front gate open and quick footsteps pass in front of the windows. Lee was facing the door when the boy came in.

He stopped when he saw her. He was tall, dressed in a lumber jacket and dungarees, with short brown hair and a hungry face. "Look," he said, as if speaking to himself, "we got company! Who let you in, baby?"

She folded her arms over the shapeless bodice of the dress and sauntered over. "Goosey let me in," she said. "He told me I could join. Who are you?"

"A dame join the Vagabonds? Are you kiddin'?"

"I just saw Julia Brink. She didn't think I was kidding."

The supercilious smile froze on his face. "You—a friend of hers?"

"I'm here, ain't I?"

The boy took off his jacket and flung it across the room. It landed on a chair. "It sounds screwy to me," he said. "The only time we let dames in here is when we—"

"Is when you what...?"

"Well—when we have blow-outs—and things." He narrowed his eyes. "You sure Goosey said you could join us? He ain't got much to say around here, you know."

"Who has?"

"Me. I'm the leader of this club." He walked into the room, taking a cigarette from an open pack in his shirt pocket, and lit it without offering Lee one. "Goosey's got his nerve," he said, "bringin' you here without tellin' us."

"It was an emergency," Lee said. "He told me you were regular guys. Otherwise I wouldn't have—"

"We're regular, all right. But dames make trouble. That's why we made the rule. Maybe you'd be smart if you listened to me instead of Goosey and scram out of here."

"Let him tell me." She held out her hand and reluctantly he gave her a cigarette. She lit it and said, "You don't think I like the idea of staying, do you?"

"You're goin' to have a hell of a time convincin' the others, sister."

"Maybe I won't have to. If you're the leader, like you say." She stepped close, and blew smoke in his face.

She put her hand on his arm and he flung it off. "Don't do me no favors!" He turned away from her, leaning on the old-fashioned mantel.

"Maybe you don't like the way I dress," Lee said. She opened the zipper at the bodice as he gaped, and slipped the dress over her head. Underneath she was wearing the familiar sweater and skirt. She laughed when she saw the expression on his face. "Like me better now?" she asked.

He shook his head, forcing a smile as his eyes went over her. "I got to hand it to you," he said. "You're miles ahead of me."

"Like me better?" she persisted. "I won't be any trouble to anybody. Especially to you. What's your name?" She was close again.

"Slip it to me easy, kid. What kind of a jerk do you take me for? My name ain't Goosey."

"I'm only trying to be friendly. I got to be. Because I want you to be on my side."

"Don't I know it? But if you're Goosey's dame you know I can't touch you. So don't play up to me."

Lee suppressed her anger and flounced away. "It looks like I'm wasting my time on you."

"You are." He went after her as she started towards the back. "Where do you think you're goin'?"

"To my room."

"To your *room?*"

She turned and faced him. "Yeah. And if you make a move to stop me I'll see you get a taste of real trouble! Goosey believes every lie I tell him! And I can lie real nasty if I have to..."

He folded his arms to his chest and said, as if to himself, "Well, I'll be a—"

Lee cut him short with a laugh. "Think it over," she said. "I'm in a tough spot but so are you. Be nice to me and we'll get along."

She walked away from him, conscious of his eyes on her back. Her nerves were on edge and at any moment she expected to feel his hands on her, to get the full blast of his words.

But nothing happened. He let her go to the room. She locked the door and after a second of dazed silence she fell upon the couch, trembling, and pressed her hands to her face.

She felt awful. Every bone in her body ached, every muscle. How long could she go on taking it, putting up a tough front when all the while she was like jelly inside, sick with worry and fear?

No money, no home, no friends; not anyone she could really depend on, that is. Mangum had already told the police; she was sure of it. Only his fear of Ricco would keep him from telling. But there was no sense in going to pieces. She had to face the truth, make the best of it. She was a thief now and nothing could change that fact. All the excuses in the world weren't strong enough. She was just no good.

If Ricco showed up this minute and offered to help her she wouldn't even think of turning him down. No matter what he asked. That was the lousy part of it. She would be willing to give without his asking. She had thrown herself at him because he was powerful and rich and could give her the riches and pleasures she always dreamt of having. Getting money the easy way, deliberately making it tough for her father and his mistresses had warped her beyond repair. Even Goosey was too good for her.

But it went deeper than that. Much deeper. Beyond the fault of her laziness, her acceptance of stealing as a solution to her problems. She thought of the blonde waitress and her father, how the image had changed after she had seen Ricco.

The hard springs of the leather couch pressed against her, and she lay there, fighting down the ever-recurring image, the bursting urgency that was more overwhelming than her fear. She knew what lay behind it all, but she was afraid...

Afraid, ever since the night she had lain here, on this very same couch, accepting Goosey's caresses, pretending he was Ricco, eager and dizzy with drink, aware of the burning response, the sudden need that gripped her with tantalizing fingers of compulsion. It had been close. Too close. She didn't want it to be Goosey. But it almost didn't matter.

When she had gotten home it was the same. She hadn't slept that night. And all the while, as she had lain in the warm bed, it was Goosey's image that impinged on Ricco's, and the faces of other boys she had grown up with. That night had been terrible and wonderful at the same time. Maybe it was the drink that had kept her dreaming, and wanting. But the sheer intensity had never been there before the undeniable longing. It was like she had become a woman overnight, within a few short hours.

It was surprising how it made her forget everything else—Mrs. Mullins' nagging, the shock of her father's flight. Even the hateful realization of having to go to work the next day.

She wanted to be loved, taken care of, and here she was, pursued by her sins, fighting alone in a world full of strangers. What kind of help could she expect, with everyone suspicious of the other, each looking after his own skin?

The Vagabonds would wander in, and soon she would hear the knock on the door, and step out into a circle of hostile faces. Goosey would be there to help her, but could he? Maybe if she went back to Mangum and threw herself on his mercy—

She heard voices near the door, and sat up.

One voice was loud and shrill. A woman's voice, familiar and edged with toughness. Lee started, unable to believe her ears.

The boy shouted back, and then the tough voice said, "I know she's here. Because the boss was told. And if you don't open up and let me speak to her he'll come here and tear the place apart!"

"All right," came the sullen reply. "I knew there would be trouble as soon as I saw her here. Dames!" he cried, and Lee could hear his angry, receding footsteps.

Someone tried the knob and then the tough voice said, "Open up, Lee, I got to talk to you. It's important."

When Lee opened the door the woman stepped in and closed it slowly behind her.

It was Madge, and she looked deadly serious.

CHAPTER SEVEN

"IT'S JUST the break he's been lookin' for," Madge ended, looking across the couch at Lee. "If everything works out all right, Goosey'll get a nice fat raise, and maybe promoted to collector. And you—"

"No! To hell with him! Let him clean his own dirty wash!" Lee could hardly contain herself. She got up, glaring at the compact girl, dark eyes burning with anger. "The whole thing looks like a frame-up to me!" An accusing finger stabbed through the gloom. "You're in on it too, aren't you, showing me how I could steal nylons so I would be caught! Maybe Goosey is too dumb to see what's going on, but I'm not!"

Madge sat back, unperturbed. "You talk too much. If you know what's good for you you'll keep quiet and listen to what I have to tell you."

"Sure, and get in deeper! Mangum was in on it too, wasn't he? Making that phony proposition to scare me away. And then coming around to the flat, to make sure that I listened to Goosey."

"You're talkin' crazy. It's just the way things broke, like I told you."

"Yeah, just the way things broke," Lee sneered. "A couple of hours after I find a hideout he sends you right to me, with a plan all worked out. But I'm not going to stooge for him, no matter what he threatens! I don't have to stay here! I don't have to—"

"If you don't do like he says, Lee, he'll have you picked up and booked." Madge got up. "Think it over." She smoothed her hair.

"I don't have to think. I made up my mind already. Now, get out!"

The small girl shrugged. "It's your funeral…"

"Let him come and tell me himself, if it's so important!"

"Maybe he will. But I'm bettin' that he won't waste his time on you. You're a fool, Lee. This is the chance you've been lookin' for. The chance to get in solid with him." She saw the sobering light creep into Lee's dark eyes, and smiled inwardly. "Frame or no frame, Lee, it might be worth havin' him, even on his own terms."

But the anger came back again, overcoming the fear. "No. I don't mean a thing to him that way. He made it clear enough at the beginning. That's just what I'll never forget!"

Madge got up. "Some guys take a lot of breakin' down. You got what it takes. You just have to keep tryin', that's all."

"And all the while he'll keep using me, getting what he wants, and after I can't help him anymore he'll be figuring other angles, getting other dames. I'm not going to spy on the old lady, and you can tell him that for me! If he thinks she's got something that he'd like to have, let him go up there and take it away from her, but he's not going to make me the sucker again!"

"I hope you change your mind, for your own sake. Nobody ever said no to him and got away with it."

"Then maybe I'll be the first one."

"Maybe…"

Lee went to the door and opened it. The tall boy was right outside, listening.

Madge saw him and laughed, brushing past with a provocative sweep of her shoulders. "I hope you heard everything," she said. "It'll give you an idea what to do with this dame."

"I knew what I was goin' to do the minute I found her waitin' here."

Madge fluffed her hair, the hard smile on her face. "As long as she ain't goin' to be of any use to the boss, it don't matter what happens to her."

The boy flexed the fingers of his hands, watching Lee intently. "Me and you both got the same ideas," he said to Madge. "If she don't understand English, maybe she understands this…" And he reached out suddenly, giving Lee a violent shove.

Madge sauntered away, laughing soundlessly. She turned and looked back as she came to the door, and saw that the boy had Lee pinned against the wall. "I didn't see a thing," she cried. "That's goin' to be my story. But be careful, Lee. Don't do anything I wouldn't do!" And she went out, the meaning of her words hanging in the air like dirty smoke.

"I'm askin' you for the last time," the boy warned Lee. "Are you gettin' out, or aren't you?"

He was very close to her, with his face only inches from hers. Lee could feel his breath on her cheek. "I'm waiting for Goosey," she said. "He brought me here and I won't leave unless he tells me to."

"That's what you think." He shoved her again and she staggered back into the little room. When she saw him close the door and lock it, her heart leaped to her throat.

"Stay away from me! If you try to touch me, I'll—"

"Goosey's had this comin' to him for a long time," the boy sneered. "Maybe this'll show him not to go big-dealin' all over the place…"

Lee shrank away, looking about wildly for an available weapon.

"Don't fight back and you won't get hurt," he cried, and lunged.

She tried to evade him but there was no room to move, and she found herself sprawling on the couch, with the boy over her.

She turned her head as he tried to kiss her and his lips found her ear. She jerked up suddenly and butted him under the jaw. He cried out and fell to the floor.

Lee staggered to her feet but he wrapped his arms about her and the force of his grip caused her to sag into him. He pushed her back so that she was half on the couch and half off, freeing one hand to caress her as she arched to keep her balance.

Lee dug her fingers into his hair, gasping, knees trembling as she strained to keep him from her. But it was no use. He was much too strong for her. Her resistance collapsed and she fell back violently, striking her head against the wooden frame of the couch.

Everything went black.

She was conscious of his every move, but Lee couldn't fight back.

She seemed to be paralyzed, filled with a throbbing pain that started in the base of her skull and fanned out through every nerve in her body.

"Please don't!" she whispered, "Please…don't…"

The boy looked down at her, hesitating. He swung her back onto the couch, panting, dizzy with exertion. A faint trickle of blood ran down his left temple, where her nails had found their mark. He put his fingers to it and when he saw the crimson smudge rage flared and he struck at her. "You lousy little tramp!" he cried, "I'll teach you to scratch me…"

Weakly she protested his violence, but he was beyond listening or reasoning. His fingers caught at her throat, holding her still as his lips found hers. Then, with deliberation born of spite and desire, he caressed her. "You lousy little tramp," he said again, and Lee seemed to shrivel at his touch.

There was silence in the room, except for his heavy breathing, and the soft rustle of his movements.

Lee, senses spinning through the swirling darkness, felt the warm air on her skin, the harsh pressure of his fingers. And then his lips.

"No," she breathed, "no…" But there was no strength in her, and she lay back, helpless with terror.

"You little…tramp…" she heard him say over and over. "You…little…tramp…"

And then the warm, heavy air seemed to creep up on her, and she struggled vainly, in her mind, to fight the knowledge of what was happening to her.

It wasn't right that it should happen this way. Not after all the dreams, the sweet fears that had held her back for so long…

His lips…and his hands… What could she do to stop him? If only she could strike back. Strike back, and squirm away… But his hands pinned her down, and his lips…

And then, as the soggy darkness enveloped her, there was something else…

The fevered touch burned through her like a flash fire, clearing her brain with the explosive knowledge of his transgression. A scream tore from her throat and she shoved him. The boy cried out and fell to the floor, writhing.

Quickly, as the room seemed to spin and rock about her, Lee stepped over him and made for the door, turning the key in the lock just as he pulled himself to his feet.

He staggered after her, his face white with pain, his hands clawing the air between them. He threw himself at her, but she stepped aside and he crashed into the door.

As he fell back, cursing, the door was flung open and Goosey rushed in. He saw Lee's torn sweater, the look of terror on her face.

"Goosey...Goosey!" she cried, but he pushed her away and swung at the swaying boy, hitting him flush on the jaw.

The lean form seemed to fly through the air, landing face down on the couch. Goosey grabbed him by the collar and hauled him to his feet, striking again and again.

Lee tried to stop him, but she couldn't.

Someone shouted from the far end of the clubroom, and a moment later the place was an uproar of voices and stampeding feet. Three boys surged in and grappled with Goosey, and the tiny room was a mass of flailing arms and clashing bodies.

It was like an eternity of horror to Lee, but the fight lasted only a few seconds. Two of the boys held Goosey to the couch while the third supported her battered assailant.

"All right," the third boy panted, "let's have it. What started all this?" He was looking at Lee.

She didn't answer at first. She stared at his ugly, pockmarked face, at the cruel line of his jaw. His shoe-button eyes burned into hers with venomous intensity. "Well?" he demanded. "What are you waitin' for?"

Lee supported herself against the wall, breathing brokenly. Then she said, pointing an accusing finger, "He—tried to attack me. I—came here to wait for Goosey. He wanted me to go, but I wouldn't. Then he pushed me into this room and—"

Goosey sprang to his feet, dragging the two boys with him. His homely, good-natured face was congested with rage. "I'll kill him!" he cried. "The lousy son-of-a—"

His arm was wrenched and he broke off, gasping. He sat down again, held by the two boys.

"Get out of my way, Brambles." The leader of the Vagabonds, his face cut and swollen, pushed the pock-marked one aside and stood over Goosey. He grabbed his hair and bent his head back. "I guess you know what this means, Goosey! I could make this a fight just between you and me, but I ain't goin' to! We'll let the gang handle it, the right way! Before we get through with you, you'll wish you never were born!"

Goosey tried to break away again, glaring up defiantly. "You ain't makin' no kangaroo out of me! This ain't got nothin' to do with the gang! If you weren't a yellow-belly you'd step out in the back yard with me and settle it right now!"

Brambles came over and looked down at him. "Lefty is our leader," he said, "and you went against his orders. No dames. That's our rule and you know it." He turned to Lee, who was standing against the wall, watching fearfully. "You were lucky," he said. "If it was me that found you instead of Lefty here, you wouldn't be standin' there now, lookin' like nothin' happened." He leered then, his shoe-button eyes caressing every provocative curve. "Maybe we should try her instead of Goosey," he said. "It would be a lot more fun givin' her the works." And he laughed. "How about that, Lefty?"

Goosey forced himself half way up by sheer bull strength, freeing one arm and lunging at Brambles. Lefty hit him in the face and he fell back, pulling the others with him. "Sit down, you lousy punk! We'll fix you quick enough!"

Lee stepped out and tried to help him. It was a mistake.

Lefty grabbed her, shamelessly, laughing as she struggled to unclamp his hand. "We'll fix him first and then fix you!" he cried. "You ain't foolin' with kids! We'll show you! The both of you!"

Brambles glanced through the door as the sound of voices reached them. "It's Ribs and Pinky," he reported.

"Keep them outside. But tell them what happened. Fix up the chairs so we can start the Kangaroo."

Brambles went out.

"When the other four come," Lefty said, still holding Lee, "you're goin' to see just how we fix punks like Goosey. He broke the rules, and we don't stand for that kind of stuff from nobody. Even me." He rubbed his jaw. "Besides, he slugged me. He's goin' to get something for that, too."

Lee was weak with fright. She didn't care how he was holding her now. It was all so fantastic, so unreal! The air seemed to be charged with madness.

She had heard about kangaroo courts. From some of the young toughs she knew, from reading about it in the papers. They might hurt Goosey bad. Cripple him maybe. They were crazy enough, and mean enough.

"Lefty," she said. Her voice came out thin and weak. "Don't hurt Goosey. Please! He didn't mean to hit you, he didn't—"

"Shut up, Lee!" It was Goosey speaking. "I'll have my say when they ask me! Don't butt in anymore! Don't make it worse for yourself!"

Lefty sneered. "Nothin' can help her now. Nothin'. She had her chance but she turned it down. It was her chance to make it good for all of us, but she wouldn't listen."

Goosey started. "What are you talkin' about? What—"

"Tell him, Lee," Lefty interjected. "Go on, tell him."

She squirmed out of his grasp and backed away. "No. No, I won't tell him."

"She says she was framed, Goosey. By the boss. With your help." He turned to her, smiling. "You'll change your mind about it when you see what happens to Goosey." He paused. "Unless you change it before."

"Maybe—Goosey wasn't in on it!" Lee cried. "But all the same I was framed! Goosey, you got to listen to me! Something happened while you were away! Something—"

"Shut up!" Lefty put his hand over her mouth. "He don't have to know about that! Not that part of it!" He fingered his jaw again, glaring. "No," he said slowly. "He don't have to know about that until after we fix him. Boss or no boss, he's got to be fixed!" He gestured to the boys who were holding Goosey. "Take him out. When the other guys come, call me."

Goosey started to say something but Lefty pushed his hand in his face and the other dragged him out. Lee made a break for it but she wasn't quick enough.

"You're stayin' in here with me," Lefty said. "Dames don't sit in on kangaroos."

Lee backed towards the window.

He followed her. "They won't need me either. Not right away. Not until they start to give him the punishment."

Lee had her back to the sill. She couldn't go any further.

"I'll—do as you say, Lefty! Only don't hurt Goosey! And don't hurt me…"

He was right in front of her now. "It's too late about Goosey. He's got it comin' to him. Even the boss would agree to that. But you—"

"Please, Lefty! Please don't touch me!"

He put his arms around her, laughing harshly. Lee went limp with fear. He pressed her against the sill. "Let Goosey sweat," he said. "Let him sweat a little before they beat the hell out of him!"

She couldn't stop him. He kissed her neck, wedging against her. "I got crazy before," he said. "I lost my head. But not this time, Lee. Not this time!"

He moved.

There was no use fighting him. Lee drew in her breath sharply, squeezing her eyes shut.

Lefty took his time. She knew what he was trying to do. It had happened to her before, with Goosey. Only with Goosey she hadn't been afraid, even in the dark hallway.

"Let him sweat!" Lefty grated again, and put his lips to hers.

But even as he trembled against her, as his breath whistled in his throat, as her awareness of him became acute, she sensed the fear in him, the fear that rose with his desire.

It wasn't like before, when rage had blunted his senses. Something was holding him back.

"Don't—be a fool, Lefty," she whispered. "I'm—not—worth it."

He didn't seem to hear.

From beyond the door came the sound of voices. Angry, accusing voices, with Goosey's frenzied pleading sandwiched in between.

Lee started to cry.

The voices grew louder, more abusive.

There was a heavy thud and Lee felt as if the room had collapsed about her. "No...no..." she whimpered. "Goosey...Goosey..."

"Shut up," Lefty grated "Shut up." His cheek was moist and felt wet against her skin.

He seemed to crouch for a minute, his head resting on her shoulder, shaking like a leaf. He dug his fingers into her arms, making little sounds. He started to talk to himself. "No..." he rasped. "No..." just as Lee had.

Someone knocked on the door and he choked back his breath, drawing away from her.

Lee opened her eyes.

Lefty looked haggard in the dim light.

"We're takin' Goosey with us," the voice said. "You'd better come along"

Lefty couldn't take his eyes off Lee. He backed towards the door, still in the grip of emotion. "All right," he said, "I'm comin'. I'm comin'." He wiped his face with his hands, and said, pointing to Lee. "You stay here. And keep your mouth shut. If you try to make trouble you'll get the same as Goosey."

He went out and locked the door behind him.

Lee sank to the couch, sick beyond words.

A faint mewing penetrated the stillness. Lee heard it but it didn't register. Not until she heard it again, when it seemed to be closer.

A cool draft eddied around her feet, and she sat up.

Looking at her, not two feet away, stood Julia Brink.

"You don't look very well," Julia Brink said. "Won't you come upstairs with me, and have a cup of tea?"

CHAPTER EIGHT

RICCO PEERED across the table at Lefty and said, "Tell me about it."

Lefty told him everything. His face was still puffed and sore from where Goosey had hit him. "You should of let me know about Lee," he said. "Until Madge showed up I thought Goosey was just a little screwy, bringin' Lee to the club. I'm afraid I scared hell out of her. He couldn't face Ricco's steady stare. "I—lost my head a little, I guess. I got so mad when she scratched me—"

"Forget it. Maybe it'll teach her a lesson." He sat back, bit off the end of a fresh cigar, and lit it. "How bad is Goosey hurt?"

"Enough to keep him in bed a couple of weeks."

Ricco's eyes narrowed. "I hope you jerks had sense enough not to overdo it."

"You don't have to worry, Mr. Ricco. Goosey will be all right."

"I hope so." He got up. "Don't forget that when I send Goosey back you should treat him right. He's got to remain a member of the Vagabonds so Lee won't get ideas of going elsewhere. She has nobody but Goosey now and I'm counting on her sticking close to him."

Lefty shifted uneasily. Ricco looked at him. "What's bothering you now?"

"The old lady," Lefty said. "If Lee tells her anything she might get mad enough to throw us out."

"She won't. Not if I know her, she won't. She wouldn't part with those fifty bucks a month if you put a gun to her head."

'I guess you're right."

"I know I am." Ricco threw a five dollar bill on the table to cover the drinks and said to Lefty, "Wait here for ten minutes until after I leave."

"Yes, Mr. Ricco."

"And another thing: Be careful of what you do to Lee." A hard smile came to his lips. "She's jail-bait and we'll all get into a jam if she starts lying about things. You had your little bit of fun. Now lay off her." He examined his cigar, decided against smoking it, and ground it into the plastic tray. He fastened his eyes on Lefty's face. "Don't ever feel sorry for her. And don't start thinking that she might be nice to you if you're nice to her. You don't need her. There are plenty of professionals around. Keep your mind on your work."

Lefty nodded silently, staring into his empty glass.

Ricco gave him a pat on the back and walked out.

Lefty waited until the ten minutes were up, zipped his lumber jacket, went to the restroom and left the *Golden Rooster* by the side entrance. He wondered how Ricco had guessed that he'd gone soft on Lee.

It was one o'clock in the morning, and Flatbush Avenue stretched into the darkness, a wide corridor of stone and silence. He started back for the club.

When he got there he found the back room empty, except for a big gray cat sleeping on the worn leather couch, purring contentedly.

The bag that Goosey had brought with Lee's things in it was standing on the floor between the windows, unopened. Lefty touched it with his fingers, went to the steampipe that ran up through the ceiling and put his ear to it. Voices. He could hear the sound of voices. So Lee was upstairs with the old lady. Talking.

He went back to the couch, pushed the cat to one side, and sat down. Before the night was over he would know whether Ricco had guessed right again, or not.

He sat there, fingering his aching face, and waited. Ricco had offered him ten to one that Lee would stay. That she would ask Julia Brink to help her. "Not with the idea of her doing what we asked her to," Ricco had said. "But she'll get around to it after a while."

Lefty had his doubts. But there was no sense in arguing with Ricco.

"The old lady might take a liking to her," Ricco had said. "And if I know Lee, she'll play up to her, cats and all, to make a place for herself there. With Goosey around she'll be satisfied for a while. We'll get to her. After she begins to hate the old lady's guts. Nobody can stand Julia Brink for long."

So here he was, waiting. Lee might not react as Ricco predicted, and it was his job to keep her there until she did.

Lefty yawned and stretched out, pushing the cat to the floor. He placed his hands behind his head and closed his eyes, thinking of how they had beaten Goosey. Funny, how good he felt after it was over. The relief he felt looking down at the battered form was almost the same as if he had gone the whole way, as if he hadn't held back with Lee. She had tied him up into knots until it seemed like he would explode. But now he was all right. All right, that is, until he started thinking about her. No...better to think of

Goosey, and how they beat him. Because if Lee came down alone later, there would be no telling what he'd do. And Ricco had warned him.

Lefty opened his eyes when his mind kept wandering back to Lee, and got up impatiently. The feel of Lee was on the couch, in every nook and cranny of the room. He went to the steampipe again and listened. The murmur of voices continued.

He walked away, jamming his hands into his pockets, wondering how women could talk so much.

But it wasn't a woman talking. In the stuffy, over-furnished confines of Julia Brink's back parlor a little man was pacing the floor, his opaque squirrel's eyes going from Lee to Julia and back again.

He moved circumspectly, carefully avoiding contact with the numerous cats lazing on the floor. He was a young man, in his late twenties. He had neat, brownish hair, cut short and parted on the side.

Lee watched him from her chair, the cup of tea gone cold in her lap. She felt as if she were living in a dream, that everything that had taken place since Mangum's discovery of the thefts was part of a mounting nightmare, that nothing was real. Soon she would wake up and find herself in the lumpy bed in Mrs. Mullins' flat, with the safe, familiar things around her...

The small-boned man with the sharply-chiseled features was all too real, however, as was his burning look of distrust. "You're taking advantage of Miss Brink," he said, halting in front of Lee. "You had no right in the first place to move in downstairs. You knew there would be trouble with the boys. You were looking to start it."

"That's not true. I had no place to go. I was broke. And I think you have a hell of a nerve busting in here like this, insulting me! Julia asked me to come up. I didn't force myself on her."

"The poor thing needed a cup of tea so badly," Julia said calmly. "The boys gave her a miserable time." She frowned at the angry man, and shook her head. "I always said that you had bad manners. Now sit down in that chair and behave like a gentleman." She turned to Lee as he sullenly complied. "You mustn't mind him too much. He always behaves badly.

Sometimes I wonder why I put up with him." She made a clacking noise with her tongue. "Even as a boy he was this way." She put down her cup and folded her arms over her withered bosom. "Sonny Pierson, Lee is waiting for your apology. And so am I."

"You can wait until you die," he said. "Can't you see what she is? How do you know she wasn't sent here to steal from you?"

Julia Brink drew herself erect. The brilliant blue eyes glittered frostily. "And just what have I got in this place that's worth stealing?"

Lee started to rise, but the old lady waved her back into the chair. A nondescript feline rubbed against Lee's nylons, begging to be petted. Sonny watched disdainfully as she put the cup aside and picked up the cat.

"Misery loves company, I see. Maybe I am mistaken about you, Lee. You could be just another stray that Julia's taken to."

"Curb that nasty tongue of yours, Sonny!" Julia was on her feet, naked hatred in her eyes. "Deliver your message and get out!"

"I'll deliver it some other time. When we're alone."

The old lady held out a firm, demanding hand. "Give it to me!"

"You're acting like a fool, Julia. Do you want everybody to find out?"

Lee rose to her feet, cradling the cat in one arm. "Maybe I better go downstairs," she said. "My things—"

"I want you to come right back up," Julia said. "I won't have you staying there alone. Not after what happened tonight. We'll have to work out something better for you, my dear."

Lee gave her a grateful glance. "Thank you, Miss Brink."

Sonny stepped aside to let her pass. "I hope you'll be as loyal as the rest of Julia's pets," he said. "She's managed to live alone all these years without running into serious trouble."

Lee stopped and looked at him. "I don't want anything from anyone, Mr. Pierson. All I want is for people to let me lead my own life."

He smiled coldly. "That applies to others as well as to yourself. Try to remember that."

She refused to let his words affect her. She turned and walked away, the cat still in her arms, and made for the basement. It didn't matter, one way or the other, what Sonny Pierson thought of her.

It was Goosey she was thinking of. Where had they taken him? What had they done to him?

Julia Brink had been kind to her, but all the while as she had fussed making tea, as the hours had dragged on, filled with aimless small talk, Lee had grown more tense, more anxious, worrying about Goosey.

Julia was hungry for someone to talk to, someone of her own sex, and she had made the most of her opportunity. Lee had hardly listened.

And then, a few minutes after midnight, the doorbell had rung. Lee had sprung from her chair.

The old lady was at her side in an instant. "It's not what you think it is," she'd said. "Please sit down. It's for me."

"But—"

The brilliant blue eyes had fixed Lee's with calm reassurance. "I'm expecting someone," she said. "A messenger."

"It—could be—something—else."

The thin, translucent hand had patted Lee's arm. "The boys would hardly use the bell. And as for the police—"

"The police!"

The dry, bloodless lips were turned upward in a sly smile. "They often come around at night. Complaints, you know. From the neighbors—about my cats in the backyard. But I'm sure it's only the messenger. I don't hear a sound from my pets, do you?"

Lee had watched as the little old lady moved under the billowing muslin, halting at the door for a final over-the-shoulder smile before descending the stairs.

Then there had been nothing but silence, and the depressing gloom of the crowded, over-furnished room.

Lee had expected something quite different from what she saw. The place was rundown, shabby. Dust was everywhere, coating the drapes, clinging to lampshades, dancing in the air in little swirls behind one's footsteps.

And the cats. The scores of lazing, staring cats. Their glistening, curious eyes followed every movement. Lee found it unnerving at first, feeling the eyes upon her, the impersonal, watchful eyes.

They were strangely quiet cats, given only to occasional mewing. Each wore a leather-and-metal collar, with the name Brink scratched on the tag. Lee got up, restless, sensing that the felines were conscious of her every move. She went to the door, listening for sounds from the lower hall.

"You're late," she heard Julia say. "Was there any trouble tonight?"

A man replied, with a nasty little twist to his voice, "Afraid I'd beat it with the boodle, Julia?"

And then the startling reply. "I wouldn't put anything past you. Even murder."

He laughed. It embellished his words with venomous significance. "I'll remember that if I ever decide that I'm tired of taking your insults."

Julia slammed the door. "Go on up," she said. "I want you in front of me, where I can see you."

The man started up the stairs. "You haven't got a knife in your stocking, have you, Julia?"

Lee moved back from the door and returned to the chair, not knowing what to make of the strange exchange.

The man came in just as she seated herself. He stopped when he saw Lee, and stared.

Lee stared, too. The resonant voice that had carried through the halls belonged to a man no larger than an outsize jockey. He was trim and well-dressed and bore himself cockily.

"Who are you?" he asked, spinning his hat toward the threadbare sofa. "How did you get in?"

Lee rose slowly at his approach. "Miss Brink will tell you who I am," she began.

A quick smile came to the sharply chiseled face. He extended a deceptively friendly hand, and said, "My name is Pierson. People who like me call me Sonny."

Lee reached out instinctively. Pierson didn't touch her hand. Before she could stop him, he had stepped nimbly forward, sweeping her into a close embrace. He kissed her full on the mouth and, as he let her go, she felt his cupped hand sting against her.

"Now I feel that I really know you," he laughed, but the next moment found him staggering back with harsh, red welts showing across his cheek.

Julia Brink came into the room just in time to witness the by-play. Her blue eyes glittered gleefully, and she cried, "Good for you, Lee! If I had my strength I'd add a few of my own."

Pierson retreated, holding his face and glowering.

"I think I'll get another cup and saucer," Julia chuckled. "You could use a spot of tea right now, Sonny Pierson."

"Never mind the tea! Get this girl out of here!"

The old lady turned her back to him and gestured for Lee to sit down again. She poured hot tea into the cold, half-empty cup and took it from the tray on the table to the girl sitting in the chair. "Drink it," she said. "It will help take the bad taste out of your mouth."

Pierson stuck his hands into his pockets and followed Julia with hot, angry eyes. "You'd better tell me why this girl is here," he demanded. "If you don't you can get somebody else to risk his neck for you, because I'll quit as of this minute!"

"I've heard you threaten that before," Julia said calmly. "And I know that the only time you'll quit is when they put me in the grave. But there's no earthly reason why you shouldn't know why Lee is here. She's alone in the world and needs to be helped. Goosey Mullins brought her to the club because she had no place to go."

"I thought so," Sonny began, but Julia squelched him with a look, and went on. "Her father ran off with some trollop and left her without a cent. It was purely an act of kindness on Goosey's part."

"I'll bet."

"Thank God she didn't fall into the hands of the likes of you, Sonny Pierson."

He shrugged. "I could have done better than bring her to a stinking cellar club." He took his hands out of his pockets and threaded his way between the cats, his opaque squirrel eyes fastened on Lee's face. "You're up here now because there was trouble. Julia isn't so free-handed and generous, even with a cup of tea, unless she finds good reason to be. What happened down in the clubroom, Lee? They started to fight over you, didn't they?" He waited for her answer.

She looked at him defiantly, but he could read the truth in her expression, and he said, smirking, "I thought so. You did cause trouble. And Julia has every reason not to want any. Not right now, anyway. So in order to be safe she invited you up here."

Julia folded her hands at her waist and regarded him with grudging admiration. "You got a brain in that head of yours, Sonny Pierson, even if it is a little twisted."

"Thank you," he said sarcastically.

It was at this point that Lefty listened at the steampipe for the second time. And now, several minutes later, Lee was groping down the darkened stairs toward the basement, thinking of Goosey, and blaming herself for everything.

CHAPTER NINE

"I THOUGHT I'd come to see how you were doing," Ricco said. "How are you feeling, boy?" He patted Goosey's shoulder and sat down near the bed.

Goosey smiled despite the pain that came to his battered face, taking Ricco's extended hand. "I got nine lives," he said, "just like the old lady's cats. It's—real nice of you to come, boss. I never expected that you should—"

"Forget it. You work for me, don't you? I sure must have a bad rep around, that people say I don't care what happens to my help." He took off his snap-brim and held it carefully in his lap, patting his sparse hair lovingly. "I just saw your old lady in the street," he said. "She was going shopping or something." He smiled, shaking his head. "You should have seen her the morning she came running over to tell me that someone beat you up. She looked like she was ready for the hospital herself. You're a lucky kid to have a mother like that, Goosey. Me, I never had that luck."

Goosey's eyes drifted towards the far corner. "Yeah," he said. "I guess I'm pretty lucky at that." He moistened his swollen lips with his tongue. "Mr. Ricco. There's something I got to ask you about—"

The easy smile appeared, and the hand patted Goosey's shoulder once again. "If you're worried about your wages, forget it. I just gave your mother the envelope downstairs, in the street. And next week, if you're still laid up, she'll get another. Don't worry about a thing."

"Thanks, Mr. Ricco. But that's not what I wanted to ask you."

"Well, shoot, kid. That's why I'm here, to see what I can do for you. What is it you want to know?"

Goosey turned his head and looked up into Ricco's face. "What happened to Lee, Mr. Ricco? Do you know?"

Ricco laughed. It had a solid, reassuring sound. "She landed right on her feet, Goosey, just like them cats you were talking about. She's staying upstairs with the old lady, I heard. With Julia Brink, or whatever her name is."

Goosey sank back with a sigh of relief. "That's—good," he said. "You got no idea how worried I was."

Ricco's face grew hard. "About those punks who beat you up, Goosey—the Vagabonds. Want me to do something about it?"

"Nah. It don't matter. What's the sense in makin' more trouble? Thanks just the same, Mr. Ricco."

"Anything you say, boy." He got up. "I'll send someone around to see them, if it'll make you feel any better. I was thinking the old lady isn't too much protection for Lee, with those guys still hanging out in the basement. If the old lady keeps her it wouldn't be a bad idea for you to join up with the punks again, just in case."

"Yeah," Goosey said, and nodded his bandaged head thoughtfully. "You got something there, Mr. Ricco."

The tall, broad-shouldered man put on his hat and walked toward the door; He turned and looked across the room at Goosey. "I forgot to tell your old lady about the doctor bills," he said. "Tell her not to worry about 'em. Just send 'em to me. I'll see that they're paid."

Goosey's blackened eyes shone with gratitude. He tried to say something but the words stuck in his throat.

"Save it," Ricco laughed. "I'll work the hell out of you when you get back." He waved to Goosey, still smiling, and made his way across the neat little parlor. The door opened just as he was reaching for the knob.

Lee stood on the other side, caught with surprise.

Ricco's smile broadened. "Well," he mocked. "It certainly is a small world! Come to see the patient, Lee?"

The pretty face was stiff with anger. "You got your nerve, coming here. It's all your fault that Goosey got beat up!"

A large, strong hand closed over her wrist. "Keep your voice down. And stop talking crazy. I had nothing to do with it."

"Sure. You had nothing to do with it. That's why Lefty got after me when I told Madge to go to hell. You tried to scare me into doing your dirty work for you—"

The fingers closed painfully, cutting off the angry words. "If you mention any of this to Goosey you'll get the same as he got, do you understand?"

"Let me go…"

He closed the door behind him, forcing Lee out into the hall. "You can see Goosey some other time. Right now you're coming with me!"

Lee didn't budge. "Let me go, Ricco. You can't scare me anymore. All I have to do is talk to the old lady and whatever you're figuring to do with her will go right down the drain. All your sweet little plans, Ricco. Right down the drain!"

Ricco thrust his face close to hers, eyes burning. "You better listen to me if you don't want your nose smashed to a pulp, and your teeth knocked out. No dame is going to tell Ricco what to do!" He shoved her towards the stairs. "Get moving…"

Lee obeyed, at once fearful and triumphant. She forgot all about Goosey, lying inside, on a bed of pain.

Ricco's car was at the curb. He opened the door and pushed her in as two kids stopped their game and gaped.

"We're going for a little ride," Ricco said. "And before we get back you're going to agree to do as I say."

Lee remained silent.

Ricco started the car and headed for Prospect Park. He drove slowly, looking at her from time to time as he kept talking. Lee just listened without answering.

They completed the circuit and were approaching the Botanical Gardens again when Lee said, "And what do I get out of it? Meals and lodging from old lady Brink? Suppose you're wrong?"

"It's up to you to find out whether I'm wrong or not. Once I get the right information we can knock her off without trouble. I could have the whole borough routed if it wasn't for her. I'm sure she's the one who's blocking me."

Lee smoothed her skirt at the knees and gave him a sidelong glance. "I'm not lifting a finger to help unless you give me a better deal. The shoe is on the other foot now, Ricco. You need me."

"Stop kidding yourself. You heard what I told you. You wouldn't be living with the old lady now if I hadn't made it come out that way. And you're staying there and following orders until I say otherwise."

Lee kept smoothing her dress. "You haven't got such a strong hand at that, come to think of it, Ricco. The old lady likes me now. She's lonely and wants someone to talk to. But I could make her hate me in nothing flat. It would be very easy, Ricco. And if she decided that she didn't like having me around, who would do your spying for you then?"

Ricco smiled. It was a thin, hard smile, and Lee instinctively drew back. "I'm taking you back to see Goosey," he said. "I want you to get a good look at him."

He turned to her and she read the threat in his eyes. She forced herself to meet his gaze, and said, "You must take me for an awful dumb broad, Ricco. It just came to me, listening to your story. If you got no other way of getting information from the old lady, you can't afford to knock me out of the picture. What would you do? Find another girl and bring her to the Vagabond Club? I don't think it would work for the second time. The old lady isn't that stupid. Beating me up won't do you no good at all. Because you'd be right back where you started from. When you get back to Goosey's street you can drop me off, Ricco. Maybe I'll see him and maybe I won't. That's just the way I feel about it now."

Ricco pulled in at the parking space behind the greenhouses and turned off the ignition. He put one arm on the steering wheel and leaned toward Lee, smiling. "You got a lot of style, kid," he said, "but no guts. You'll do as I say. Remember what Lefty did to you? Or tried to? He's practically living in the basement now, isn't he? And do you know why? Because I told him to. Because he's there to see that you carry out my orders. Nobody has to know about me, that I had anything to do with it. Be a sensible kid, Lee, and don't get yourself hurt."

"I'll go along with you on one condition."

"Still think I'm bluffing, huh?"

"Maybe you are and maybe you're not. I'm not sure. But you could make it all very simple by letting me visit your apartment."

"And let myself open for a real dirty charge?"

Lee put her hand on his arm. "You know I'd never do that, Ricco. Never…"

He sat back. "Yeah, sure. How many times have I heard that before? And right after the first visit there would be more, until I found your clothes hanging in my closet, and you telling me what to do! No dice, sister. Ricco runs his own life."

Lee held him with her eyes. "I want to live with you—sure I do. Don't you know why? How dumb can you be? And how blind? I'm in love with you, Ricco! I'd do anything for you if you'd only be decent to me. I'd never want to hurt you. Can you understand that, Ricco? Can you?"

"Then prove what you're saying by helping me. You love me! All I get from you is a lot of words but no action. I told you how high the stakes were. If I lose my delivery contracts on account of her, I have no business, I have no legitimate cover-up for my taxes."

A look of misery came into her face. "You'll only make a fool of me, take me for a sucker, if I help you. You haven't given me as much as a promise, Ricco. You've done nothing but threaten me."

He shook off her hand angrily. "It's the only way I can handle it," he said. "If I let you have your way I could kiss everything I own goodbye. All that would have to happen is for your old man to find out, or for the old lady to write a letter to the police." He sat back and started the car. "I'll give you a couple of days to make up your mind, Lee. I'm not promising nothing, but if you pull this off for me I'll give you enough to keep you living high for a couple of years. That's my final offer."

They rode in silence until they came to Goosey's block. The car pulled up at the curb, and then Lee said, "I changed my mind about seeing him. I better get back to the old lady."

Ricco didn't drive up to the house. He stopped at the farthest corner and waited for Lee to get out. She didn't. Instead, she moved closer. Then, before he could stop her, he found her arms around his neck, and her lips pulsing against his.

He tried to push her away, but she clung like a leech.

When she finally let go there was blood on his lip.

Lee evaded his angry lunge, and slipped out. "Remember what I told you," she cried. "I'll be waiting for your call…"

She laughed then, brazenly, and adjusted her shoulder bag, flouncing away as Ricco glared after her.

From the opposite corner, emerging from the drug store, a little man with mouse-brown hair and opaque eyes watched Ricco put his handkerchief to the bleeding lip.

With cool deliberation he took a cigarette from the fresh pack in his hand, igniting it as he followed the flouncing hips.

The gun he carried seemed to burn under his armpit.

CHAPTER TEN

JULIA BRINK was in the kitchen feeding her army of cats when the phone rang. She told Lee to put down the bowl of milk and answer the call. Lee was only too glad to get away, forcing an aisle between the mass of mewing, greedy felines with cautious steps, taking great care not to step on a stray tail or foot.

It had happened once, quite accidentally, and the squalling had hardly subsided before the frail old lady was at Lee, berating her for her carelessness. "Cruel, callous girl!" she'd cried, "watch your clumsiness! How can you be so thoughtless? These poor creatures depend on us for love and protection. How would you like it, never to feel safe, to be subjected to intense pain without the slightest warning? Carelessness is a cardinal sin if it causes pain, and for that you ought to be punished! You'll sleep on the floor tonight, just like these poor creatures, and perhaps it will penetrate…"

Lee hadn't answered back. Little old ladies were entitled to have queer notions, she thought; but she was unpleasantly surprised when she found the door to her room locked tight. Julia Brink had been quite serious.

Following her terrible experience in the basement club, the first few days spent in Julia Brink's shabby apartment came to Lee like a gift sent from heaven. Despite the disorder and the dust and the eternal cats underfoot, the even flow of empty, useless hours was just the tonic her frayed nerves needed.

Julia set a frugal table but the food was good. She didn't ask Lee to clean up or cook or use the old-fashioned washtubs. The food was ordered by phone, the laundry picked up and delivered.

"I haven't set foot in the street for nigh on to fifteen years," Julia told her. "I get enough excitement from just reading the papers. You don't have to visit a madhouse to see that the people in it are really mad, now do you, dear? That's just how I feel about the outside world. I am quite content to stay right here, away from the senseless cruelty, the hatred, and the greed. I have my darling pets and they have me. What else does an old lady need?" And the blue eyes glowed brightly, waiting for Lee's approval.

The cue was there and Lee took it. Julia was pleased. "Of course, it does get dull talking to the poor, dumb creatures," she added. "Occasionally one does long for an answer, the sound of a human voice. Lee, dear, if you'd care to humor a lonely old lady for a little while, I have an extra room—"

It was a pleasant room, Lee found, though a little run-down from neglect. But with a little fixing up it could be the nicest room she'd ever had.

She had spent her first night on the shabby sofa in the living room, and the prospect was far from pleasing. But it was better than staying in the basement, not knowing, from one minute to the next, what was going to happen.

Lefty had given her a fright when she'd gone down to get her bag, standing silently in the dark. He refrained from touching her, though his questions had been peculiarly sharp.

"Are you sure you're tellin' me the truth?" he'd demanded. "You're not sayin' that about the old lady, just to get out of here, so you can go upstairs and sneak out over the roof?"

"Why are you asking? Do you want me to stay here so I can't talk about what you did to Goosey?"

He didn't say much after that, and Lee took it as the reason for his strange apprehension. But now she knew different. The little pieces of the jigsaw were beginning to fit together. Ricco himself had added the finishing touches by what he had told her this afternoon.

"Now watch where you're going!" Julia warned again. "I'm sure you wouldn't want to sleep on the floor tonight!"

Lee kept her thoughts to herself, picking her way between the unheeding animals gingerly.

The phone rang; she answered it.

She didn't recognize the voice at first, as it came to her over the wire. Then, after a brief pause, the man laughed and said, "Julia must be feeding the cats. I timed it just right, didn't I, Lee?"

"I wouldn't know. Why did you call?"

"To speak to you," Sonny retorted. "I saw something very interesting this afternoon. I'd like to discuss it with you."

"Not now. I'm busy."

"Wait…don't hang up." The tone had changed abruptly. "You better listen to me if you know what's good for you. I want to see you tomorrow night, Lee. At the Beechmont Hotel. At nine sharp."

"If you want to see me you can come here."

There was a slight pause. "All right, I'll come. If you don't care about Julia hearing that I saw you with Ricco. And how you kissed him in the car."

Lee stared into the mouthpiece. She couldn't speak.

"You're up to something dirty," Sonny said. "And I want to find out what it is."

"You—don't know what—you're talking about. Ricco and me—"

"I know that Goosey works for Ricco. But I know too that nothing much happened until you came along. The whole thing was a put-up job, wasn't it? Ricco got you in here so you could spy on Julia!"

"It's a lie. It's not true…"

The twisted laugh drifted over the wire. "If that's the case then you got nothing to lose. Tell Julia I'll be over to see her tomorrow night."

"Wait! Sonny…listen to me."

"I'm listening…"

Lee drew a deep breath. "I—was only asking him to help me. You know the fix I'm in. Goosey works for him, and—"

"Stop lying and make up your mind which way you want it. You'll be back on the street after I speak to Julia. I think you know that, Lee. Are you meeting me at the hotel or aren't you?"

Lee hesitated. She shut her eyes, groping vainly for some way out of it.

"Well?" Sonny cried again.

"I'll—meet you," Lee said. Her words were barely above a whisper.

"Good. Now you're being sensible. Tomorrow night at nine. Ask Julia to come to the phone now. It will save you from explaining."

Lee pulled herself together and walked into the kitchen. "It's Sonny Pierson," she said to Julia. "He wants to talk to you."

Julia stopped what she was doing and gave Lee a bright, searching smile. As she went to the phone, in passing, she said, "I hope you won't keep that appointment with him. Sonny's up to no good. He'll try to get back at you for the slap you gave him." And she sailed out, still smiling.

Lee was to recall her warning the very next evening. But she wasn't quite prepared for the shock she got when she saw Sonny in the lobby of the Beechmont Hotel.

She had just passed into the magnificent green-and-gold lobby when a small man sitting on a bench near the main desk broke away from his companions and approached her. She didn't recognize him at first, unprepared as she was to see him wearing such flamboyant clothes.

But it was Sonny Pierson all right, wearing the gaudy attire of a bellboy.

He laughed as she stood in stunned surprise. "What's the matter?" he jibed, "Don't you like the way it fits me?"

Lee was completely, upset. "What is this?" she cried. "Some kind of joke? Why—"

"This is what I do for a living," he cut in. "Have I disillusioned you, Lee?"

She glared down at him. "What are you trying to pull? If you've dragged me here just to play games—"

"You'll find out whether it's a game or not." The smile was still on his lips but his eyes had grown hard. "Come on. Follow me and keep your voice down."

He started away. Lee didn't move. He came back, his expression cold as death, and said, "Stop acting like a fool. Unless you want Julia to know about you and Ricco."

Lee followed him into one of the bronze-and-glass elevators waiting on the main floor.

"Fifteen," Sonny said to the operator, and a few seconds later he was showing Lee down the ornate onyx hall toward the corner room.

"Nobody knows whether you belong here or not," Sonny explained. "That's why I had you come without a bag. I have the key to this room and it could just as well be yours."

"But—"

"No questions now. Wait until we get inside."

He unlocked the door and switched on the light. Lee stopped at the threshold, staring.

Sonny grinned. "Go on in, country girl. I'll bet you never saw anything like this in your life."

She moved slowly, taking in the expensive decor with wide, awestruck eyes. "It—it must cost a fortune to live here," she said.

"It does. But for you, Lee, not a cent." And he laughed. He took off his pillbox and sent it sailing across the room. "Look around," he urged. "Make yourself at home." He sat down on a damask-covered sofa and slouched back, crossing his legs. "In there," he said, pointing, "you'll find a combination bath-and-dressing room. Go in and take a peek. Hollywood hasn't got better."

The place seemed to hypnotize her. She walked around as if in a dream. Then, as she stood in the center of the room, bathed in the mellow glow of the crystal lights, she put her hands to her face and started to cry.

Sonny hurried to her side. "Easy, baby," he said. "Take it easy. I know exactly how you feel."

He took her elbow and led her to the sofa. His arm was around her but she didn't mind. She put her head to his shoulder, her gleaming, blue-black hair running down the scarlet of his uniform like a fall of burning jet.

"Even Ricco couldn't offer you this," he said softly, and his words broke the spell.

Lee drew away and sat up, holding back her tears. "Tell me what you want so I can go," she said. "Why did you bring me here? Why—"

"I want to speak to you about Ricco, I want you to tell me what he asked you to do."

"He didn't ask me anything. We're—just friends, like I told you. Goosey introduced us."

Sonny curbed his anger. "I wish you'd stop lying. Ricco's a dangerous man, a gangster. He's trying to get certain information. Information he'd give his eye-teeth to have. This has been going on for a long time, Lee." He moved close, opaque eyes shining like glass beads. "He's never come close to finding what he wants to know—until now."

"I'm trying to make sense of what you're saying."

"Come on, stop kidding me! You know what I mean. In all the years he's been trying, he never found out about me. You did. Does that make sense to you?"

Lee stared. "But why is that so important? You must have been seen going in and out of the house."

He laughed mirthlessly. "I've never seen Julia except at night. And always between one and four in the morning. You would like to know why, wouldn't you? And so would Ricco." He tapped the back of her hand with his finger. "He has no idea who I am, or that I even exist."

He reached out suddenly and grabbed her wrist. "Did you tell him about me in the car? Did you?"

"Let go of me! Let go of my wrist!"

His fingers tightened. "Answer me! Did you tell him, or didn't you!"

"No—I didn't! Now—will you let me go?"

He spoke through clenched teeth. "If I find out you lied to me—"

Lee wrenched herself free and sprang up. "You little fool!" she cried, "if you had any sense you'd stop nagging me! I didn't tell him because I didn't think it was important. I only met you once—the night I had the trouble. I didn't give you a second thought!"

He looked at her. "Sure. You even forgot that I kissed you. You forgot that you slapped me!" The opaque eyes were glittering now.

She regarded him coldly. "I made myself forget because I didn't like you. Because I took you to be a mean, nasty, little man."

Pierson rose slowly. The expression on his face caused Lee to retreat before him. "Maybe that's enough reason for you to tell Ricco about me!"

"No," Lee said. "I won't tell him. Just because he wants to know. I'll never tell him, I'll never spy for him!" Her voice started to spiral. She stopped.

The slight man in the gaudy red uniform watched her closely, peering as if he meant to read her innermost thoughts. "I'd like to believe that," he said.

"I want you to believe it," Lee said. "Because I know he only wants to use me. Because if Julia throws me out he wouldn't lift a finger to help me!"

Sonny stroked his cheek thoughtfully, his eyes not for one moment leaving her face. "Why do you hate him? What has he done to you to make you feel this way?"

Lee took a deep breath. "He threatened me. He seems to think that I'm no better than the other riffraff he knows."

"But still you kissed him."

Lee didn't answer. Her cheeks grew warm with rising blood.

Sonny watched her as the silence grew. Then he said, as if he had made up his mind, "I'll treat you better than Ricco. I'll give you anything you want. Look." He unbuttoned his jacket and came out with a wallet.

When he held out the three bills to her, fanwise, she saw that each was a fifty.

"Take them," he said. "There's plenty more where these came from."

She stepped back, as if the bills were aimed at her like a deadly weapon.

"Just don't say anything to Ricco," he said. He smiled then, and his sharp, well-defined features softened into friendliness. "You're a beautiful kid, Lee. And in spite of everything, pretty decent, too. You'd be crazy to get yourself involved with a guy like Ricco. You can have a nice, quiet life with Julia. She's a little bats, but where else would you find a place to stay, with no questions asked? Will you take a bit of friendly advice from me?"

Lee followed the fluttering green of the bills as he let them fall from his hand. They landed on the seat of the sofa.

Sonny put the wallet back in his pocket and secured the row of brass buttons. "Don't see Ricco anymore," he said. "Don't even speak to him on the phone. If he threatens you again, tell him that you'll go to the D. A. He won't risk losing his trucking license. It's his biggest paying racket."

Her eyes drifted to the three bills nestling on the sofa.

Sonny smiled to himself. "I'm a pretty generous guy when it comes to women, Lee. Especially the kind who cooperate. You won't regret taking my advice."

She looked up at him. "You must be in some kind of racket yourself, to be so generous with your money."

"I am. But I don't have to strong-arm or threaten people the way Ricco does. I don't have to...in my racket." His hands went to the red jacket fondly. "Go on, Lee. Pick up the bills. They're yours. I'm no piker. Ricco never pays off. But I do."

Lee couldn't take her eyes off the money. The very sight of it seemed to melt her resolve, to kill the gnawing fear within her. She thought of what it could buy for her, of all the things she'd dreamed of having— And there would be more...

But then there was Ricco, and what he meant to her...

Sonny picked up the bills, rolled them up and stuck them in the neck of her sweater. She started to protest but the words never passed her lips.

"All I want is that you play fair with me," Sonny said. He went to the door, unlocked it and held it open. He waited, smiling, for Lee to precede him. "Someday you're going to change your mind about me. All that stuff about my being mean and nasty. And it'll change sooner than you think. Because it's suddenly become important to me." He paused for a moment, and his voice dropped. "More important," he repeated, "than anything else in the world."

CHAPTER ELEVEN

"I'M BEGINNING to wonder about you," Julia said, watching Lee as she cleared the dinner table. "And I'm beginning to worry, too. I'm not a very good influence, am I, dear? I didn't mean when I took you in that you should pattern your life after mine. I didn't mean that at all. A young girl like you should go out occasionally, and have a little recreation." The fine, patrician hand went out and caught Lee's arm. "Put down the dishes a minute and listen to me. You've been working too hard, Lee, working yourself ragged trying to straighten out this mess of a place. I don't care if it never gets dusted, if the windows never get washed. Look at you! There isn't a bit of color in your face! Why don't you want to go out? I'm not an invalid, I can take care of myself. Just because I board you here doesn't make you my slave."

The china-blue eyes shone with gentle reproof. "I've caused enough unhappiness in my day, and I don't want you to become another victim to my selfishness. Why don't you take off that apron and see how Goosey is getting along? I'm sure he misses you."

Lee's face did not reflect the chiding smile. "I suppose he does," she said. "But his mother doesn't. I'm—perfectly satisfied with the way things are right now. You haven't heard me complaining have you?"

"Not in so many words. But there's something about the way you look. Lee, what's bothering you? Why have you been so nervous and jumpy lately?"

The dark, expressive eyes contrived to look blank. "I don't get you. There's nothing wrong with me."

Julia shook her head. "My dear, you're not fooling me one minute. But of course, if you don't want to tell me—"

"It has nothing to do with you," Lee said bluntly, and went out with the dishes.

But Julia didn't let it rest there. She followed Lee into the kitchen, trailed by several cats, and said, "That boy Lefty hasn't left the clubroom for almost two weeks now. Has it something to do with him? Is that why you're afraid to go out?"

"No. Why should I be afraid of him?"

Julia folded her hands at her waist—tightly. "Will you go downstairs now and tell him for me that I don't want him sleeping there?"

The silence that followed grew heavy with tension.

"I'm waiting for your answer, Lee."

Lee took off her apron and hung it neatly over the chair. She seemed strangely grim. "I'll go," she said. "What else do you want me to tell him?"

Julia studied the pale, set face. "Only that I mean what I say. They can have all the meetings they want, but nobody is to remain overnight."

The girl hesitated, shrugged, and started for the stairs. Julia went with her to the landing. "I'm sure," she said, "that this will mark a change in your behavior." Lee kept on going. She wasn't thinking of Julia now, but of Lefty. And Ricco. The blood started singing in her ears.

When she reached the nailed-up door she made a sharp turn and walked through the short hall towards the stairs leading into the back yard. It was pitch black outside. She felt her way down the wooden steps and entered the basement through the rear door.

Lefty jumped up as she came in. He threw down the magazine he had been reading and sauntered over to her, his thumbs hooked into the slanting pockets of his dungarees. "It's about time," he said. "What've you been tryin' to do, make a marathon of it? Why didn't you come to see me sooner, like the boss ordered?"

Lee ignored his question. She kept her distance, tensely alert, and said, "Julia doesn't like the idea of your sleeping here. She said that it's final. You have to get out."

Lefty stared. "Is that all you come to tell me?"

"Yes."

He laughed, rocking on his heels. "This is really something! What makes her think I'll listen?"

"You'll listen. Because Ricco will tell you the same thing. I'm set upstairs, Lefty. I'm not running away and Julia has no idea of throwing me out. You can go and tell him that, if you want."

A look of relief crossed his face. "I get it. So you decided to play along with him." He shook his head. "You had me worried for a minute, the way you spoke." He slipped a loose cigarette from his shirt pocket and offered it to her. Lee took it and he held a match to it. "The boss'll be glad you made up your mind," he said. "Is there anything else you got to tell me?"

"Yeah. I got plenty to tell you. But you wouldn't like the sound of it!"

"Still sore about what we did to Goosey, huh?"

"What do you think? Why did Ricco make you do it, Lefty?"

He tensed. "Ricco? He had nothin' to do with it. Maybe we wouldn't of been so tough on Goosey if he hadn't hit me. When a cluck like him gets ideas about runnin' the gang—"

"He didn't have that idea at all! But I'm wasting my breath talking to you. Now you better go, before the old lady gets more suspicious."

Lefty didn't move. He looked at the glowing end of his cigarette, and said slowly, "It ain't my idea to beat Goosey's time with you, but how about lettin' me take you out one of these nights? I'm sorry for what I did, Lee. The way you talked to me, I thought you were just another one of those pickups."

Lee smiled scornfully. "Who are you trying to kid? We grew up in the same neighborhood. You've known me all your life."

"I remembered you only as a kid. Not—the way you look—now."

"Sure. But you're going to remember plenty about me, aren't you, after what you tried to do."

"You should of said something. You didn't know who I was either—until later."

Lee laughed harshly. "I'll never forget you, Lefty, for the same reason. Goosey saved me just in time. And you have the nerve to stand there and ask me to go out with you!"

"I told you I was sorry."

"Sure. You're sorry...now. But as soon as you get another chance to—"

"Look," he cut in. "I don't blame you for not trustin' me. But things are different now. I had a lot of time to think. I could do a lot more for you, Lee, than Goosey. Because the Vagabonds do like I say—because Ricco has a lot of confidence in me."

Lee watched him. There was a strange look on her face. She stepped up to him in the gloom, fixing him with coldly calculating eyes. "Suppose I told you that there was more to Ricco's deal than you know? That stooling for him is only part of my job?"

"I—don't get what you mean. What are you talkin' about?"

She smiled, queerly. "Come on, Lefty. You're not that dumb."

He waited, tensely, his gaze wavering over the lush figure, the hard, attractive face.

"You followed me to the Beechmont Hotel the other night, didn't you?"

"I'm—supposed to. That's part of my job."

"Do you know who I met there, Lefty?"

He shifted uneasily. "Yeah," he said. "I know…"

Lee's heart stopped beating. She couldn't bring herself to speak.

"The boss was supposed to be out of town that night," he said bitterly. "But he wasn't. He was there all the time, wasn't he, in his room—with you."

"Lefty—"

"Oh, I don't blame you. There was nothin' you could do about it, I guess. As soon as I saw you walk in through the door I called up his room, just to check. Nobody answered." He turned away. "When you took so long to come down again—"

A feeling of wild elation swept through her. Then Ricco didn't know! Then nothing had happened to Sonny—

Sonny. It gave her pause for thought, to realize how clever he was. Working as a bellhop in the same hotel with Ricco, where he, could watch his coming and his going, time his every movement. And all the while Ricco not knowing about him, not knowing that he worked for Julia Brink, who was blocking his deal to take over every paper route in the borough! The nerve of Sonny, asking her there, right under Ricco's nose, under the watchful eyes of Lefty!

"Well," Lee said slowly, "now you know. But he's not kidding me. Not one minute, Lefty. He's only using me, just like he's using the rest of you."

"I wish I could believe that." He faced her again, hopefully. "If I thought that he would be willin' to let you go—"

"Damaged goods," she said cruelly. "You'd be willing to take Ricco's cast-off?"

"There's no other way I can get you, is there?" he asked softly. "You can't change what happened. But you can forget it." He came close again. "I'm pretty good at forgettin'," he said, smiling crookedly, "as you know, Ricco might even give me a bigger break, later, for takin' you off his hands. Did you think of that, Lee?"

She drew back as he tried to touch her. "It's a stinking thought! A lousy-rotten thought! That's the difference between you and Goosey. He—would never consider it!"

"Maybe. But he doesn't know that it happened...yet."

She grabbed his arm. "Lefty, if you tell a word of this to Goosey, I'll—"

"You'll what?" He laughed, but there was no mirth in it. "He can't do nothin' to me, and he can't do nothin' to Ricco, either. He's just a big, dumb cluck, like I told you. Sure, I know what you're thinkin'. That's he's crazy enough to make trouble if he finds out that Ricco crossed him, that he took you." He threw his unfinished cigarette to the floor and ground it out with his heel. "If that happened, Goosey would be a dead duck." He stuck his hands into his pockets, and said, "Maybe it's something I should keep in mind."

"No, Lefty. If you want to get to first base with me, you better forget it. As of now."

"But you just said—"

"Goosey got enough already. Why rub it in? I need friends, Lefty. A lot of friends. Ricco doesn't hand out guarantees for anything. If trouble comes, he might blame me. I don't know. Dames always get the blame whenever anything goes wrong. If I could feel that you and Goosey—"

Lefty cut in with heavy sarcasm. "And all of the Vagabonds too, I suppose? What are you tryin' to give me? Ricco's my boss! He takes care of m...!" He lifted his hand in a threatening gesture towards her.

"Yeah, he takes care of you. Like he took care of me. He forced me into a deal and then let me have it from the bottom of the deck! I'm not forgetting how he got me that stinking job, how Madge set me up so I got caught by Mangum! He knew where Goosey would take me! And then to finish it off nice and neat, he sends her here to put a bug in your ear! Did you ever stop to wonder, Lefty, how it was that Goosey came so soon after Madge left? Just in time to find you on the couch with me? Maybe you don't think that Ricco sent him over?"

He threw his hand at her. "Don't give me that! He never figured that far!"

"Think, Lefty," Lee persisted. "Goosey got beat up, didn't he? He got put out of the way without even knowing that Ricco was behind it. And now I'm living upstairs with old lady Brink, trying to get the list he wants, and the name of the political boss who's behind her."

"So I still don't see—"

"You will," she said darkly, "If Ricco gets tired of playing around with the old lady and tries to force the information from her. That's where you'll come in, Lefty. And the Vagabonds. You'll be doing the dirty work, you and the gang of kids. So if anything bad happens, Ricco will be clean. All the cops'll see is a bunch of kids looking for loot in a strange old lady's house. Everybody thinks she's rich; everybody in the neighborhood thinks she's got dough stuck in every corner and crack. Do you think, if the old lady gets hurt, that you'll convince the cops that Ricco was behind it? With maybe a good percentage of them on his payroll?"

Lefty flared. His smug assurance was gone. He looked bewildered, and upset. "Just what the hell are you drivin' at?" he demanded. "Why are you tellin' me all this?"

Lee was very close now. A feeling of evil seemed to permeate the darkened room, underlining her persuasive words. "Goosey was his fall guy once," she said, "and now he's made me one. Ricco's after big stakes. Loyalty doesn't mean a thing to him. Not from his side, anyway. If he has to wipe out you and me and all of the Vagabonds to get what he wants, he won't think twice about it. That's what I'm trying to tell you, Lefty. We can only trust him so far. Our only protection is to stick together, to forget our differences. You and me and the rest of the boys. And take care how far we stick out our necks for him."

Lefty took his hands from his pockets, made as if to hold her arms, then lowered them stiffly. "Maybe I shouldn't trust you either," he said. "How do I know you don't want to use me for a stooge?" His voice grew hard. "You could of sold out to the old lady. I don't know. You could of told her about us workin' for Ricco, just to feather your own nest. He grabbed her then, and cried, "Did you? Did you?"

Lee didn't struggle to break free. She looked up into the pale suspicions of his face, and said, scornfully, "Sure. I sold out. For a crummy bed. To be a nursemaid to a houseful of cats. Just because I felt sorry for a stingy miser of an old lady."

Lefty could feel her breath on his lips, the firm warmth of her pressing against his chest. "If I thought for one second that you were playin' both ends against the middle—"

"I could forget what you did to Goosey," she said. "I could forget that Ricco got you wrapped around his little finger, if you promise to stop tailing me. If you let me work this out my own way—"

"Yeah. And what am I supposed to get out of it? Make like the *Three Musketeers* and die for a smile from the queen?"

Lee made a slow, studied movement. As she heard him draw in his breath, she said, "Maybe it'll be more than a smile. Maybe it'll be a date, just like you want."

"Lee—"

"Down here, some night. When the old lady's asleep."

He kissed her. Suddenly. Violently.

Still she remained in his arms. "Me and you and the Vagabonds, Lefty. Sticking together. Just in case."

"And Goosey?"

"He's a dumb cluck, like you say."

He was sweating now, with the yielding firmness of her under his hands, with the soft, exciting smoothness of her only a fraction of an inch away.

"Lee," he said again, and his voice sounded strained and tense. She let him, just for a quivering, ecstatic second, and then broke away. "Ricco can force me," she said, "because of what he knows. But you, Lefty. You got to wait for my favors."

"Lee...don't go! Not yet..."

She was a bold, tantalizing silhouette in the gloom, as she stood by the door, holding him with her burning glance. "You better go now, she said, so the old lady can see you leave. The rest is up to you, Lefty. We need each other. Think it over. Long and hard."

And then she was gone, with the scent of her lingering in the air, with the feel of her against him still warm.

His eyes drifted to the couch, his thoughts to the night he had held her there, seeking, and finding. If only he could trust her!

His lips twisted bitterly. Everything for Ricco and nothing for him! That's the way it was always going to be. Unless— Unless—

He closed the door to the little room behind him and walked through the dark silence of the narrow clubroom. Ricco had made a point of getting Goosey back into the Vagabonds. His reasons seemed wise at first, but now, thinking it over—

How deep a game was Ricco playing? If he could only figure it out, Lefty thought. After what Lee had told him, he wasn't sure of anything anymore.

Except what she had come to mean to him.

Cripes! If he could only get her to care for him! If she only knew what the touch of her did to him!

Days and nights without end he had prowled the damp and lonely basement, thinking of her, dreaming of her! Waiting for her footstep on the stair, listening to the sound of her voice…

And then…the night she left the house…

It was the worst night he'd ever spent, thinking of her with Ricco, in the big, expensive hotel, with her in Ricco's arms…

He could have killed Ricco that night. Ricco, the big-time operator, forcing a kid just because she couldn't help herself, taking her fresh, young body, and—and—

But he was crazy, thinking like this. Lee would never be his. Not the way he wanted her. All the way, for all the time…

It was cool out in the street, cool and clear, and Lefty took deep, sucking breaths. His head was so hot he felt like he had a fever. To think that a dame could make him feel like this! Him, Lefty, the Big Wheel, the leader of the Vagabonds!

During those few brief moments when his fingers knew the pulsing warmth of her, the incredible smoothness… Cripes! It was enough to make a guy blow a fuse!

She had kissed him tonight. She had let him, moving against her, trace the soft, flaunting curves of her, responded to the slow, unfolding growth of his desire...

Maybe...if he did like she said...

Lefty glanced up at the stars and strode away, his hard heels echoing on the pavement, his fists balled deep in his pockets, trying to contain the quivering that started at the back of his knees, shooting upward with a pain he had never before experienced...

Yeah boy! he thought, *I got it bad! Real bad...*

CHAPTER TWELVE

IT WAS the same room, on the same floor. Sonny looked the same, too, in his scarlet uniform, with the same, knowing smile on his face.

The difference was that she didn't feel afraid, as she had the first time. The furnishings were even more beautiful than she remembered, the glowing crystal lights more mellow.

It made you feel good, even if you knew it could never be yours, just to sit and look, to feel the beautiful silk under your hand, catch the soft warm colors with your eyes, and let everything sink in.

It was almost like making love, embracing everything with your senses, filled with an aching desire to call it all your own, to possess it with your body, as you would a lover... But the difference was, too, that the thrill would never wholly die; it would linger on, long after the caresses were forgotten, long after the sharp explosion ebbed and eddied away. That was the difference...

Sonny was grinning at her now, familiar and friendly, pouring the chilled wine into long-stemmed glasses. He had taken her into the kitchen before, showed her the ice-bucket placed deep in the refrigerator, holding the swoop-necked bottle with the French label like a mother tenderly cradling her baby.

"The best," he'd said. "The best is none too good for you. So you found out about Ricco, hey? You must have thought me crazy, asking you to come with him living in the same building, now, for the second time!"

"I did, at first. But then it came to me that he must be away again, like before. Still, you're taking a hell of a chance, Sonny—"

"I like to take chances. That's what makes life interesting. Do you think I'd be working for Julia if there wasn't any risk? She hates me as much as I hate her—but that serves to add to the interest."

Then he'd taken the bucket into the big, beautiful living room and set it into the folding stand that had come along with it. And now she had the glass to her lips, watching him over the rim.

"Like it?" he asked, and she nodded, wrinkling her pert nose as the bubbles danced about.

He sat next to her on the sofa, glass in hand, and caressed her face with his eyes. "It's a good thing Julia took you in with her," he said. "If it weren't for you coming along right now, she'd have found herself fighting Ricco alone. I was all set to throw up the sponge."

"You're kidding me," Lee said. "You're priming me with a little soft soap."

He flicked her chin with a chiding forefinger, and said, "It always helps, doesn't it? But what I just told you happens to be true. I'm tired of doing her dirty work for her, sneaking around like a two-bit private eye lugging a gun under my armpit."

Lee placed her glass on the little side-table. Her eyebrows rose. Then she laughed, and said, "Now I know you're kidding me! You wouldn't even have room to hide a gun, a little guy like you, now, would you, sonny-boy?"

Sonny laughed with her. "You'd be surprised what they say about us little guys."

"But why the gun? Is it on account of Ricco?"

"Partly. He and his mob are not the only ones who'd like to get their hands on the messages I carry for Julia."

"Now," Lee said pertinently, "you're expecting me to ask you why."

"Of course. Isn't that what Ricco wants you to find out?"

"I suppose so."

He leaned close. "What other information did he ask you to get?" When Lee didn't answer, he tapped his scarlet jacket significantly, and said, "Are you still on my payroll or aren't you?"

Lee held her breath. "You mean—you want to give me more?"

"Didn't you come hoping I would?"

She lowered her eyes. "I guess I did."

He tapped her chin again. "That's my girl. At least you're honest about it," He raised his glass. "Drink up. A toast to us, Lee." She took the glass from the table, and he went on, "To hell with Ricco and Julia and all their conniving ways!" They touched glasses and drank.

"Before we go any further," Lee said, "I got to tell you something." She paused, biting her lips. "I was crazy about Ricco once. I left myself wide open for this because I tried to force myself on him. I—I'm still not quite sure, that if he wanted me, that I wouldn't—"

She broke off, unable to go on.

Sonny's opaque eyes grew wary. "I get it. You're warning me not to tell you too much."

"Yes."

He got up, filled his glass again, and drained it dry. "I should have brought something stronger," he said, and poured again. "What about you, Lee? Want some more?"

"No, thank you."

He finished the drink and sat down next to her. "Maybe I could make you forget about Ricco," he said, and took her hand, fondling it gently with his own small paws.

"I—wouldn't like you to try. Not—yet—Sonny."

He dropped her hand and leaned back on the upholstered arm. "You've just talked yourself out of a nice chunk of dough," he said. "Unless you change your mind before you leave."

She started to rise, eyes flashing. "Maybe I should leave right now!"

Sonny reached out and she sat down again. "You sure got a temper to match those burning eyes! Take it easy! You should know that this is all part of the game. All of us are out for what we can get. The difference is how much each is willing to pay for what he wants." His fingers caught hers again. "With you," he said softly, "I'd be willing to risk everything. On one throw of the dice. Remember that when you start losing your patience with me."

"I don't trust you. You or Ricco. You're both using me."

"It's not true in my case. But I can't stop you from thinking that way."

"You can if you keep this on a business basis. Strictly. I could have told Ricco about you long ago. I didn't. Because—"

"Because there's a lot more for you to find out. About Julia and me. About the list of newsstands she owns, and the name of the guy who's keeping Ricco from monopolizing the delivery routes." He watched her. "You could sell yourself to Ricco with that information, couldn't you?"

"I'm not selling myself to anyone..."

Sonny smiled. "I've delivered two messages to Julia since I first met you. Were you careful enough to put down the dates? It's very important, you know."

She snatched her hand away. "I'd throw up the whole stinking business if I had someplace else to go!"

The smile grew broader. "I gave you a hundred and fifty bucks last time. It should have been enough to make you independent for a while. Long enough for you to duck away and get a job somewhere. Why didn't you leave us, Lee? Ricco with his threats and Julia with her crummy living, and me—"

"You're forgetting Goosey, aren't you? He got into this trouble on account of me. He's the only decent man I ever knew. You, and Mangum and Ricco—and my lousy old man—not one of you is fit to polish Goosey's boots!"

"You make it sound so nice and noble, Lee. But you don't believe it yourself. You don't give a damn about Goosey. You don't give a damn about anybody but yourself. And that's the truth!"

Lee got up. "I'm going home. I've had enough of this."

"We haven't finished the wine yet, Lee."

"Finish it yourself!"

He started to unbutton his jacket. Lee stood over him, not moving.

"I'll give you another hundred and fifty," he said. "I'll help you get out of this stinking mess if you let me set you up in a nice apartment somewhere. Or if you'd rather make it a hotel—"

Her lips curled. "Didn't you know? I'm jail-bait. I could have you thrown in the can for even meeting you here! And you talk about setting me up!"

He got up, matching her scorn with his. "I'm not a guy called Ricco. I'm not afraid of losing what I have. Besides it would be more than worth it, to take the chance." The buttons were opened and the bills were in his hand.

She swung hard, hitting his knuckles, and the folded bills fell to the floor. "I'm tired of being treated like a tart!" she cried. "If you ever try that again—I'll go straight to Ricco and tell him everything I know!"

Sonny kept his temper with an effort. He picked up the bills, sighing, and put them in his back pocket. "You still don't know enough to make it worth his while. He'd still need the list, and—"

"But he'd have you. And a good beating by his gorillas would get him all the information he wanted!"

The opaque eyes grew steely. "You're talking out of turn, Lee. You better watch your tongue, if you know what's good for you!"

"I know what's good for me, all right. But it isn't you!"

"Sit down."

"No!"

"You better do like I say. We got to settle this matter here and now."

"As far as I'm concerned, it's all settled!"

Sonny's hand snaked out and smashed the words against her teeth. Lee tumbled to the sofa.

He grabbed her hands as she tried to get up, and held her down.

"I don't like to play rough," he panted, "but you forced me. You got to make your decision now, Lee. Me or Ricco. I don't care what happens to Julia. I've been her stooge long enough. If you send his boys after me, I'll get back at you if it's the last thing I do…"

"Let—me go. I didn't mean it. You got me mad—"

"Sure. You got me mad, too. But I don't let things like this get by without putting a cork on it. Who's it going to be, Lee? Me…or Ricco?"

"You're treating me like a tramp!" she cried savagely. "At least Ricco didn't!"

"He did worse. Only you didn't see it. He didn't treat you like you were anything. Not even a tramp. He didn't consider you as a woman. You were nothing to him. Do you understand that, Lee? Nothing!"

"Shut up! I won't hear any more! Shut up and let me go home."

"The truth hurts, don't it, Lee? He gave you a phony story about jail-bait because what you had to offer didn't interest him. He used you like a crook uses burglar tools, to chisel his way into something he needs badly. Sure, every crook loves his tools, but not the way you want to be loved, Lee. Not by Ricco!" His fingers were crushing hers now, his voice lashing out like the snap of a bull whip. "I can see it in your face," he cried, "that you hate him for it! That's why you're here with me, tonight. Because of your fear, because of your hate! Lee—"

She jerked one hand free and pummeled his chest, striking against the hard brass buttons until her flesh stung with pain.

Sonny didn't stop her. He sat there, laughing, laughing at the violent show of frustration, at the tears that came to her eyes, at the foul words that came from her lips.

"Nothing…" he mocked again. "You're nothing to Ricco. Not even a tramp!" And she struck at him again, until the pain killed the meaning of the words.

She went limp then, crying in his arms, and Sonny held her, stroking her hair with cool, sardonic fingers. "That's my baby," he said. "Let the poison out. Every time you think of him, let the poison out, like this." And he smiled into the soft, blue-black waves, knowing the texture with his lips.

It was good to feel his arms about her, to let the tears come. It was good to cry, to pretend that it would make things right again. Crying didn't come easy now. It never had, even as a little girl. Her pride was fierce and neglect had sharpened its razor's edge. But there was nothing left now, not even pride. Ricco had seen to that. So she cried.

It came to her then, as she lay against him, feeling his fingers in her hair, that she wanted it to be this way. She had cried on her first visit too, when the beauty of what she could never have stabbed at her heart, and Sonny had taken her in his arms. And now, for the second time—

It was comforting, the feel of him close to her, the knowledge of his affection, the affection of his desire. Lee wasn't being deceived. And she didn't deceive herself. But could it ever be any other way? Even with Goosey, who thought he loved her with a pure, burning light…

"Anything," she heard him whisper. "I'd do anything to have you love me…"

And she huddled to him, the tears still trembling in her eyes, conscious of his growing boldness.

"Lee," he whispered again, and kissed her.

She waited, not giving, not protesting.

His hand was cool where it touched her skin, hesitantly uncertain, anticipating the violent, negative reaction. But the girl didn't move.

A long drawn sigh came from Sonny's lips as he caressed her. Lee was like a docile kitten in his arms, warm and soft and reticent. Gently, he bent forward. The suede pump made no sound as it hit the rug. The other followed.

Sonny's drifting caress took her back to Madge, and the nylons——and Mangum's search as he held her in his arms. But it was all so far away now. It wasn't real. As if it had never happened. A half-remembered dream, best forgotten… Yes, that was it… A half-remembered dream, best forgotten…

Sonny…

The room grew dark because she willed it so. The mellow light caught at her fluttering lids, prying gently, but it was better in the dark, in the warm, enveloping dark.

She drew herself, kitten-like, into a shy, retreating crouch, leaning backwards to his urging.

His breath caressed her ear, flowing down, like a gentle stream, along her pulsing throat.

She whispered his name again, cradled in the dream, resisting momentarily.

His cheek, lips and fingers, trembling with longing, fever-hot, reverent yet profane in their containment, their possession… It wasn't enough.

She wanted to be hurt, to match the pain in her heart…yet, it wasn't right…to surrender…like this…to await, breathlessly, the final encroachment… There was no violence, no demanding greed… Nothing…like it would have been…with…with…

She pressed her lips together as resistance sprang within her like a coiled spring! She mustn't! She mustn't! She mustn't surrender now! She didn't love Sonny! It was Ricco she wanted, Ricco…

Ricco, the man who didn't want her… Who thought she was nothing… Not even a tramp…to be taken…and cast aside…

Not even a tramp…

"Lee." The intense whisper grated in her ear. "Don't—resist. Don't—fight back… Please… It has to be… It has…to…be…"

And then, as she fought against herself, against the throbbing urge that beat in every nerve and fibre, the delicate, resistless knowledge was upon her, brooking no denial.

The hungry, eager flowering… It was like nothing she had ever experienced before… The hungry, eager offering…and the slow, ecstatic unfolding… It was more than she could bear…

"Sonny!" she cried, and the sound of it pierced him like a leaping flame.

"Always… Forever…" he, mumbled, and then his words were lost in the shattering resurgence of her pride, the will to crown her affirmation with the only weapon at her command… Her beautiful body…

CHAPTER THIRTEEN

THE NEWS DELIVERY TRUCK was parked a few feet down from the Vagabond Club, its motor running. Lee didn't know that it belonged to Ricco until she saw the placard fastened to the body paneling.

It was past midnight. Every window in the street was dark. The sound of her heels on the pavement reflected the echoing loneliness, the plaguing insecurity of a woman walking home late at night.

She chose to walk along the curb, away from the shadowy doorways, the gloomy-black wells of basement approaches. The dim headlights picked her up as she continued on directly toward the truck.

She slowed her gait appreciably, at once tense and alert. The presence of the truck puzzled her. She tried to think of a sensible reason for it being there. She couldn't.

From a distance, with the lights shining in her eyes, she couldn't tell whether it had a driver or not.

She pressed her shoulder bag to her side, painfully aware of the crisp new bills pinned to the lining. Lee swallowed her heart and kept on going, ready to run at the slightest warning.

The white placard caught her eye as she moved abreast of the truck, the large white placard with the red and green lettering, proclaiming the virtues of the *New York Press*.

This time her heart refused to go down. Ricco, she thought. Ricco had grown impatient, and—

A hand touched her from behind, and she stifled a cry.

"Kinda jumpy, ain't you?" She turned to see Goosey smiling at her.

Lee flared. "What's the matter? You crazy, or something? You scared the life out of me!"

"I didn't mean to," he said. "I just came out of the club. It's my first day out. I wanted to look around."

"What did you expect to find this time of night?"

"I was lookin' to see if they threw my stuff out. Jeez, you ain't mad at me, are you?" His voice was edged with disappointment. "I was goin' nuts, waitin' to hear from you. Why didn't you write, or something? I would of come after you sooner, only they wouldn't let me out of bed. What's happened, Lee? Are you up against it? Can't you stand the old lady?"

"I'm doing all right," she said. "I never had it so good in my life."

His hulking form loomed over her, filled with joy at the very sight of her, tremblingly anxious to hear a good word. "I'm glad, Lee. You got no idea how I kept thinking of you, even through the pain, and the dope they gave me."

She smiled up at him, and patted his arm. But suddenly it came to her that she was talking to a stranger, that she didn't give a damn about Goosey at all. The thought made her shiver.

"You're cold," he said quickly. "The night air is too cold for you! I'll leave in a minute, Lee! I—just wanted—to make sure—if you know what I mean, that you were still here, even though Ricco told me. I got the funniest feelin' layin' in bed, thinkin' of you all these weeks. Like something terrible had happened. You sure you're all right, Lee? That there's nothin' I can do?"

She laughed, hoping that he hadn't caught the quirk in her voice. "Still the same old Goosey, huh? Clucking around me like I was a precious china egg. I'll survive, Goosey, in spite of everything. And you can tell that to Ricco, too."

He cocked his head like a puzzled St. Bernard. "Tell Ricco? What for? I don't get you."

"Never mind. I was just talking."

"What about seein' you soon, Lee? Makin' a date together? I—missed you so bad I still can't believe I ain't in bed, imagining all this…"

She moved towards the stoop. "The old lady don't like me to go out too often, but I'll talk to her. Give me a ring sometime." She started up the stairs.

"Lee?" He was right behind her, touching her elbow. "Ricco raised my pay. He made me a driver. Tonight was my first time out. That's why I had to come to tell you." He waited for her to say something.

She just stared.

"What's the matter, Lee? Ain't you glad?"

"Sure! Of course I am! It—it came as such a surprise!"

Goosey laughed. "Yeah, a real surprise, huh?" His free hand held the other elbow now. "You said once it would happen like that, but it surprised you just the same, didn't it? I'll be a collector yet, you'll see!"

"It's—just wonderful, Goosey! I'll bet your mother was glad, too!"

He grinned, uneasily. "I ain't told her yet. I don't know whether I should or not. She'll want the extra dough. And I want to save it—for us."

Lee felt her lips go stiff. "For us," she echoed.

GANG MOLL

"Yeah. Like Ricco said, there's nothin' like havin' a little house, and raisin' a nice family. It's always what we wanted to do, isn't it, Lee," he pleaded.

The words wouldn't come. How could she tell him now, that she didn't care? The shoulder bag seemed to burn against her side, weighted with guilt.

She saw Goosey go tense. "Lee," he said. "You ain't changed your mind? You—"

"I never made it up," she smiled. "You know that as well as I do, Goosey."

"But I thought, with the raise, and everything—"

"We have time, Goosey, plenty of time to talk it over. But not here, not right now."

His fingers tightened. "You made up your mind already didn't you—to forget about me—to—"

"Please, Goosey! That isn't so at all!"

"Then why are you hedgin'?" His voice rose. "I can't take it much longer, Lee! Why don't you come right out with it, and say yes or no!"

"It isn't—that simple. You got to believe me, Goosey!"

He was on the step with her now, standing close, gripping her painfully. "Swear that there's no one else! If that's the truth, swear it!"

She felt sick inside, sick with the knowledge of her shame. Yet anger flared, and she pushed him away, hating him for making her feel unclean. You're crazy!" she cried, "talking like that to me! I don't have to swear to anything! What did they do to you, knock your brains out?"

"Maybe... But if they did, it was on account of you! Now you listen to me, Lee—"

"I ain't listening to nobody! Nobody's going to run my life for me, you or Ricco or the old lady upstairs or anybody, do you hear? I'm sick and tired of being pushed around! What the hell brought you here anyway, snooping around so late at night? Did someone tip you off? Did Ricco send you to check up on me?"

The venom of her words bit into him, snake-fanged, and he stared down at her, shocked into silence.

She turned away and walked to the top of the stoop. Goosey didn't follow. He just stood there, crushed beyond words.

Contritely, she whispered, "Goosey. I'm—sorry. I didn't mean it that way." The corrosive guilt still burned within her, the feel of Sonny's hands on her body, the final possessive caress. If she could only make herself believe that she hadn't given herself because of the money! If she could only say, "It was because I was lonely, because of my frustration!"

He ascended reluctantly as she held out her hand, and took it.

"Goosey, don't go away mad. It isn't right, that it should be like this, after everything that's happened. I didn't mean to jump on you like that. It hasn't been too easy for me, either, living off the old lady's charity, not knowing from one day to the next, what—"

"Sure. I understand. I guess—I sort of beat the gun myself, flyin' off the handle without thinkin' how you must feel about it. You been havin' it pretty tough, too, worryin' about Mangum and everything." He ran his fingers through his hair, smiling ruefully. "That's one of the things I meant to tell you, right off. Ricco paid him, so you don't have to worry no more. Mom let Mangum in to see me. He wanted to know where you were. Then Ricco came and gave Mangum what he asked. He was swell about it, Lee. He said I didn't have to pay him back all at once, but just so much a week. That's why he gave me a better job. That's—" He broke off, staring. "I didn't get you, Lee. Did you say something?"

"No, Goosey. It's all right. What—what else did Ricco say?"

"Well, like I told you. About seein' that the two of us were taken care of." Goosey hesitated. "That's what I meant when I said—"

"Ricco," Lee said queerly. "So that's the way it is!" She saw through him now, what lay behind his strange behavior. He wasn't impervious to her attraction. He had wanted her all along. But without the risk. If he could get her to marry Goosey—

"What's the matter, Lee? Did I—"

"I was just thinking of Ricco, Goosey. How funny it is that he should take such a personal interest in us, a big deal like him. Didn't it ever make you wonder, too?"

"Should it? That's just the kind of a guy he is, that's all. A swell guy, like I told you all along."

"Yeah. A real, swell guy."

"You sound like you don't believe it."

Lee smiled in the darkness. "Oh, I believe it all right. Him and Santa Claus. Twin brothers. Only with him it's always Christmas." She snickered.

Goosey laughed. "Yeah. Ain't it so? Always doin' things for people." The laugh faded off, and he said, "But I still got to know, Lee. Tell me the honest truth. There ain't anybody else, is there, Lee? You're not stallin' me because you met another guy?"

"Did Ricco tell you to ask me that, too?"

"No, but—"

"But what, Goosey?"

He shifted uneasily. "I got a letter sayin' that I should keep my eye on you."

She felt as if the wind had been knocked out of her. "A letter?" Lee repeated. "Who sent it?"

"That's—the funny part of it. I don't know. It wasn't signed."

Her fingers dug into his arm. "Where is it? I want to see it!"

"I—tore it up. I got so mad when I read it—"

"What else did it say? What—"

"Nothin' else. Just what I told you. You sound like you got an idea who wrote it. Have you?"

"No, Goosey, I haven't."

"I figured it was one of the gang," Goosey said. "Maybe Lefty. He hates my guts. Lee, I hate to ask you again, but—"

"Come closer, Goosey, and put your arms around me."

He encircled her waist as they stepped into the vestibule. "Lee—"

"Kiss me, Goosey."

Their lips met. She clung to him, mouth parted, breathing into his. Then she said, drawing away. "Does that answer your question?"

He embraced her again, trembling all over. "Lee! Then you didn't forget me! Then you—" He found his breath forced back in his throat by the violence of her caress.

She held him close, her cheek to his, filled with a black rage. Would there be no end to it? Why did people hate her? Why did they want to hurt her? Why, why, why!

Goosey gave a gasping sigh, conveying his love the only way he knew how. Choked with emotion, inarticulate, he pressed her to him, his dry hot lips reading her face.

Lee was close to tears, galled to madness. They were all against her, everyone of them, Ricco and Lefty and Mrs. Mullins—even old lady Brink, with her childish, domineering ways. Any one of them could have written the letter, each for his own reason. Only Sonny Pierson could gain nothing by it... Sonny, who was willing to pay for his love, who risked Ricco's wrath, who stood to lose everything by defying old lady Brink...

She felt no shame now, in having given herself to him. She felt glad, and proud. Sonny wanted her for herself. He wanted her for no other reason than that he desired her, that he loved her.

She was glad now, that it hadn't been Ricco. Or Lefty. Or even Goosey. Goosey, with his crude, fumbling ways, with his childish, desperate greed, grasping and grasping and demanding as if she were an exotic food, to be consumed in one choking gulp.

But let him. It didn't matter. Let him believe that she cared for him, let him know her for a few brief, ecstatic moments. Let Ricco, too, be deceived into thinking that possession was not far off, that she would ultimately tell him all he wanted to know, and bring about the ruination of Julia Brink...

When the time came, she would tell Goosey, reveal Ricco's real reason for wanting them to marry. And then she would stand by, laughing, as disillusioned Goosey struck back...

And if she couldn't do it through Goosey, there was always Julia Brink, and the power that was hers, to confiscate Ricco's license. She had only to tell Julia the truth, testify before the commission that Ricco planned to monopolize the delivery routes, that he had threatened her into forcing her to spy for him...

When the time came...

But for Goosey the time was the present, moving to her like a needle to a magnet, crushing the breath out of her with his surging embrace.

Let him, let him, she thought, and the memory of Sonny's subtle caresses smoldered in her mind. Poor, childish Goosey. He doesn't know any better. It will always be the darkened hallway with him, even after marriage, the darkened hallway... Not...the way...Sonny knew... Not...the gentle approach, the gradual building up, the slow, creeping fuse, the mounting tension, the delicate, febrile caress...

But there was a limit, a limit to the pity she could feel for Goosey. Beyond that limit...

"No," she said, but Goosey smothered her protest with his lips, deep in the throes of rising emotion, shaken by the sudden pulsing contact. "No!" Lee cried again, tearing her lips away. "Goosey, no!"

He didn't seem to hear. Lee found herself jammed into the angle of the wall, with Goosey against her.

For an intense, breath-bated second he locked her in his arms, rocking as she sought to thrust him from her. Then, fighting off the response that seemed to gnaw at her very vitals, she forced her hands between them and Goosey, with a moaning cry, sank back, shuddering fitfully.

"Lee," he said, and turned away, looming tall and rigid in the gloom. He kept his back to her, digging his heels into the tiles, clenching his hands against his thighs. "Lee..."

She stood behind him for a moment, a warm, trembling shadow in the dark. "Don't—turn around, Goosey. Let—it be good night...this way."

She stopped at the foot of the stairs as the door closed behind her, pressing her hands to her face, listening to Goosey's uneven shuffle as he left the vestibule.

Overcoming the weakness that dragged at her knees, she started upward, the bag clutched tightly to her side. She was afraid now, filled with a singing vibration that stemmed from the very core of her being.

And it frightened her.

What was happening to her? She should feel ashamed, degraded. Only a short while ago the devastating knowledge had come to her, the sweet, secret knowledge that she had longed for through all the painful maturing years. How many times had Mrs.

Mullins warned her, how many times had she seen in the movies, or read in the magazines the inescapable punishment meted out to the transgressor? She was unclean, disgraced, contaminated in the eyes of the world. Yet the heavy hand of guilt was not upon her.

What would Goosey say if he knew? And Julia Brink?

What would they say if they could read her mind, if they could witness the kaleidoscopic pictures of joy flickering with the still live embers of desire? She wasn't sick or ashamed or pained with grief. She didn't despise herself, or hate Sonny.

Because of Goosey she wanted him all the more. Was it such a terrible thing, so hard to understand?

Lee halted at the second floor landing and groped in the bag for her key.

It didn't matter anymore what anybody thought of her, least of all, herself. There was a meaning to existence now, where there had been no meaning before, only fear and sweat and struggle. Now she had found compensation. Now she had found the answer to many things: the lonely bitterness of Mrs. Mullins, the hectic, recklessness of her father.

But marriage to Goosey wasn't the answer she was seeking, nor the indefinite giving Sonny would demand of her. Maybe Ricco was right. It was a horrifying thought, low and mean and contemptible, just like Ricco himself. Long ago he had known her for what she was. It was as if the same devil dwelt in both of them, controlling every thought and action.

Ricco...

She turned the key in the lock and opened the door.

The lights were on and Julia was there, moving in the rocker, waiting for her.

The china-blue eyes were undimmed by the lateness of the hour, the thin hand as steady as ever as she stroked the cat in her lap.

"I forbid you to see Sonny again," she said. "I know you've been to the hotel. I told you once before I have no use for girls who trouble themselves with men. If I can't have your promise now you'd better prepare to leave."

She got up, gesturing Lee to silence with a wave of her hand. "Don't bother to deny it. I may be old but I'm not blind and I'm not a fool. Will you tell Sonny to his face the next time he comes that you refuse to see him again?"

"But I don't see any harm in—"

"Will you or won't you?" Julia cut in sharply. "The matter is very important to me!"

"And it's important to me, too! How can you expect me to give an answer on the spur of the moment?"

The blue eyes narrowed. "I see. So it has gone that far already." She lowered her arms and the cat jumped to the floor. "I'm telling you this for your own good, Lee. Because I want you to stay. Sonny is a conniving little cheat! He's dishonest and insincere! He'll only bring disgrace and shame upon you!" She drew in her breath. "And I won't have it! Not in this house, do you hear? Do you want him to ruin your life, to bring grief and trouble your way? Get married if you have to, but don't make yourself the pawn of men!"

Lee turned on her heels and walked toward her room. She stopped at the door and faced Julia Brink across the room. "What makes you think that he won't marry me?"

"Because he has nothing he can call his own. Nothing, do you understand, Lee? Without me, he would be a nameless thing, walking the streets, grubbing for food! Everything he has he owes to me, his job, his life, his loyalty!"

"But—"

"Remember my words, Lee! I consider him beneath contempt! Don't waste your youth on him!"

The silence rose to a quivering tension.

Lee saw with a start that there were tears in Julia Brink's eyes. A cry escaped her lips, and she stepped forward.

Julia waved her back. "Go to your room, you little fool," she quavered, "before you make me regret my words!"

And she moved away, followed by the mewing cat, her frail shoulders trembling, but ramrod straight.

CHAPTER FOURTEEN

LEFTY SAW her step into the telephone booth and when she came out he called to her and Lee stopped in her tracks. He walked to where she was standing, carrying his smile clear across the drug store, and said, "I thought you turned into the invisible woman, or something. What have you been doin' with yourself? I been wantin' to see you ever since that little talk we had."

Lee, conscious of his curious eyes upon her new outfit, caught her reflection in the glass of a showcase and instinctively fussed with her dress. "The old lady's been pretty cranky," she said. "She just don't want to be left alone. I'm getting pretty sick of the whole thing, to tell you the truth. The only reason I'm here is because I had a fight with her. I don't know what's got into her."

"Maybe I can tell you," Lefty said. "But we'll let that go for now. You promised me a date, Lee. What about keepin' it? Tonight."

"Some other time, Lefty. I—"

"Tonight would be a good night," he said, "The Vagabonds are holdin' a meetin'. About lettin' Goosey join up again."

"I got a date," she said, "for tonight. You saw me make the call." He looked at her. "It ain't with Goosey. Because he's goin' to be at the meetin'." The smile had left his face. "Who is it, Lee? Ricco again?"

"I don't think I ought to tell you."

Lefty swore silently. "I should of known it! That's why he wanted the meetin' for tonight! To get Goosey out of the way, and me! How many times you been to see him, Lee?"

She kept her eyes lowered. "I don't think I ought to tell you that, either."

"I was wonderin' about the fancy duds," he sneered. "So you're still playin' along with him, after that long spiel you gave me!"

"I can't help myself. You know that. Now you better let me go. I don't want to be late."

They walked to the street, with Lefty still holding her arm. "Let him wait. I got to talk to you."

"Lefty—"

"Shut up. I ain't forgot what you told me. About all of us stickin' together, and everything. He's gettin' pretty fed up himself with the old lady. If he wants us to do a job on her what am I goin' to tell him? If you back down on us where will we stand? The way it looks to me now is that you changed your mind, that you like the color of his money!"

"No, that's not true…"

"I suppose the old lady gave you the money? In the pig's eye, she did!" He thrust his face close to hers. "You sold out to Ricco, just like the rest of us, didn't you? That's why the old lady's scared, that's why she don't want to be left alone!"

"No, it's nothing like that at all! Ricco wouldn't need you or the Vagabonds if I told him what I knew! Or are you too dumb to understand that?"

His fingers tightened painfully. "You better make up your mind how it's goin' to be," he said grimly. "I ain't riskin' my neck for nothin'. If you don't put it on the line for me I'm pullin' out and Ricco can do what the hell he wants with you!"

Lee didn't shake him off. She stood there, her dark eyes at once angry and pleading. "You got to go along with me just a little while longer, Lefty! Stall Ricco off if you can. And if nothing else works—"

"Yeah, go on. If nothin' else works?"

"Well—I'll put it to him straight. That we know what he's up to. That for our help he'll have to give us protection—and a cut."

Lefty looked at her and laughed. "You'll get a cut all right, tryin' to shake-down Ricco! Right across the throat! So he's goin' to be a-scared of you!"

Lee spoke quietly. "Not a-scared, Lefty. I'll just walk out on him. And rather than let me—"

His lip curled. "You still think you're the Queen of Sheba, huh? Maybe he thinks so. He would know better than me. But if I don't get the chance to find out soon I'm lightin' a fire under Goosey! Remember that!" And he let her go.

She hurried away, forgetting Lefty no sooner had she turned her back. He could be of use to her but right now she had more important fish to fry, and she made her way to the rendezvous with Julia's warning blotting all else from her mind.

She hadn't slept much since the night of Julia's ultimatum. Sonny had become the most vital thing in her life. Up to the time of her acquiescence, security mattered more than anything else she could think of. Except having Ricco. But having Ricco would have meant having security, too. A sort of left-handed security, that is—as Goosey's wife, with Ricco playing the benevolent benefactor; and paying clandestine visits while Goosey was at work.

No…it wasn't what she wanted at all. If she was going to sell herself it would be with no strings attached.

The pressure, however, was becoming too much for her. She was getting it from all sides now. From Julia, and Goosey, and Ricco. And her desire to keep Lefty and the Vagabonds as the ace-in-the-hole was beginning to boomerang. Her false promises somehow had to be made good. She had to make a decision. Soon…

The more she thought of it, the more impossible the situation became, and by the time she met Sonny outside the Century Theatre on Flatbush Avenue her mind was in a seething turmoil.

He greeted her anxiously as she approached, wasting no words as he took her hands. "You look as if you haven't slept for days. Julia really put the knife into you, didn't she?"

"I told you what she said. What are we going to do, Sonny?"

"Easy now… We'll think of something. Just don't get panicky, that's all. It isn't as black as it looks." And he gave her a queer, hard smile.

She watched as he purchased the tickets at the window, wondering at his calm assurance, whether his words had any real significance. She found out after he took her to a corner of the large, ornate lounge.

He seated himself next to her on the gaudy imitation Empire sofa, his eyes sweeping the dimly-lit interior with casual penetration. "These places always remind me of an undertaker's reception room," he said. "Even the spray they use smells like formaldehyde. Maybe it's done deliberately, to deaden the minds of the customers, so they won't object to the junk they've paid good money to see." He shook his head. "It's a fit place for the dead, all right, a fit place to discuss Julia and what we're going to do about her." His voice was grim.

Lee sat erect, her eyes fastened to his pale, calm face, not daring to analyze his words.

He turned to her, the queer smile still on his lips, and said, "I've given a great deal of thought about what to do with Julia. Years and years of thought, long before you appeared on the scene, Lee.

And like a miracle, Julia took you in and solved everything for me. For *both* of us, rather." He took her hands in his and leaned close, his voice barely audible in the oppressive stillness. "You've come to mean a great deal to me, Lee. I want you to know that before I say anything else. I trust you. Together, the both of us can have a wonderful life. But first I have to know just where you stand. He paused for a moment, strangely hesitant, and questioned her with his eyes.

She watched him, not knowing what to say, filled with a creeping uneasiness.

"Do you love me, Lee?" he asked. "How much do I mean to you?"

"But—what's this got to do with Julia? What—"

"It's got everything to do with Julia. If I can be sure of you, as sure as I am of my feeling for you, then—then Julia won't be any kind of problem at all."

"You're making it sound like a conspiracy, or something." Lee frowned vexedly. "What's the build-up for? You know how I feel about you. You've been the only man in my life."

"That's just it, Lee. I want it to stay that way."

She held her breath, waiting.

"How would you like to be rich, have all the money you can spend, run the old house as if it belonged to you?

"I'd like it fine," she said. "But just what would I have to do to get it? Kill Julia?"

He laughed. Mirthlessly. "Not exactly. Just take better care of her, that's all. See that she's kept strictly to herself, with no visitors, no outside contacts." As he saw the doubt rise in her eyes, he went on quickly, "She's threatened to throw you out, hasn't she? You don't have to waste any sympathy on her. She's been a callous, domineering wretch her whole life. She's made it miserable for scores of people. It's a wonder to me that she wasn't taken care of long ago!"

Lee shook her head, drawing away as if Sonny had slipped poison into her hands. His smile had vanished now, and in its place was such a look of venomous hatred that Lee felt herself go cold all over.

"I don't know myself," he grated, "how I've put up with her all these years! I was just about at the end of my rope when you came along, Lee! Julia owes her life to you, believe me! And I—I owe you my sanity, and my freedom—"

Lee looked about wildly, fearing that they had been overheard. But the dim lounge was almost deserted, except for a necking couple huddled behind a potted palm, yards away.

Sonny emitted a deep, rasping sigh. "I know," he said. "I must sound like I'm crazy to you. But I have the best reason in the world for hating her, the best reason for taking over what really belongs to me..." His opaque eyes were burning now, burning with an emotion that came from the primitive roots of his being. "She wants to deny me everything, Lee, everything! That's why she threatened you. Because she knows what you mean to me. But it's not going to be that way this time. We're going to put a stop to it, Lee, the both of us, once and for all!"

She edged away from him, at once fascinated and fearful, watching the play of emotion on his face.

"I brought a fortune into that house," he said. "Month after month, year after year, she's been stashing away those long manila envelopes, hiding them in every corner of the house. Do you know what was in them, Lee? Those so-called messages I collected at her newsstands every two weeks?"

Lee nodded weakly, wetting her lips with her tongue. "Money," she said. "There was money in them—"

"No, not money, Lee. She was too smart for that. They were negotiable notes. That was part of my job, to go to the bank with the cash and buy up these notes. God knows how many big business houses she controls now, just through that simple little practice. And among those notes, Lee, are several Ricco would give his eye-teeth to get back. The fate of his delivery business, with a few more added to her collection, would be a foregone conclusion!"

"It—it's just too hard to believe! My God, and all along I kept thinking of her as a harmless old lady, messing around with cats because she was lonely!"

His lips were drawn tight against his teeth. "She's lonely, all right. And before we get through with her she'll be lonelier still!"

He snatched her hands. "Lee! You got to help me! You got to stay with me! Don't you see how easy it will be? We can cash in the notes. We can force her to sign them and every once in a while I'll go to the bank and get the cash. And whatever I collect from the stands will stay in our pockets—yours and mine! All we have to do is cut off the phone, and be tough with her! You can do it, Lee. You got guts! I knew we could work together the minute I laid eyes on you…" He pulled her to him. "We won't have to worry about anything then, about coming or going as we please, with no one telling us when we can make love or we can't. Lee, I'm not asking you to do anything wrong, believe me! Everything she owns belongs to me, but if I don't get it now, I never will! The cats will get it, Lee, or some lousy charity, if she dies! We'll keep her living as long as we can! You see now, don't you, that what I'm asking is not so bad?"

Caught in the web of words, Lee sat there, head spinning. The room seemed to swim before her eyes, swirling with the sound of Sonny's voice, sucking her down into a whirlpool of crime and madness.

She squeezed her eyes shut, trying to deafen herself to his entreaties, the flow of golden promises that acted upon her senses like strong drink.

There were so many things she wanted to ask, but all she could say was, with striking bluntness, "Julia said you would never marry me."

Sonny's fingers closed on hers spasmodically, but he said nothing.

Lee opened her eyes. "If you're willing to have me share in all these things you claim belong to you, why won't you marry me?"

His face was like a mask. It had the look of death upon it. Through bloodless lips, he said, "I'm a man without a name. If I marry at all before Julia dies, I'll have no claim to anything. Officially, I don't exist. Only Julia has the power—through her sworn statement—to recognize me as a living person." His eyes bored into Lee's. "That statement will never be filed if I marry you—or anyone else." He broke off then, the grinding bitterness of his words hanging in the air like a suspended sword.

"But—I don't understand!" Lee cried. "How can she control that? How—"

"I'll tell how," he grated harshly. "Because I'm her son! Because I was born to her in a shuttered winter bungalow, with no one around to witness the disgrace..."

Lee gasped. "Then—there was no record—no one who—"

"The one person who knew is dead. The woman she paid to raise me. But I was never registered."

Lee was struck speechless.

"A pretty story, isn't it? Blue-blooded Julia Brink hiding her shame in the cold, stinking dark! Discarding her brat without a tear, without even having the decency of acknowledging his existence!" He laughed, soundlessly, jabbing a forefinger against his chest. "That's me, Sonny Pierson, her collector and gunman, the fool who's protected her all these years."

Lee couldn't meet his eyes. "Your father—" she said quietly. "Did you ever find out who he was?"

"Yes, I found out all right. From my dear mother herself. Because she wanted him to pay and pay and pay! He's the very same man Ricco would like to find out about, the big deal politician who licensed all of Julia's newsstands, the guy who's standing in Ricco's way!"

Lee stared down at her stiff, tense fingers. "Then—then it all ties in— It all makes sense now—"

"Rotten, stinking sense, Lee! The one thing I've got to have is her sworn statement, her acknowledgment! Then I can go to the tramp who was my father, and force him to—"

"But Julia! Why didn't she? Why doesn't she let you—"

"Because she hates us both! It's twisted her mind and made a mad woman of her! My father is the symbol of obscenity and I am its product—something evil and dirty to be stamped out, no matter how. He's never married, and neither shall I. Not in her lifetime. Because she refuses to permit the further propagation of evil! 'Foulness begets foulness.' That is her answer to both of us!"

He turned away, his eyes bleak and haunted. "But it isn't the end, as she thinks. I'll get what is rightfully mine. And I'll take it in front of her very eyes, and she won't be able to stop me!" He drew a deep, shuddering breath and took Lee's hands again. "We'll wring every last nickel out of her, Lee. We'll take everything she's scrounged and saved and denied herself for and spend it like water! We'll fix that miserable wretch, the two of us, Lee! You'll do that for me, won't you, Lee? Won't you?"

The thick, offensive stillness pressed around them, clouded with the smell of death. *Like a funeral parlor*, Lee thought. Sonny had sensed it because in the back of his mind the suggestion was already there, growing from his festering hatred of Julia Brink.

Death. There was the smell of death in the air.

Lee shivered, her face as white as paste. She got up, seeing the image of Julia in front of her eyes, stretched out on the floor, stiff in death, the mewing cats prowling around the body—and the fixed, china blue stare, watching her, watching her…

"No," she whispered. "I could never go through with it, Sonny. You—mustn't ask me to. Never again."

And she started across the soundless carpeting like a lifeless automaton, the once warm and pulsing blood frozen cold in her veins.

"Lee!"

Sonny sprang from the sofa and hurried after her, raging wordlessly.

He caught up to her in the marble and onyx lobby and laid an angry hand on her arm.

Before he could say a word he was grabbed by the shoulder and swung violently around.

"All right!" Lefty cried. "What's the pitch? Who are you and what are you doin' with Lee?"

CHAPTER FIFTEEN

SONNY DIDN'T bother to explain. He sized up the situation within a matter of a few seconds, because he recognized Lefty.

He turned to Lee and cried, "So you were working for Ricco all along! You got me to talk and now you're walking out on me! But I'll fix you for this, you little tramp!" His hand shot out and caught her squarely across the mouth.

She fell against Lefty and Sonny bellowed an obscene name, exploding with rage. "You won't get away with this!" he shouted. "I'll get you if it's the last thing I do!"

A few dawdling movie-goers froze in their tracks, gaping as Lee struggled to keep Lefty from going after her assailant.

"No!" she cried. "He's got a gun! Let him go! Let him go!"

But Lefty pulled away from her and ran in the direction of the street, his hard heels echoing in the oblong shell of the lobby.

She called out again but Lefty didn't even look back.

As he barged into the milling crowd outside the theatre, Lee pulled herself together and walked along the polished marble wall, holding herself erect with a supreme effort. Her knees had turned to water and her stomach was crawling with pain.

She couldn't think. It had all happened so quickly that nothing had quite registered. She stopped under the brilliant glare of the marquee, staring at the flowing human stream. It had come together again, after the scattering penetration created by the headlong flight and pursuit of the two men, like blood coagulating along an asphalt crack, absorbing the sound and the fury with jellied resolve. Sonny and Lefty had disappeared completely, swallowed up by the headless monster. She must will herself to set her body in motion.

Lee forced her way to the curb, grateful for the numbing daze that insulated her mind against thinking.

"Taxi," she said, and the tall, uniformed street-usher blew his whistle and the cab came.

When she got out in front of the familiar house she saw that the lights were still on in the Vagabond Club. The meeting, she thought. Lefty hadn't even gone to the meeting. He had followed her. And now he knew that she had lied. He would tell Ricco about Sonny. He would—

The crawling pain started again and she halted at the foot of the stairs, pressing her hands to her stomach, filled with a growing fear. She had to act, and act fast. Before Lefty betrayed her, before Ricco could force her to give the golden prize to him.

She started up slowly, fear sharpening her wits, greed pressing the weapon into her hands. She had to follow through now, with everything that Sonny had told her...

Julia wasn't in the room when she let herself in. But the light was on. Lee took off her white tam and dropped it on the frayed, dusty chair. She went into the kitchen, searched for something strong to drink, gave up, and came back. Julia was waiting for her, the inevitable feline cradled in her arms.

"You've been to see Sonny again," she said.

Lee sat down and started a cigarette. Her match hand began to tremble and she cupped it with the other, holding it steady.

"Have you seen him for the last time, or have you decided to leave here?"

Lee fanned the match out and returned the china-blue stare with insolent defiance. "I don't know whether I'll see Sonny again or not," she said. "You may not either, for a long time to come."

Julia's muslin petticoats whispered as she moved across the room. She stood over Lee, the cat still in her arms, the fine, slender fingers digging into its pelt. "Why won't I see him? What have you done to him?"

"I've led him to the slaughter," Lee said, and she smiled bloodlessly. "Ricco will know all about him pretty soon. And if he makes Sonny talk, he'll know all about you, too."

The old arms sagged as the weight of the cat became too much for them. The animal landed on its paws and padded away. "Explain yourself!" Julia cried. She clasped her hands under the formless bodice, her frail body straining with anxiety.

"It happened accidentally," Lee said. She crossed her legs, holding her knee lightly, the cigarette projecting from between her fingers. "We were followed," she went on. "Sonny ran away but he may have been caught."

Julia groped behind her for a chair and sat down. Her face was the color of melted wax. "He won't tell them! He mustn't! He mustn't!"

Lee bent forward. "Look, Julia. I want you to get one thing straight. I wasn't working for Ricco. He wanted me to, but I turned him down."

Julia didn't seem to be listening. Her gaze was far away, and glassy. "Sonny won't tell them!" she whispered. "He hates me too much for that! He won't tell them no matter what they do!"

"I hope you're right, Julia. For my sake, as well as yours."

The blue eyes ground toward her painfully, like glass beads turning in a doll's head. "He'll hate you for this, too, as much as he hates me!"

"I suppose so. But I don't care." Lee drew on her cigarette and let the smoke drift through her rose. "I might have, once. But not anymore. He's a stinking little punk, Julia. And you're not much better. If I didn't have so much to gain it would make me very happy to see Ricco take the two of you over." The round blue eyes remained expressionless. Lee tapped the muslin-covered knee. "Did you hear me, Julia?"

"I heard you."

The pounding of her heart had subsided now, and Lee experienced a strange, growing calm. Lefty would come to her first, before he went to Ricco. She was sure of it. And she knew how to take care of him. But the pressure had to be kept on Julia. Relentlessly.

"I want you to tell me about Ricco, Julia. If you want me to help you, you better tell me everything."

"Help me? You're offering to help me after what you did to Sonny?"

"You'll need help, Julia. What I did to Sonny happened because of you. You're too old to know what you're doing. You hate-twisted your mind until you couldn't think straight. You drove Sonny right into my arms, Julia." Lee stopped talking. She ground her cigarette against the sole of her shoe and dropped the butt into the plate of soured milk near her feet.

Julia glared. "You just made this up about Sonny being caught by Ricco's men. You're lying to me, trying to draw me out..."

Lee ignored the accusation. "I've decided that me and you should become full partners," she said. "I want you to tell me where you hid all those business notes and give me a list of all the newsstands you own."

It dawned upon the old lady then, that Lee knew more than she was telling. The thin fingers plucked at an invisible seam on her sleeve, trembling as they revealed her fear, pinching the cloth in an expression of anger. "You got Sonny to talk!" she cried. "You lured him and—"

"It doesn't matter how you put it. But you like to think of it happening like that, don't you, Julia? Because, as you say, 'foulness begets foulness.'"

Lee sprang up in alarm as the old lady slumped forward in the chair. She grabbed the bony shoulders and held her erect, shaking her as the china-blue eyes rolled up in her head.

"Julia! Are you all right? Julia, sit up!"

The thin, faint voice seemed to reach her from the grave. "Take—your dirty—hands off me…"

Lee fell back as if she had been slapped.

The old lady sat up, gasping, her face twisted with hate and frustration. "So…he told you…" she breathed. "He…told…you!"

The dark eyes smoldered. "They showed their hatred nakedly, matching the venom of Julia's words.

The laughter that grated past Lee's lips was pitiless, hard beyond description. "Sweet little Julia Brink," she mocked. Each word was like the slash of a knife, ripping the last vestige of decency from the trembling old body. "Sweet little Julia Brink, writhing in the stinking dark, giving birth to the shameful product of her lust. Alone in the stinking dark, Julia, hating herself, hating the baby, hating the man who used you! A beautiful picture, isn't it, Julia? And through all the years you kept it hidden, shutting yourself away with your guilt in this house, blackmailing the man who betrayed you, punishing Sonny by keeping him nameless, living on the hatred of your own flesh until you relished the poison, the filthy stew that kept you going! You've reached the end of the line, Julia. You're going to step down and let me take over!" Lee shook her, vengefully. "It ought to make you even happier! Now you'll have someone else to hate, Julia. Me!" And the unclean laughter spewed from her lips again.

The old lady slumped in her hair, a pitiful rag-doll of a woman, with no life in her, no resistance. The tears that came to her eyes were as unreal as the bright china-blue eyes. She cried without making a sound. She just sat there, the tears running down her cheeks, beaten down to nothingness.

"You're going to tell me everything, do you hear?" Lee persisted. "If you want to hold on to what you have I got to know!

116

I'll help you keep off Ricco. I'll see that he isn't told about Sonny! But I got to be told everything…"

Julia didn't move. She stared dully at the floor, at the plate of soured milk with the burnt-out butt swimming in it.

Lee started to speak, broke off then, shrugging, and slipped her arm under Julia's shoulders. "I'm putting you to bed," she said. "When you feel better you tell me what you want to do."

The old lady refused to get off the chair. She looked up at Lee, disengaging herself, and said, "Where's your father?"

Lee gaped. She put her fingers to the wrinkled forehead. Julia thrust the hand away. "I'm not sick," She said. "And I'm not going mad, if that's what you're thinking." She took a deep, heaving breath, forcing herself erect, and said, "We're going to settle this now, Lee. Tonight."

Lee sat down again. A feeling of uneasiness came over her, coupled with a deep distrust.

"I'll tell you about Ricco," Julia went on, blotting out the tears. "It can be told in a few words. He's a vicious brute who wants to take over all newsstand distribution. In this borough and all the others. He's brought most of the dealers under his thumb by violence and intimidation. Every one of them but me. He's made a fortune but he still wants more." She blew her nose and stuffed the tiny square of linen under the cuff of her arm-length sleeve. "He brought me to the verge of bankruptcy several times, by making short deliveries and refusing me credit on returns. But he hasn't got a full list of all the stands I own. He's got to have that list, and soon. He's got to wreck me before the renewal of his license comes up, so he can be big enough to shut everything down if—if it is refused him." The firm voice wavered. The blue eyes sought out the plate again, unable to meet Lee's penetrating gaze. "Do you—understand what that would mean? If—Ricco could shut everything down, the commissioner would be forced to resign, and a new one appointed. The hold I have over him—would be gone. Ricco would continue to operate, and smash my holdings…" The words trailed off, choked back by the resurgence of her emotion.

Lee sat quite still, studying Julia's face. The beaten look had faded, and in its place, once again, was the maddening assurance, the hard, hidden arrogance.

A grudging admiration rose in Lee, tinged by a warning of danger. The old lady wasn't licked yet. She could see it in her eyes, in the sound of her measured words.

"But you're holding some of Ricco's notes," Lee finally remarked. "Sonny told me. Enough, he said, to—"

"Cancel him out? No, I'm afraid that isn't quite so. Their maturity follows the renewal date of his license by several weeks. Postponement of the renewal is the real threat he faces—but if he gets the list first, and—and finds out about my past—" She clamped her lips together and pressed her hands against her knees. "Lee—who was it who followed you? Who—"

"You don't have to know his name. It won't matter anyway, if he runs to Ricco with the news. But if he doesn't—"

Julia leaned forward tensely. "If he doesn't?"

Lee rose slowly. "If he doesn't—it won't be much trouble at all, to keep him quiet." And a bitter smile came to her lips.

Julia watched as Lee caressed the side of her hip, as her glance went to the ripe, thrusting bosom. She looked away, her face stained with blood. "Foul," she muttered, and Lee heard it and laughed.

"The list," Lee said. "I want the list."

The old lady got up, supporting herself on the back of the chair. She had the look of a mummy, dry and withered.

Perversely now, as Julia shuffled across the threadbare rug, Lee felt the pangs of conscience. *Foul,* she thought. *Dirty, filthy foul! Julia's right! And Ricco was too, all along! But there's no going back now! Only deeper, and lower...*

She followed Julia into the bedroom, watched as she unhooked a dusty picture from the wall and took a yellowed slip of paper from behind the frame. "The list," Julia whispered, and held it out in a trembling hand.

Lee took it. She creased it into small squares without once glancing at the row of notations, and placed it in her bosom. "And now his name," she said.

Julia shook her head. "Not—right now. Please, Lee! Please!"

"All right. I guess it can wait."

"Thank—you—Lee— You're—a good—girl—"

"Sure. As long as I go easy on you. Don't start lying now, Julia, and cringing. It's making me sick to my stomach."

The old lady lowered herself to the edge of the bed, her jaw hanging loosely. "I'm afraid," she said. "You'll never stop Ricco, Lee. Who's—going to collect now? Protect—my people from his gangsters? Sonny was shrewd, and brave. But now that he's known—"

"Forget about him! He was nothing but a no-good louse anyway. You're lucky to get out of this alive!"

"I guess I am, Lee. I guess I am."

She turned away. "I'll look in on you later. To see if there's anything you need. You better get to bed now. You look all in." Lee started for the door, and, stopped.

Someone was outside, in the hall, brushing against the panels. She threw a quick glance at the old lady on the bed and saw that she too, had heard it.

They listened, not a word passing between them, waiting with tense immobility.

The sound came again.

Julia put her hand to her mouth, stifling cry.

They heard the creaking of the hinges then, as the door swung open.

Lee forced herself to move. An eternity seemed to pass before she finally set foot outside the bedroom. Slowly, she turned her eyes toward the front door. The threadbare rug, the dancing motes of dust, every little detail seemed to register in the camera of her mind as she looked across the room. Clearly outlined in the curtain of hazy light, the furniture stood, fearful, waiting, as if suddenly arrested in flight.

And then she saw the thing move along the open door, drifting down and projecting itself, laboriously, across the worn lip of the rug and stop.

It was a hand.

Lee felt the floor slip from under her. She grabbed for the table, reached it, and held on.

Painfully, she pulled herself erect.

When she looked again, the hand was still there, limp and un-moving. And there was blood on it.

As in a dream, with maddening reluctance, she found herself moving toward the door. It seemed to take an hour to negotiate each step.

Julia emerged from the bedroom just as Lee pulled back the heavy oak frame.

They saw Sonny lying there, beaten to a bloody pulp, looking for all the world like a carelessly disposed bundle of dirty clothes, except for the faint movement of his breathing.

CHAPTER SIXTEEN

BRAMBLES WAS mopping the floor of the little back room when Lee walked in. He stopped when he saw her, leaning on the handle, and said, "Look who's here, Lefty! Old lady Brink's little helper! Itchin' for more trouble? What do you want with us?"

Lefty got off the couch and snatched the mop handle from Brambles. "Beat it," he ordered. "And don't come back for a couple of hours…"

He stared. "Hey now! Just a minute! That's breakin' the rules! You can't—"

Lefty's swollen hand slipped inside his lumberjack. "I can't what? I'm the guy who makes the rules around here, Brambles. This is special business. Now do like I say and beat it!"

Brambles glowered. "Ricco's goin' to hear about this! What goes on around here, anyway?"

"This," Lefty said, "goes on around here!" And he pulled out the gun. "Now, scram!"

The boy with the pock-marked face moved away. "Packin' a rod!" he muttered. "You better watch your step, Lefty! That's all I can say." His shoe button eyes took in Lee from head to foot before he left, and he jammed his hands into his pockets sullenly, taking his own sweet time as he walked down the length of the narrow room.

They heard the door slam, and Lee said, not taking her eyes off Lefty. "I know that gun. It belongs to Sonny." She held out her hand. "You better give it back to me."

Lefty returned it to his pocket with a deliberate motion. "You'll get it back after you keep your promise." A crooked smile came to his face. "It might come in handy, in case Ricco gets rough with us."

"Don't give me that! You're not bucking Ricco. You told him about Sonny, didn't you? And he had you beat him up to find out what he knew!"

Lefty waved her accusation aside. "Don't be a jerk. Ricco laughed when I told him. I beat him up myself, the little runt. And him with a gun on him!"

Lee couldn't believe her ears. "Ricco laughed? About—what?"

"That you should fall for a runty bellhop! I knew who he was after I took a good look at him. He looked different in the movies, with other clothes on. Cripes," Lefty cried, "the nerve of you! Meetin' this guy at the same hotel where Ricco was stayin'!"

Lee didn't know what to say. She went limp with relief. Lefty saw her lean against the doorjamb for support, her hand to her breast. He let go of the mop handle and it fell to the floor with a dull report. "The runt had it comin' to him," Lefty said, "for tryin' to slap you around. What kind of a racket was he in, that he had to carry a gat? Was the old lady payin' him to tail Ricco?"

"No. She doesn't even know who he is."

Lefty gave her a penetrating look. "He's still upstairs, ain't he? Why is she keepin' him there?"

"Because he can hardly move!" Lee cried. "Were you crazy, beating him like that? And why the hell did you drop him in front of the door?"

"You're a smart dame," Lefty said. "Guess."

"I don't see what sense it makes!"

"This is what sense it makes..." he cried, and lunged suddenly, grabbing her. "You played me for a sucker and now you're goin' to pay!"

He held her arms pressed close to her side, while he laughed harshly into her face.

She tried to get away from his lips but they found hers in a bruising kiss as he pressed her against the wall.

"You had me thinkin' all the while you were layin' for Ricco, and I was afraid to touch you! You were lettin' this runt take you, laughin' behind my back, linin' me up against the guy who was always my friend!"

He dug his hands into her, into the firm soft flesh, and she cried out. He laughed, wildly. "This time Goosey won't be here to save you, you lyin' little tart! I'm goin' to use you, just like you said Ricco was goin' to use me!"

He grabbed her by the hair and flung her toward the couch, his narrow, good-looking face distorted with rage. "I ought to beat you like I beat the runt!" he shouted. "Me—fallin' for a dame like you, gettin' all kinds of crazy ideas!" He lashed out savagely, and Lee crashed down on her back, bouncing against the leather-covered springs like a punctured rubber ball.

"I'll teach you to make a sucker of me!" he cried, and snatched at her.

She twisted away but Lefty put his hands on her, and the heel of her shoe caught him on the cheekbone, knocking him to his knees.

His fingers found her wrist and she was forced to turn to him as he pulled back her arm in a painful hammerlock. "Now," he gasped, "you little tramp! See if you can break out of this!"

He spanned the couch with one leg, pinning her down, and Lee couldn't move. "This—" he panted, "is just the way—I want it—" Crudely, his hand moved, and Lee cringed convulsively. He laughed, shaking his head crazily. "I'm not a runt! I'll show you what a real man is like!" And the violence of his caress seemed to shrivel her spine.

For a sickening moment everything went black. But then her fingers curled around the butt of his gun, closing spasmodically as she found it, and fearfully, as he raged, she drew it from him.

She raised it over his head to strike, but Lefty saw it coming and the gun crashed harmlessly against his shoulder, jumping out of her hand at the impact and spinning to the floor.

He laughed again, spanning her jaws with the fingers of his free hand, squeezing. "Thanks!" he grated, "for gettin' it out of the way!" And he increased the pressure.

He found the pulsing artery under her ear and Lee lay helpless as the creeping darkness came upon her. "I knew you'd come lookin' for me," she heard him say, "after I dumped Sonny at your door. It paid off this time, waitin' for you…"

She couldn't move now. It was terrifying. She tried to raise her arm, to ward him off, but it remained useless and dangling, hanging down over the edge of the couch. And her legs were quivering as if shot through with high voltage.

As her receding consciousness flared for a brief, flickering moment, she sensed the hovering, alien presence close by, the stealthy approach... And the approach, too, shamelessly, of Lefty's desire...

It happened just as the final darkness descended, as the savage surge of him broke the barrier of her defense...

Lefty cried out, strangely, and seemed to leap away, only to fall heavily, clutching at the air as he rolled from the couch and hit the floor.

Lee heard the faint mewing before she passed out, felt the familiar caressing contact of the soft, warm pelt across the back of her dangling hand, and sank into the grateful darkness.

The coldness of the water brought her to. When she opened her eyes she found herself in Julia's arms, half-sitting, half-reclining on the leather couch, her disarranged clothes decently in place.

She looked into the old face but Julia's attention was riveted elsewhere. Lee followed the hostile stare and saw Lefty, his right temple streaked with blood, sagging against the window sill.

"You're clearing out right now!" she heard Julia cry, "and you're never to come back, do you understand? Every last one of you!"

Lefty kept staring at the barrel of the gun, his face white and working. "You can't throw out the Vagabonds," he said. "Ricco won't let you! Ricco—"

Lee felt herself sinking back as Julia drew away. She pressed the flat of her hands against the leather and held herself erect, watching as the tiny, muslin-clad figure glided towards Lefty, the gun held firmly between the translucent fingers. "This is my answer to Ricco," she said, and raised the muzzle slowly.

Lefty started to sweat. He waved his hand at her, weakly. "All right," he said. "But you ain't heard the end of this. And she hasn't either!" The gun followed him as he moved towards the door.

"Remember!" Julia warned. "This property belongs to me. Let Ricco just try to force his way in!"

Lee got to her feet and followed Julia down the long narrow room as she prodded Lefty before her. Not a word was spoken. There were no more threats, no more warnings. To each of them the picture was crystal clear. The decision had been reached, the choice made. Lefty stood with Ricco. And Lee—

"I'll never forget this, Julia," she said. "You could just as well have let him—"

"Nonsense, I've got other plans for you, my dear, and Lefty was not a part of them." She held out the gun. "Here, take this ugly thing away. And come with me."

Lee followed meekly; her head still swimming from the frightful ordeal. In the dank gloom of the outer hall, she watched as Julia stopped in front of the cellar door. Julia turned then, a queer smile on her face, one hand resting lightly on the knob, and said, "Look behind you."

An involuntary gasp sounded in the stillness as Lee caught the shadowy movement of the high wooden paneling as it seemed to melt away before her very eyes.

"It's really quite simple," she heard Julia say, "the way it operates. You just have to put your foot in the right place on the right floorboard. My father was a very ingenious man, Lee. He built this house. Solid as a fort it is, and as safe, if you want it to be. Downstairs there is a vault as strong as any you'll find in the largest bank. Someday I'll show it to you, after we rid ourselves of Mr. Ricco."

Lee felt Julia's hand at her back, urging her forward. "When you reach the top of the stairs, Lee, just lean gently ahead. The wall will give and you'll find yourself in my bedroom, behind the clothes hung in the closet."

"But."

"Go on up, my dear. You needn't be afraid. I want you to know about this passage just in case that Mr. Ricco decides to pay us a visit. I understand that he can become quite violent at times."

The thin, quiet voice kept rambling on as Lee took one step at a time, her eyes following the streak of phosphorescent paint that hung in the gloom like a jagged ladder, ascending into the endless dark.

"There, you see?" Julia said, "There are the markings, plain as day, right on the wall. Push between the two vertical lines and we'll be safely back in the apartment."

The old lady found Lee sitting on her bed as she stepped out of the commodious closet, the automatic flung carelessly on to the counterpane. She picked it up and placed it in the dresser drawer.

"Now you know most of my secrets," she said. "There isn't much else for you to find out."

Lee took a deep breath. Reality seemed a far way off. It seemed that she would never disentangle herself from the cloying web of fantasy, the persistent, clinging nightmare that had haunted every waking and sleeping moment since the flight of her father. The little old lady surely didn't exist, Lee told herself; she was just a figment of her nagging, relentless dream, the confused jumble of a disordered mind. Sonny and Ricco and Goosey—all of them— Lefty and Mrs. Mullins and the blowsy blonde waitress brushing her hair in her father's room—they would all disappear, dissolve in smoke as soon as the fear left her, the fevered, crawling fear of being put away, of being left, alone and unloved, in a world full of uncaring strangers. If only someone would love her! Warmly, as a little girl longs to be loved! Lee put her hands to her face, rocking on the bed, and started to cry.

Julia watched, smiling to herself. She helped Lee from the bed then, and said, "Come. I've got something very important to tell you. And I want Sonny to hear it too." She led Lee into the room that had once been hers, and Sonny looked up from the bed, his battered face robbed of all expression. Only his eyes, his strange, opaque eyes, revealed his emotion. Lee looked beyond him, unable to meet his silent accusation.

He raised himself painfully, as Julia doubled the pillows behind him, and said, "Why did you bring her here? Why didn't you throw her out, like I told you?"

Julia smiled. "I'm sure you'll change your mind after you hear what I have to say." She drew up a chair near the bed and sat in it, motioning Lee to follow suit. She looked at one, and then the other, as Lee settled close, and said, "I've decided to stop fighting Ricco. I'm too old, and too tired—"

Sonny jerked erect, unmindful of the pain, incredulity twisting his face into a grotesque mask. "Before you say another word," he cried, "I'm warning you, if this is a trick of some kind—"

"I suppose you could call it a trick," she cut in smoothly. "But it's a trick that may save my life, and yours. I haven't much longer to go, Sonny, and I want to live the rest of my days in peace. Let the jackals fight over my fortune. It—it's become meaningless to me now. All I want is to be left alone." She turned slowly, and fixed her eyes on Lee. "The decision rests with you, my dear. Whether Ricco gets his way, or you get yours."

Lee waited, sensing there was more to come.

"It could be," Sonny interjected coldly, "that I'll be the one who'll make the decision!"

"Ultimately, perhaps, but not right now." She folded her hands in her lap, and said, with deliberate distinctness. "I've written a new will. Leaving all my monies, properties and holdings to Toledo Sissle, providing she consents to become my adopted daughter."

Silence.

It dropped, tangibly, like a first act curtain charged with coming drama.

Sonny sat frozen on the bed, stunned beyond protest. Lee could only shake her head, numbly, as no words came forth.

Julia's soft laughter floated on the silence like a mocking, disembodied spirit. With great relish, she said, patting Lee's lifeless hand, "If we can get your father to consent, my dear, you'll stand to inherit more money than you ever thought existed. Of course, now that you know the fortune is going to be yours, you'll never surrender the list to Ricco, will you, or tell him about my past?"

Sonny came to life, suddenly, like a marionette roused by a mad manipulator. He pounded his fists against his knees, and cried, "You're insane! Stark, staring mad! Everything you have belongs to me, it's mine! I won't let her take a dime, do you hear? Not a dime!"

Julia watched him calmly. "And how are you going to prevent it?"

Sonny ignored her challenge. "You fool!" he shouted. "Can't you see what you're doing? You'll be signing your own death warrant! Do you think she'll wait for you to die? She'll run right to Ricco, and together they'll plan your death!"

"I think not. I'm counting on her greed to keep her from going to him. Why should she share her fortune with him, after the way he's abused her?" She turned, smiling, to Lee. "Isn't that so, my dear?"

Her head was throbbing so that she could hardly think. "You don't mean it," she said. "You've never been good to anyone in your whole life! You have no reason to love me! You—"

"Let us say that I understand you, at least. I don't blame you for what you are, Lee. Just—as by the same token—I was not to blame. My father was too busy, always, to care about what I was doing; lost in his work just as yours was lost in women and drink. It's the common bond that draws me to you, Lee, that makes me pity and understand. But more than that, I know you'll protect my name, keep my secret—that you'll fight for what is yours—against Ricco or anyone else—once the realization comes that I am giving you my fortune, that it will be yours."

"And do you think I'm just going to sit back and let her walk off with everything that belongs to me?" Sonny was beside himself, trembling with rage.

"I'm afraid you can't do anything about it." Julia smiled. "Unless, of course, Lee finds it in her heart to forgive you."

Sonny controlled himself with an effort. He sank back, cradling the back of his head with linked hands. "So that's it..." he breathed. "So that's your little game. So now I'm to go crawling to her, just as I did to you all these years, debasing myself, scheming, planning, hoping for a few crumbs of kindness—" He squeezed his eyes shut, appalled by the depth of her hatred. "I can't believe it," he murmured, "that you can hate me so much! Julia—"

The old lady got up, blue eyes glittering with a strange light.

"There's nothing further I can add. The next move is up to Lee. I'll write out my will as soon as I get her answer. Lee, I want you to give me your word that you won't leave this house until you've made up your mind. There's no telling now what Ricco may do. Have I your word?"

Lee nodded dully. "You have my word."

"Good! I'll call my lawyer and prepare him for the shock." She chuckled. "The poor man will be relieved to find that my fortune won't be wasted on cats! He may even believe that I've actually become sane!" She walked to the door, still prattling. "Of course it may take some time to locate Tom Sissle, but the sooner you make up your mind, my dear, the sooner we'll find him." She halted for a moment, and faced them, the shrewd, knowing smile starting hundreds of tiny wrinkles in her skin, like a stone thrown into a placid pond. "There is one final condition," she said. "The name of Sonny's father shall remain a secret. Forever. Are you agreed to that, Lee?"

Sonny rose slowly on the bed, as white as death, waiting for Lee's answer.

Lee raised her head. Her eyes sought the far corner of the room, and she said, not looking at either of them, in a voice that was hardly above a whisper, "I agree."

Again there came the silence as of the lowering of a curtain. But behind the silence, as Sonny sank back grimly; as Julia retired with a crisp "Thank you!" rose the ghostly sound of a match being struck near a powder keg.

The end, it seemed to say, was not yet.

The tenuous fuse had only begun to smolder.

CHAPTER SEVENTEEN

"I THINK it's about time," Ricco said, "that we settled this thing." He took a dime out of his pocket and handed it to Goosey. "You got the number. Call her up. And tell her that you want her to meet you here at the *Golden Rooster.*"

"But maybe she's still sick, like the old lady said." Goosey turned the dime over in his palm and looked at Ricco.

"And maybe the old lady just don't want her to see you anymore. You know what a screwball she is. Since she threw out the Vagabonds, you're on her blacklist the same as the others."

Goosey took a sip of his beer. "I wish to hell I knew what it was all about. Was Lefty really carryin' a gun? Did he really try to stick her up?"

Ricco leaned back in the booth, his rugged, handsome face showing signs of impatience. "You heard what Brambles said. He saw the gun. If it was any of my business I would have gone up to see the old lady about you, I mean—but all this is between you and Lee, and she might think I'm a pretty tough looking cupid. Look, Goosey, I'm only trying to do you a favor. I got better ways of spending my time."

"Yeah, I know, Mr. Ricco. But we sort of—well—got out of touch with each other since she had the trouble you patched up with Mangum. And then her not bein' able to visit me on account of my old lady—it made her like a stranger."

"I suppose so."

"And now this crazy thing, with the old lady not wantin' her to see me. Jeez, it's just like a conspiracy or something, that I shouldn't get married to her..."

Ricco laughed. "I wouldn't be surprised if it is that! But go on now...call her up. If she answers the phone and stalls you herself then you really got something to worry about. But she won't, you'll see. If I know anything about dames, she'll come over with bells on..."

Goosey got up. There was a look of hope on his homely face. "Okay, Mr. Ricco, I'll give it a try. Should I—should I tell her you're here, too?"

"If you think it'll help."

Goosey trotted toward the phone booth, jiggling the dime in his closed fist. When he came back Ricco saw that he had a big smile on his face.

"She's comin', boss, just like you said!" He sat down, grinning from ear to ear, and tossed down the remainder of the beer with joyful abandon. "You were right, too," he said, wiping the foam from his lips, "about the old lady bein' mad at all the Vagabonds. And what do you think Lee said besides?"

Ricco bit off the end of a cigar and put it in his mouth. As the flame of the match danced to his inhalations, he smiled at Goosey and nodded for him to continue.

Goosey said, "She wanted to know whether you were lookin' to be best man at the weddin'. Can you beat that, boss? She must of smelled you were behind it!"

The cold eyes flickered. "She's a smart kid. But I hope she appreciates what I've done for you. You weren't due to be a collector for a couple of years yet."

"Oh, she liked it fine when first I told her you made me a driver! It knocked her for a loop, it did. She could hardly believe it. But wait until she finds out that I'm a real big deal now!" A flood of gratitude poured from the jubilant Goosey. "Mr. Ricco, I'd do anything for you, you been so swell to me. If you asked for my right arm this minute—"

"Cut it, Goosey, you're drooling. All I want is that you should do a decent job. Just keep in mind that you're working for me, and not for that dame you're so crazy about."

Goosey laughed, beckoning the waiter. "These drinks are on me, boss. You got to let me pay you back some way!"

They had four refills before Lee showed up. Goosey knew she had arrived when Ricco, facing the entrance, straightened in his seat and put his hand to his balding head self-consciously.

Goosey met her halfway down the floor, trotting out and grabbing her hands in his as she stopped between the bar and the fancy archway leading into the back room.

"Jeez, look at you!" he cried. "I didn't expect you to dress up! You look like a million bucks!"

She acknowledged his all-engulfing, hungry glance with a fond squeeze of her fingers. "A million bucks," she said. "That's just what I feel like, too! I got wonderful news to tell you, Goosey. Wait'll you hear!"

"You mean you're goin' to marry me? Is that what you mean?"

She slapped his cheek playfully. "Maybe something even better than that! Come on, I see your boss wigwagging us. Let's go over and give him an eyeful…"

"Yeah," Goosey laughed, and looked at her again. "He's gettin' an eyeful right now. I never seen him stand up like that before, to give a dame the double-O!"

Smiling with the brazen knowledge of what the skin-tight satin dress revealed, Lee linked her arm in Goosey's and sauntered down the aisle, feeling every eye upon her. The firm, clean thrust of her seemed to fascinate the onlookers, daringly unsupported as she was, provocative with pointed suggestion. The snug hipline, following the rhythm that ran in rippling highlights from the audacious curves to the soft resolve of molded, flaunting contours, moved with the breath-catching grace known only to dancers.

Ricco, a set smile on his face, offered her his hand as they came to the booth. His words were prosaic but the catch in his voice belied his front of hard-boiled sophistication. "Nice seeing you again, Lee. Had it tough for a while, hey?"

"For a while," she agreed, and sat down. "But luck has a way of changing."

"I'm glad to hear it." He signaled the distant waiter. "I ordered a champagne cocktail for you," he said. "I remembered you liked them."

Goosey laughed. "Yeah, I remember that too." He sat close to her, grinning into her pretty face. "One night you liked them too much though, huh? Boy, will I ever forget that night!"

She slapped his arm. "You better, Goosey. You came damn near close to losing your head."

"Who wouldn't, the way you looked?" Ricco smiled at her through the cigar smoke. "I remember that night, too. You had on almost the same kind of dress you're wearing now. And I got you mad because I called you a pest, or something, for hounding me about a job. Yeah, a lot has happened since that night, a lot of things have changed." His eyes drifted over her. "But you haven't, Lee. You're still the same nervy, hot-looking dame—except that you've learned a lot since then. How can I tell? By the look in your eyes...the adding machine look."

The waiter came and Ricco lifted his glass to her. "I'm glad you learned what the score was. I'm rooting for Goosey, you know. When are you going to put him out of his misery and marry him?"

Lee gave Goosey a lingering smile. "You still in such a hurry, Goosey? Afraid I'll spoil, or something?" Part of the smile was rewarded to Ricco. "Don't you think I'm too young for that, Mr. Ricco?"

"Not if it's done legal," he smiled back. "There's a difference, I've heard."

Goosey laughed. "Go on, say some more, Mr. Ricco. That was real good."

"Sure, that was real good," Lee repeated. But her words held an undertone of mockery. "If things ain't legal they're just no good for Mr. Ricco. Are they, Mr. Ricco? He don't like anything unless it belongs to somebody else, legal. Like newsstands and delivery routes." Lee smiled as she saw him stiffen. "Even women. He likes them to belong to somebody else, legal. That's why he never married. It gives him a nice, cozy feeling, to play Santa Claus and then collect back his presents— Especially if the bait's got no hook on it, nice fresh bait without the jail-hook waiting to catch him."

Goosey laughed. Then he said, innocently "I don't get it."

"You will," Lee said, "if I marry you."

Ricco said nothing. He just looked at her.

Goosey didn't know how to take it. He stirred uneasily, flushing.

"That ain't no way to talk to Mr. Ricco, Lee. I mean, about you and me, gettin' married, and me—gettin' it. It—it ain't nice."

Ricco flicked the ash of his cigar into the empty glass. "You're too sensitive, Goosey. You ought to be glad that Lee is so open. Coy dames make for trouble. When you marry Lee, you'll know where you stand, exactly. That's one thing I always liked about her. No bluff."

Lee's mocking smile did not diminish. "Gee, thanks again, Mr. Ricco. Do you really mean it?"

"I never say anything unless I mean it." He fixed her with his eyes. "Sometimes people forget that. People like old ladies and young dames who should know better."

Goosey felt that he was on the outside now, looking in. He caught the waiter's attention and called for more drinks. Just to let them know that he was still around.

"I thought we were goin' to talk about me, Mr. Ricco," he complained. Then he slipped his arm around Lee's waist and snuggled close, winking at her. "About us gettin' married, and the raise to collector's job Mr. Ricco gave me."

"How nice," Lee said, and pecked him on the cheek. "I expected he would do something like that."

"Jeez! Is that all it rates?" Goosey's disappointment was tinged with anger.

She patted his arm. "I was saving the rest for later." Lee paused then, deliberately, and took out her compact.

As she held the mirror up to her face, Ricco said, "All right, Sarah Bernhardt, now that we're all set up for the punch line, what is it?"

"I'm going to inherit a fortune," she said, and dropped the compact into her open bag, *plup!* The gesture was timed perfectly. It had the effect of a gambler throwing down the final, winning trump card.

Goosey's eyes snapped open. He gaped, glancing from Lee to Ricco and back again. "A fortune..." he repeated. "You hit a number, or somethin'? Lee, what—"

She laughed, her eyes still on Ricco. It had the sound of glass being ground underfoot. "No, Goosey," she said. "It's something much bigger than that. Julia Brink just made out a new will. She's leaving all of her money to me."

Ricco took it without a murmur. He put the cigar to his lips, drew, and let the smoke drift slowly through his nose.

Goosey scratched his head. "What money?" he wanted to know. He turned to Ricco. "Boss, Julia Brink ain't so rich, is she? She must be levelin' with Lee, sayin' that."

The cigar came out of his mouth, and Ricco said, "Oh, she's rich, all right. But not as cracked as Lee seems to think."

Lee jerked erect. "Cracked? What are you talking about? She's got more brains than you and me put together!"

"That I don't doubt at all. That's why I figure there must be some strings attached." He waited for Lee to speak.

"Well—it's nothing really important. She wants to adopt me first..." A tight smile came to her face, "...legally. My old man has to sign his consent."

"That means you got to find him first."

"Yes."

"I suppose old lady Brink hired an agency to search for him?"

"Over two weeks ago."

"Congratulations," Ricco said, and turned to Goosey. "I guess I should have told you before, but I wanted all the good news to come at once. Your promotion, and everything. You see, I knew about this all the time." He sat back, sighing smugly, his eyes on

Lee. "The old lady called me up and told me right after you made up your mind to take it."

Lee sat as if turned to stone. Her face was granite-grey.

"Like you said, Lee," Ricco went on, "she's got more brains than the both of us put together."

Goosey seemed completely devastated. "That—don't mean—" he stammered, "that you won't marry me, Lee?"

"I don't know what it means!" she cried testily. "You'll just have to wait, that's all, until we find my old man, and get the papers signed!"

"Jeez, but suppose they never find him?"

"Will you shut up, and stop talking crazy? They'll find him all right!"

Ricco smiled at Goosey, with mock sympathy. "You waited so long, you can wait a little longer. I would...for a rich young chicken like Lee, here. You should be happy instead of sad. Come on, let's drink on it!" He raised his glass. "To Lee's fortune!"

They all drank, in a stiff silence.

As the piped-in music seeped into the vacuum, Ricco added, "I hope it all turns out right. Like you said before, Lee, luck has a way of changing."

Goosey groused, making wet circles on the cloth with the bottom of his glass; Lee watched him, unable to conceal her uneasiness. Something was in the wind. She could feel it. The taste of her anticipated triumph had turned to ashes in her mouth.

Ricco pulled back the sleeve of his jacket and looked at his wristwatch. "You better get a move on, Goosey," he said, "or you'll be late. You still got your week to finish out as a driver."

Goosey didn't budge. "Yeah, I know."

Ricco then said, "I'll take Lee home. I got my car outside." He got up. "Coming, Lee?"

She glared at him. "What's the hurry?"

"No hurry. I don't want you to get back too late. It might spoil it for you with the old lady." He smiled, thinly. "You got to think of that now."

Goosey got up with Ricco, respectfully. He was still frowning. He said again, as if to himself, "Suppose that they never find him? How long can a guy wait?"

Lee gave him a dirty look, but said nothing. She rose slowly. "Some good time!" she remarked bitterly, and walked out, followed by Ricco.

The three of them squeezed into the front seat of the convertible and Ricco dropped Goosey off at the nearest subway. As Goosey stood at the door of the car, wavering and reluctant, Ricco said, "So long, you lucky dog! When you marry into the dough maybe I'll sell you a piece of my business." And he laughed.

Goosey responded weakly. He peered into the dark interior for one last look at Lee, and waved goodnight, ambling away dejectedly.

Ricco put the car in gear and started away. Lee moved as far over as she could. The silence quivered about them like a snarling dog straining against an inadequate leash.

After a while Lee said, looking out of the window, "This isn't the way back. Where are you taking me?"

Ricco met her with a smile as she pivoted on the seat. "I want you to meet a friend of mine," he answered. "At the Beechmont Hotel."

"To hell with your friend! Take me home!"

"I wouldn't think of letting you go back to Julia without seeing my friend."

"You don't want me to meet anybody! You're just itching to get me into your room!"

He laughed. "It's not the bellhop I'm talking about, Lee, so you don't have to be afraid."

"I know it's not the bellhop. But I don't care who it is! You're sore because I got you licked. Because you won't get one splinter of Julia's holdings. And now you're trying to strong-arm me!"

He reached out, and put his hand on her knee. "What's the matter, don't you love me no more? There was a time when you did everything but tie me down..."

She flung off his hand, angrily. "Sure, there was a time when I didn't know any better. I wouldn't touch you now with a ten-foot pole!"

Ricco's laughter was infuriating. "Boy," he cried, "How money does go to some people's heads!"

"Cut the malarkey and take me home!" Lee snapped. "I don't want any part of you! I'm wise to what you're after—but I'm sticking with the gang, see? Nothing you can do or say will change it!"

He gave her a quick glance.

"I wouldn't be too sure about that, Lee," he said softly. "Me and you...we belong together. Our minds run alike, along the same channels. You caught on without my even telling you. And do you know why?" he went on. "Because in the back of your mind that's just the way you want it. Everything safe, everything respectable," He took a deep breath, as the thought of having her fired his imagination. "That bellhop," he said. "When Lefty told me about him I felt like sending one of the boys to give him the works. But maybe now you'll appreciate me all the more, after we—"

Lee cut in harshly. "I don't need you now, Ricco. With the dough I'll be getting I can have my pick of men—and I won't have to tie up with any two-bit gangster like you!"

"You're kidding yourself, Lee." He turned the car off the busy avenue and brought it to a halt in a dark side street. "Let me show you what I mean," he said.

Lee protested but it happened before she could stop him. He put his hands on her, on the proud, audacious curves, and kissed her. She struggled momentarily but his possessive caress tore her resistance to shreds. It was just like she always dreamt it would be. Like a bolt of lightning out of the blue. Just the feel of him, holding her.

"Ricco..." she gasped.

Her skin was smoother than satin, firm, yet giving. She moved urgently, driven by instinctive impulse, guiding his hand. As she gave a shuddering sigh he drew away, fighting his own desire.

Lee slapped him, then, sharply, grabbing his shoulders and shaking him in a rage of disappointment.

He pushed her away savagely, and she fell back, overcome with emotion. The car started and Ricco brought it to the Beechmont Hotel.

"Get out," he said, and she followed his command.

When they got to his suite he put the key in the lock and opened the door. He pushed her in, pale and shaking, blinking at the blaze of light. And then she saw the other woman. Sitting on the sofa, with her legs crossed, smoking a cigarette. Lee stared.

Heavy-breasted and tall, with crude languor, the woman stood up. "Hello, Lee," she said, and patted her blonde, peroxided hair.

"Tell her," Ricco said, and spun his snap-brim across the room.

"Your old man's dead," the blonde waitress said. "He's been dead a long time."

Lee took one step forward, and slumped into Ricco's arms.

When she came to, she heard the rest of the story.

"He got it in a ginmill in Chicago," the blonde said. "Got into a fight with a longshoreman and the guy sunk the hook into his neck. I moved back to where we lived before, here in town. I searched all over for you. I thought you'd come back some time, just to ask, like the landlady said, about mail and things. But you never did. I'm sorry, Lee."

Ricco told her to get out.

After she left, he said, still holding Lee in his arms, "Julia knew that your old man was dead. That's why she suggested that phoney deal with you. She sent someone to the house and found out, the same way I did, when she told me about the will and the adoption."

Lee said nothing. She lay back, eyes closed, trying hard not to cry.

"It was a sweet scheme," Ricco said. "I never would have touched you. It wouldn't have done me any good, with the license renewal coming up so soon. I guess you know what would have happened to you after that."

Lee spoke without opening her eyes. "Yes, I know," she said.

"What are you going to do about it, Lee?"

She sat up then, and reached for her bag. When her hand came out she was holding a piece of yellow paper. "Here," she said to Ricco. "Here's the list you always wanted."

He read it, carefully, then refolded it and put it into his wallet. She watched him as he went to the phone and dialed a number. After he got the connection, he said, "Lefty? This is Ricco. I got the list. Listen." And he repeated it from memory. "Get the boys together and meet me on the corner of Fulton and Schermerhorn tomorrow night at ten. We got a lot of wrecking to do."

When he turned from the phone he saw that Lee was at the bedroom door, waiting for him.

He went over, put his arms around her, and said, "I guess it just had to be this way, baby." And he kissed her.

They went in then, and closed the door behind them, softly.

CHAPTER EIGHTEEN

"JULIA THOUGHT you ought to be told about it," Sonny said. "Lee didn't come home last night. She's still at the hotel with Ricco."

Goosey stood at the foot of the bed, gripping the board with aching fingers. "You're makin' it up!" he cried, "You're lyin', both of you! Something's happened to her! An accident—"

Julia met his accusation with a china-blue stare. "You know I wouldn't lie to you, Goosey. Why should I? I knew how it's been with you and Lee all along, before I took her in to live with me. It was because of what you told me that I decided to help her. And now you tell me that I'm lying, after all I tried to do for her, and for you, too." She shook her head, looking aggrieved.

Goosey pressed his fists together and cried, "But—but it's crazy, don't you see? Why should she take such a chance after everything was all set, after she knew what you were going to do for her?"

The old lady shrugged helplessly. "I don't know, Goosey. I thought I knew her better than anyone. I suspect she's been seeing Ricco secretly for a long, long time. Look what happened to Sonny, just because Ricco wanted to keep him from talking! Dumping him right at my door, a boy I didn't even know!"

Sonny laughed, bitterly. "It was just his way of telling Lee to keep her mouth shut, too. That's the kind of a guy he is. Maybe I deserved to get this beating, trying to act cute with him, but next time I'll know better."

Goosey spread his arms in anguished appeal, looking from one to the other. "But she said she was goin' to marry me. Only last night, she said, as soon as they find her old man—" He broke down, pressing his hands to his face, and turned away.

Sonny permitted himself a sly, vengeful smile. "All I know," he said, talking to Goosey's trembling back, "is that she's been seeing this guy regularly, at the hotel. I work there—or I used to. It was easy to spot her going in and out. I don't have to tell you how pretty she is, and how she walks—"

Goosey pounded his fists together. "Shut up, shut up! I heard enough! The lousy little tramp! The lousy little tramp!"

Julia reached out to him, but he shook her off.

"Ricco's more to blame than she is," Julia said. "He must have kept after her like a dog, filling her full of promises. After he got her the job, and then paid off that horrible man, as you told us, maybe in a moment of weakness, she—"

"No!" Goosey cried, "It ain't so! That ain't the way it happened! They made it up between them a long time ago! I remember it now, how they insulted each other, how they made out they couldn't get along! Always when I was there, just to fool me! All along, all along they been doin' it, while she kept puttin' me off, and he kept bribin' me with better jobs! I was crazy blind not to see it, but it was there, all the time, right under my nose!"

"Goosey—" He evaded her outstretched hand as she saw him make a move towards the door. "Wait! Where are you going?"

"You know where I'm goin'! To the hotel! And if I find them together, like you say they are, I'll—" Goosey stopped as he found Julia blocking the door.

"Don't be a fool, Goosey. Even if it's true, what can you do? You can't fight Ricco. Look what happened to Sonny. You got your mother to think of too, and your job."

Goosey's voice rose to a shout. "My job! Do you think I could work for that bastard now? After what you just told me?"

"But getting hurt won't—"

"He's the one who's goin' to get hurt. Ricco! I'm big enough to take care of him! I'll show him…"

"Sure," Sonny jibed, "You're big enough. Big enough to walk right into a few bullets! Do you think he's just going to stand there and let you beat him?"

Goosey couldn't move. He glared at Julia, across the room at the man lying on the bed, shaking with a rage that was terrible to see. He put his hand to his pocket, as if reaching for the weapon he didn't possess.

Then Sonny said, with proper grimness, "I'd like to see you do a good job on him too—for what he did to me! But you'll get yourself killed if you can't disarm him first. Goosey…" He paused, raising his arm slowly and pointing to the dresser drawer, "…there's a gun in there. My gun. If you want to use it…"

Goosey was at the dresser even before Sonny had a chance to finish, pulling at the drawers wildly.

He found the gun and jammed it into his pocket.

"Goosey! Don't!" Julia pleaded again, but he pushed her aside and rushed out of the door, swearing under his breath.

He couldn't know, as he hurried toward the hotel, that Julia was mocking him, making her peace with Sonny. All that he knew was that Lee had betrayed him, that Ricco had played him for a contemptible fool, that they were laughing at him behind his back. *Sure, get married to Goosey, Ricco must have told her—marry Goosey and I'll send him here and there and keep him away whenever I want to pay you a visit. The poor jerk will never suspect. Not Ricco, the guy who promoted him, who gave him a big raise so he could marry you!*

He kept running, the rain slashing against his face. It was dark out, the streets were deserted, except for the heavy cab traffic.

He stopped running when he realized that the Beechmont was a long way off, that Lee might be gone by the time he reached there. If he missed her, if he didn't catch them together, then he would never know—they could keep on denying it and he would have no proof—and all the while they would go ahead with their plans to make a bigger fool of him—

He stepped off the curb and right into the path of a skidding taxi. He caught himself just in time and jumped back, just as the fender brushed his leg.

The hackie started to curse him, shouting in a hard, coarse voice. But Goosey didn't bother to listen. He saw that the flag was up and opened the door and got in.

"The Beechmont Hotel," he cried. "Shut up and step on it!"

He dried his face with his handkerchief as he sat back, panting, feeling the hard barrel of the gun against his hip, cursing again as he thought of Ricco.

The hackie drove recklessly, egged on by Goosey's constant urging and they reached the hotel in a matter of minutes.

Goosey threw him a bill as he leaped out, not even thinking about the change. He caught an elevator just ready to rise as he ran through the lobby, ducking ahead of the sliding door by the fraction of an inch.

The boy told him the number of Ricco's room and Goosey made straight for the door as he was let out on the fifteenth floor.

Goosey could hear the sound of the elevator grinding upward again when Ricco answered the angry persistence of the buzzer. Goosey took his finger off the button as the door swung back and shouldered his way in, pushing Ricco back on his heels.

Ricco was wearing pajamas and slippers, and he stumbled, losing one slipper as it caught against the nap of the rug.

"Where's Lee?" Goosey cried. "Where have you got her?"

Ricco swung at him but lost his balance, and Goosey gave him a violent shove that sent him crashing into a big wing chair.

"What is it?" A shrill voice cried from inside. "Ricco, what's the matter?"

It was Lee's voice.

The sound of it stabbed out at Goosey, and he seemed to buckle, his breath oozing out in a long, painful gasp. He stopped, staring through the open door of the room.

He saw Lee, her dark hair flowing down to her shoulders, her hands crossed protectively in front of her.

Something seemed to explode inside him. He rushed in, flailing at her, crying over and over again, "You lousy little tramp! You lousy little tramp!"

She fell down and he continued to hit her.

Ricco ran for the holster hanging over the night table and pulled out the gun. "You crazy loon!" he shouted. "Stop, do you hear? Stop, or I'll shoot!"

Goosey whirled, crying out foully, and reached back. Lee grabbed his hand just as Ricco pulled the trigger.

The big, hulking body jerked erect as the bullet hit, and a look of surprise showed on Goosey's face. Then, slowly, his eyebrows still arched in pained amazement, his knees gave way and he pitched forward.

Lee suppressed a scream, staring down with vacant eyes.

Ricco didn't even look at Goosey. "All right," he said to Lee, "get dressed!"

He hurried through the rooms to the outer door and opened it, scanning the halls and listening.

Nothing.

He closed the door again, grimly, and hurried back. Lee was still dressing. He gestured with his gun and said, "Roll him under the bed. I'll get Harry up here to help me."

Lee touched Goosey with her foot and drew back. "I—I can't," she said, and Ricco snarled, "Then for Cripe's sake, pick up his gun! Don't just stand there."

It was as she was reaching down that Goosey moved. She jumped away, screaming. Screams that seemed to rend her.

Ricco was passing through the door, on his way to the phone, when he heard her. He swung around and saw Goosey sitting up, holding his stomach, the blood seeping between his fingers. And then he saw him raise the gun and pull the trigger.

When Lee got to Ricco he was dead, with a neat round hole showing between his eyes, and Goosey sitting there, laughing, waving the gun, trying to point it at the sprawling, screaming girl.

But the gun fell from Goosey's hand, and then he sat there for a moment, wobbling on his haunches, falling on his back as Lee got up and rushed him.

A horrible feeling of emptiness came over her as she saw the accusation die out of his eyes, as Death looked back at her with a cold, triumphant stare. "Goosey!" she cried. "Goosey!"

Smoke curled from the muzzle of the gun, strong and acrid. It caught at her throat, choking off her hard-won breath as with creeping, ghostly fingers.

Goosey's fingers…

"Goosey…" she whispered.

And then she saw the gun. Sonny's gun. The gun Lefty had taken from him, the gun Julia had snatched from the floor of the small back room.

Julia...

Lee bit her lip to keep from screaming. She pressed her hands to her temples, shutting the sight of death from her eyes, feeling the sickness well within her as she stumbled out of the room, blind to everything but her own need.

The phone rang.

It kept on ringing. Urgently, frantically.

When she came out of the bathroom she saw by the clock on the table that it was ten minutes past ten.

The phone kept ringing.

She put the receiver to her ear, hanging on to the table by sheer nerve.

It was Lefty.

She listened as he started to talk in an excited voice but his words made no sense to her at all. He stopped.

Then she said, just before she hit the floor, "Ricco—says—for you—to go ahead. You—got the list—Orders—Lefty— You got—to go ahead—without—without...him... Smash everything. Every...thing...!"

THE END

If you've enjoyed this book, you will not want to miss these terrific titles...

If you've enjoyed this book, you will not want to miss these terrific titles...

ARMCHAIR SCI-FI & HORROR DOUBLE NOVELS, $12.95 each

D-171 **REGAN'S PLANET** by Robert Silverberg
SOMEONE TO WATCH OVER ME by H. L. Gold and Floyd Gale

D-172 **PEOPLE MINUS X** by Raymond Z. Gallun
THE SAVAGE MACHINE by Randall Garrett

D-173 **THE FACE BEYOND THE VEIL** by Rog Phillips
REST IN AGONY by Paul W. Fairman

D-174 **VIRGIN OF VALKARION** by Poul Anderson
EARTH ALERT by Kris Neville

D-175 **WHEN THE ATOMS FAILED** by John W. Campbell, Jr.
DRAGONS OF SPACE by Aladra Septama

D-176 **THE TATTOOED MAN** by Edmond Hamilton
A RESCUE FROM JUPITER by Gawain Edwards

D-177 **THE FLYING THREAT** by David H. Keller, M. D.
THE FIFTH-DIMENSION TUBE by Murray Leinster

D-178 **LAST DAYS OF THRONAS** by S. J. Byrne
GODDESS OF WORLD 21 by Henry Slesar

D-179 **THE MOTHER WORLD** by B. Wallis & George C. Wallis
BEYOND THE VANISHING POINT by Ray Cummings

D-180 **DARK DESTINY** by Dwight V. Swain
SECRET OF PLANETOID 88 by Ed Earl Repp

ARMCHAIR SCIENCE FICTION CLASSICS, $12.95 each

C-69 **EXILES OF THE MOON**
by Nathan Schachner & Arthur Leo Zagut

C-70 **SKYLARK OF SPACE**
by E. E. "Doc' Smith

ARMCHAIR MYSTERY-CRIME DOUBLE NOVELS, $12.95 each

B-11 **THE BABY DOLL MURDERS** by James O. Causey
DEATH HITCHES A RIDE by Martin L. Weiss

B-12 **THE DOVE** by Milton Ozaki
THE GLASS LADDER by Paul W. Fairman

B-13 **THE NAKED STORM** by C. M. Kornbluth
THE MAN OUTSIDE by Alexander Blade

If you've enjoyed this book, you will not want to miss these terrific titles…

ARMCHAIR MYSTERY-CRIME DOUBLE NOVELS, $12.95 each

B-16 **KISS AND KILL** by Richard Deming
THE DEAD STAND-IN by Frank Kane

B-17 **DANGEROUS LADY** by Octavus Roy Cohen
ONE HOUR LATE by William O'Farrell

B-18 **LOVE ME AND DIE!** by Day Keene
YOU'LL GET YOURS by Thomas Wills

B-19 **EVERYBODY'S WATCHING ME** by Mickey Spillane
A BULLET FOR CINDERELLA by John D. MacDonald

B-20 **WILD OATS** by Harry Whittington
MAKE WAY FOR MURDER by A. A. Marcus

B-21 **THE ART STUDIO MURDERS** by Edward Ronns
THE CASE OF JENNIE BRICE by Mary Roberts Rinehart

B-22 **THE LUSTFUL APE** by Bruno Fisher
KISS THE BABE GOODBYE by Bob McKnight

B-23 **SARATOGA MANTRAP** by Dexter St. Claire
CLASSIFICATION: HOMICIDE by Jonathan Craig

ARMCHAIR SCI-FI & HORROR DOUBLE NOVELS, $12.95 each

E-5 **THE IDOLS OF WULD** by Milton Lesser
PLANET OF THE DAMNED by Harry Harrison

E-6 **BETWEEN WORLDS** by Garret Smith
PLANET OF THE DEAD by Rog Phillips

E-7 **DAUGHTER OF THOR** by Edmond Hamilton
TALENTS, INCORPORATED by Murray Leinster

E-8 **ALL ABOARD FOR THE MOON** by Harold M. Sherman
THE METAL EMPEROR by Raymond A. Palmer

E-9 **DEATH HUNT** by Robert Gilbert
THE BEST MADE PLANS by Everett B. Cole

E-10 **GIANT KILLER** by Dwight V. Swain
GOLDEN AMAZONS OF VENUS by John Murray Reynolds

ARMCHAIR SCI-FI & HORROR GEMS SERIES, $12.95 each

G-21 **SCIENCE FICTION GEMS, Vol. Eleven**
Rog Phillips and others

G-22 **HORROR GEMS, Vol. Eleven**
Thorp McClusky and others

A GORY MURDER WITH A TRAIL OF TWISTED CLUES

Tom Ritchie was a hard-working investigator for the District Attorney's office, slaving away day after day on an endless menagerie of routine cases. Then one day the murder case of a lifetime dropped into his lap. It was the gruesome killing of Dr. Victor Unger, a seasoned psychiatrist known to have many friends and few enemies. Unger's headless body had been found in a downtown alleyway by two screaming girls. In the spotlight of suspicion were four of the doc's ex-patients, one of which was married to a wealthy financier who had a bad habit of standing in the way of the cops. But could anyone, including the DA himself, sew together the scattered clues in such a twisted murder case as this? Only time would tell, and Tom Ritchie soon found himself under the gun to figure out the who, the when, and the why of it all before someone got away with murder.

POLICE LINEUP:

TOM RITCHIE
An investigator for the D.A.'s office and a straight-forward kind of guy. He could solve just about any crime he was put up against.

SIMEON FIELD
This tough as nails DA found himself under unyielding pressure as he tried to crack the biggest case of his career.

MRS. AMERY
A shy young lady with a troubling past. But getting the help she needed would soon land her in a sticky web of murder.

WALTER AMERY
Wealth, power and a young wife was all he had. He would do anything to keep it that way.

OLIVER THORNE
He was a respected attorney who always won his cases. What a surprise when he ended up being the key figure in a new crime.

VICTOR UNGER
Found dead, naked, and beheaded! Would one of his four patients turn out to be the killer…?

TIP YOUR HAT TO DEATH

By
H. B. HICKEY

ARMCHAIR FICTION
PO Box 4369, Medford, Oregon 97504

CHAPTER ONE

THE two stenographers skirted a small puddle and started up the alley on their shortcut to work. The all-night rain had stopped at eight and the sun was now breaking from the last lingering clouds. Halted by a larger puddle the girls turned left to slide along the back platform of the wholesale butchers' building that was second from the alley's mouth. Perhaps it was the pinkish hue of the water that brought them up short, or the stained cleaver in, their path, but a second glance froze them. Mouths agape, they stared at the figure now revealed beneath the platform. It was a man, completely nude! And where the head had been—was a stump!

TOM RITCHIE had sat in the D. A.'s chair for seventeen years—at least until the District Attorney got down to work. Ritchie had originally been loaned to a D. A. by homicide. His ability to get along with a moron, which his first D. A. was— and thieves, which the next two were, plus his long time knowledge of the city's gang structure had lengthened his tenure as chief investigator.

At the moment Ritchie's feet rested on the D. A.'s desk, and as, with one hand, he picked his nose reflectively he cogitated on murder in general and the one which the photos in his other hand depicted, in particular. He was a deceptively mild-looking man with rusty hair and twinkling blue eyes.

He stopped picking to look at the clock and then watched the door expectantly. Nine-thirty! The door swung open and Tom Ritchie grinned and got his feet under him as he rose to greet his boss.

"Morning, Chief. Going to be a beautiful day!"

It was good to feel *honest* cordiality.

Simeon Field stopped for a second. He was two inches shorter than his gangling assistant, but heavier. Under a broad

151

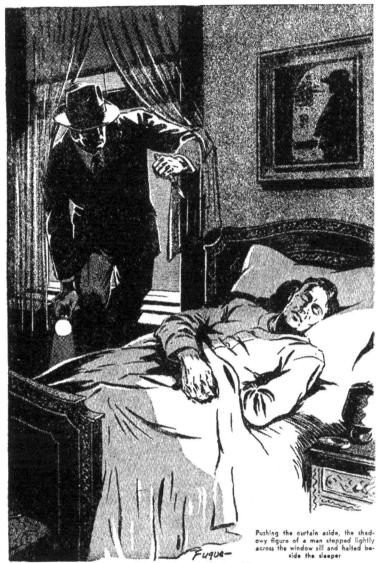

Pushing the curtain aside, the shadowy figure of a man stepped lightly across the window sill and halted beside the sleeper

Illustration by Robert Fuqua

forehead dark brows met in a straight line to almost hide his piercing black eyes. The straight nose and wide mouth were granite chiselled above a jutting clefted chin. A hard man, an ambitious man, but a brilliant man, his features said. How else like a machine to become district attorney at thirty-five?

Field was glum. "What's so beautiful about it? I've got a murderous headache."

Ritchie's smile was wry. "Well, here's one guy's been spared your trouble." He showed the picture's to his chief.

"Ugh! What the hell is this?"

"Apparently, boss, you can't see well this fine morn. This is a man who's lost his head."

Field sat down in the chair Ritchie had vacated and hefted an ash tray.

"You'll lose yours if you don't stop fooling around. What's the dope?"

"All right, Chief. Don't shoot. You know that wholesale meat place on Clark, just south of Van Buren?"

At Field's nod he continued. "Well, a couple of girls found him under the back loading platform about an hour ago. He's been dead since about ten-thirty last night."

"How do you know?"

"Because the doc says so and because the ground under him was dry. The rain didn't start till ten forty-five. Before ten-thirty the platform lights were on so the watchman would have seen him. Simple?"

"Yes. Identification?"

"None. Clothes missing along with his head. He'd been stabbed once through the heart and that would have been enough without the cleaver."

"*What* cleaver?"

"The instrument of decapitation, my dear sir. One of the butchers forgot it out there when they closed yesterday," He anticipated the next question. "No prints. Sorry."

"You look so different when you're sorry."

They both smiled. Field had forgotten his headache.

"Now how about the instrument of death, *my* dear sir?"

"Again no soap. It was probably a long, narrow, double-edged weapon."

"Is that all?"

"That's all!"

FIELD was serious. For several minutes there was silence as he pondered over Ritchie's review of the situation. Finally he looked up.

"How big was the victim, Tom? And how old?"

"About a hundred thirty or so. And about your age, Chief. It's possible for a woman to have done it, if that's what you're thinking."

"So what? Until we find out who the man is we're still no place."

"I was just thinking, Chief, it's queer. On the one hand it's a type of murder which is seldom cold-blooded: a stabbing; and on the other we have a murderer who took the time—and had the nerve—to undress the body and then lop off the head. In other words we find heat and coldness, reason and the supreme irrationality strangely mixed. If and when we crack this case we'll find a very interesting mind behind it."

" 'A most ingenious paradox', eh? Well, Tom, I guess we'll just have to wait for a lead."

The phone rang and Field answered it. It was the mayor. His honor's voice was unctuous.

"Good morning, Field. How's everything? Ah, that's fine! Wonder if you would do something for me? Oh, nothing much, really. I'd like you to drop that bookie case."

The D. A. repeated the mayor's last sentence and saw Ritchie's head bob up and down rapidly. Into the phone he said, "I think we can do that for you, your honor. That's all right, glad to oblige."

He slammed the phone down and turned to his aide. "Why are you so anxious for me to oblige that fat oaf?"

"He may be fat, Chief, but he's no oaf, and he wields power. In politics you've got to take a little, leave a little, if you want to get along."

"I beat them once."

"They underestimated you, but they won't any more. How to be honest, though in politics, *there's* a paradox for you."

Field grinned. "We'll try to do just that, Tom."

"Under my guiding hand you can't miss."

The phone rang again and the D. A. scooped it off the cradle. "Yes...you have? Where? Fine!" He was beaming as he picked up a pencil and started writing while he listened. Tom sat on, the edge of his desk.

"Okay. Give me the address again. Fine, I've got it. Good work!" The D. A. hung up and swivelled toward Tom.

"There's our lead. Couple of kids just found the head and clothes in some park bushes."

"Swell, Chief, now all we have to do is find out who he was." Ritchie was eager for action, but Simeon Field held up a hand.

"Whoa, Tom. We know who he is—or was. His wallet was in his clothes," Field paused but his assistant was impatient.

"Come on, give out with the dope. Who was he?"

"His name was—" the D. A. referred to his notes "—Victor Unger, a resident doctor at a sanitarium for the mentally ill. He also had an office at 317 South Clark Street."

"Whew! A psychiatrist! Remember what I said about the killer having an interesting mind? Looks like I was right."

"We'd better not jump to conclusions. I think we'll go up and take a look at his office before we do anything else. It's only a few blocks from here."

TEN minutes later Ritchie slid the big Buick to, the curb in front of the "Arts and Professions" building. Inside, a steady stream flowed into and out of the battery of elevators. Field shot a quick look at the building directory, then motioned Ritchie into an elevator. He gave the operator the floor number and a moment later the two were disgorged with several others.

For a second they studied the floor plan opposite them. "It's 1806, Tom, so we go left," the D. A. told his assistant.

The office was the second from the corridor's end. There was a single door with frosted glass on which was lettered simply the number and "Victor Unger, M. D." Tom reached into his pocket and brought out a ring of keys. On his second try the door opened and they found themselves in a small anteroom, empty except for two chairs and a little table. The door to the inner office was closed but not locked.

Tom cast a critical eye about him. "Doesn't look like he was doing much business, does it?"

The desk was bare of anything but the large blotter. A couch stood at the left and a small chair beside it. The walls were devoid of pictures and there was no drapery on the one outside window. The room was uncomfortably warm. It was obviously not the office of a successful practitioner.

There was little enough to see but Ritchie's intense gaze drank it all in. When he was through looking he turned to Tom. "Let's go through the desk."

The top drawer held two pencils, the second was empty and the bottom drawer, double size, was locked. The D. A. looked at Ritchie expectantly and the lanky detective fished out his keys again.

"Don't know why they bother to lock these when it's so easy to open them," he said to Field as he pulled out the drawer.

Open, it revealed an alphabetical file of cards and papers. One card was only half in and they could see the name written on it. Tom's eyes popped.

" 'Mrs. Walter B. Amery', it says here!" He looked up at Field. "Maybe he was doing better than I thought. Let's see the others."

The file disclosed only three other patients, but each name brought another whistle from Ritchie's lips. When they were through there was a small pile on the desk before them.

"That's all, Tom. We've got everything we're going to get here." The D. A. looked thoughtful, then: "Maybe we'd better take this stuff to the office where we won't be disturbed while we go over it."

They locked the drawer, then left after relocking the outer door.

"PENELOPE REED, Mrs. Walter B. Amery, B. O. Thorne, and James Craig. Why should four big-shots like that go to a small fry like Unger, Tom?"

Ritchie looked up from the card before him. "You know, I was wondering at that myself. But apparently they came for psychoanalysis, if these cards tell the truth. Could it be, Chief, that four of our leading citizens are crazy?"

Field could not repress a smile. "Not quite, no. But they certainly must have some quirks."

Ritchie lifted a sheet of paper from the pile and started to read aloud. " 'Sunday, June 13: I found myself in a large room in which there were rows and rows of toilets. I knew I had to clean them all. Something made me hold back, though, so I asked a large shaggy dog to help me. He said he would and...!'

"Holy smokes! What the hell is that?" In his bewilderment Ritchie was shouting.

"Pipe down!" Field shushed him. "It's just a dream Penelope Reed had on the date mentioned. Don't you ever dream?"

"Yes, once in a while. Nothing like that, though. My subconscious must be in good shape."

"Lucky fellow. Well, you'd better get out and see if you can pick up any leads. I've got to stay here and get that Muller case ready for trial tomorrow."

Tom hesitated. "Look, Chief. This murder may involve four of the most influential people in the city. If it does—we'll run into trouble."

Field's mouth tightened. "Just remember one thing, Tom. You do whatever you think is right and I'll back you to the limit! I don't care who's involved. I want this murder solved!"

"Swell! Now before I go I'd like to know a few things. Besides his wallet, what else did Dr. Unger have in his coat pockets?"

Field looked puzzled. "Nothing. Should he have had something else?"

"Yes. Keys for his office and desk! They were locked, weren't they?"

The D. A. stared at him. "I never thought of that! What do you think it means?"

Tom shrugged. "Maybe I'll be able to tell you when I get back."

CRAIG kept Ritchie waiting only a few minutes before having him shown in. The bank president looked as though he had been hewn from the same grey stone as the building his institution occupied. Ritchie felt sure that Craig's glance could have frozen anyone but a man with a diamond-studded collateral.

"My secretary tells me you are from the District Attorney's office," Craig said.

"That's right." Tom flashed his badge. "It's in connection with the murder of Dr. Unger," He kept his eyes glued on Craig's face. The face remained immobile but the eyes told of the inner struggle to retain composure. Was there a component of fear in the struggle?

"I...I didn't know," For a brief second there was uncertainty in the voice and then mastery came and it was the same solid voice that assured the listener that nothing on earth was wrong enough to shake either Craig or the Second National Bank. "When did it happen?"

"Last night. His body was found this morning."

"That's too bad," Tom could picture the same tone being used to tell a customer that his loan couldn't be renewed.

"When was the last time you saw him, Mr. Craig?"

"Yesterday evening. I came at nine-fifteen and left at ten-fifteen."

"You're sure of the time?"

"Positive. It was soon after that time that he was murdered?"

"About ten-thirty." Ritchie had a hunch that Craig wanted information as badly as he did. What information did he want?

"In his office?" The banker seemed satisfied to do the questioning.

"No. It was a block away. We went to his office as soon as we discovered who he was and found your name on file there. That's how we knew you were his patient."

"I see. Could it have been robbery?"

Tom decided to see if he couldn't get a show of emotion. "No. After he was killed the murderer chopped off his head and carried it away!"

The cold blue eyes didn't blink.

"That's strange. Somebody must have hated him intensely to do a thing like that," The heavy voice was almost disinterested. "Does there seem to be any apparent motive at all?"

"Not so far. We're looking for one," Tom waited for the next question.

"I see. You found my name among his patients and are hoping that I might be able to help you?"

"That's all we did find: the names of four patients and some dreams they had," Tom had figured out what Craig wanted to know. Now that he had given him the information he'd see what happened. The banker loosened up. The change was almost imperceptible but it was there all right!

"Well I'm afraid I can't help you much. Dr. Unger was a very kind man, hardly the sort to have many enemies."

"Uh-huh. Would you care to tell me what you did and where you went after leaving his office? After all, you seem to be the last person to have seen him alive."

Craig's answer was unhesitating. "I always sent my car home on the evenings when I had an appointment with the doctor. When I was through I took a cab home."

"And that is what you did last night?"

159

"That's right." The banker grew a bit more confidential. "You see, it might not be a good thing for the bank if it were found out that its president were seeing a psychiatrist. Unless it is absolutely necessary I'd rather my name did not enter this investigation."

Ritchie assured him it wouldn't. "There is one thing more, Mr. Craig. Do you happen to know the names of Dr. Unger's other patients?"

There was just the hint of hesitation. "No, I do not."

Ritchie's tone was deceptively quiet.

"Mind telling me just why you were consulting a psychiatrist, Mr. Craig?"

CHAPTER TWO

THE banker allowed himself a mirthless laugh. "Strangely enough, because I had developed migraine headaches! My own physician could discover no reason for them—that is, no physical reasons—and suggested I consult a psychiatrist."

"Had he been able to help you?"

Craig spread his hands. "I had only been seeing him for three months, twice a week. He informed me that it might take a long time before my analysis was completed."

The banker was obviously getting impatient but Ritchie took his time. "And how did it happen that you selected such an obscure man? I should think you would have sought someone better known. His office indicated that he did not have much of a practice."

Craig grunted. "If he charged his other patients as much as he was charging me I can assure you he could have afforded a fine suite. My opinion is that psychiatrists are as crazy as any of their patients. He insisted that the reason he charged so much was to give me more of an incentive to get well quickly. He seemed to think that money was the least important thing in life. And his ideas! Why, the man talked like a communist!"

It was plainly the worst thing that Craig could think of to say about any man.

Ritchie repressed a grin. "Well, *I* won't take up any more of your time, Mr. Craig."

"Not at all." The banker was being civic-minded now. "If I can help you in any way be sure to let me know." His handshake was cool and he didn't bother to smile.

Ritchie was thoughtful as he walked from the bank building. There were several things that were troubling him. Craig had been afraid that he knew more than he did. More about what? About his analysis?

Then the banker had lied when Ritchie asked him whether he knew the identity of any of the other patients. Why?

Ritchie pondered those questions while he drove to the exclusive Michigan Boulevard hotel in which Thorne, the lawyer, lived. For the present at least he had to let them go unanswered.

THE lawyer greeted him with a warm handshake. The two had been on opposite sides of the fence in several cases and each had a healthy respect for the other.

The detective had been wondering why he hadn't seen Thorne around for awhile. The grapevine had it that the lawyer had refused several big cases and was thinking of retiring.

"Haven't seen you in a while, Tom," Thorne smiled. He was a short, heavyset man with warm brown eyes and thinning brown hair. He wore a brown foulard robe.

"Been trying to dig up some clients for you," Tom grinned. "In fact, that's why I'm here now. This is a professional visit."

"You're lucky to find me here. I'm opening my home on the lake shore up north for the summer. I was going up there today but some business matters will delay me until tomorrow." Thorne became serious. "What's up."

The detective told him and watched Thorne's mouth open in incredulous shock.

"Why! Why, that's impossible! I can't believe he had an enemy in the world! I can't think of anyone wanting to kill Unger…" His voice trailed off.

"Why not?" Ritchie asked.

"Because…because he was such a *fine* man. Because he was such a *good* man! There are few people you can say that about but he was one of them. It's impossible to believe that he could harm anyone!"

"Maybe he didn't," Ritchie said.

"But he must have! Otherwise why would the murderer want to mutilate his body? If it were just a murder I could see where in a moment of anger someone might have killed him. But to do such a grisly thing…"

"Don't forget that he was psychiatrist. One of his patients might have been a homicidal maniac."

Thorne shook his head. "I don't know, Tom. He never discussed any of his other patients with me. I knew that he had only three others. He saw us each two hours a week. My appointment was always at five-thirty. It lasted an hour. He allowed fifteen minutes between patients."

Ritchie checked it over on his fingers. "That means he saw his second patient at six-forty five, his third at eight, and his last one at nine-fifteen. Maybe he did that so that you wouldn't run into each other. Most people would rather not have it known that they were seeing a psychiatrist and I can tell you it wouldn't have helped the social standing of Unger's patients."

"It wouldn't have helped my professional standing any, I'm sure. Most people think of psychiatrists as treating people who are out and out lunatics. Not that it would make much difference. I'm giving up my law practice."

"That's what I've heard," Ritchie said. "Does it have anything to do with your visits to Dr. Unger?'

"Yes. I don't mind telling you why I went to him. About six months ago I began to get violently ill every time I entered the court house. It became impossible for me to try a case. Knowing something about psychiatry, I decided to consult the best man I could get. I was sure my trouble was psychological. Dr. Unger was recommended very highly."

"DID you find out what was making you sick?" Ritchie asked.

"Not quite. But a strange thing happened. The doctor told me that for some reason he couldn't get down to the roots of my trouble. He said that I had something covered up so deeply that it was impossible to get at it in an ordinary way. When he saw me the visit before the last he asked if I would mind him hypnotizing me. In that way he felt he might be able to break the wall I'd built up. I consented."

"And he found out?"

Thorne shook his head slightly and bit his lip. "I don't know! And here's the strange thing. When I left his office the other evening I felt easier in my mind than I had in ages. Although I've never shown it I've always worked under a great tension. That tension was gone!

"The next morning I went down to the court house to see someone and I didn't get sick! Whatever it was he found out, it cured me. I had asked him what it was and he said he would tell me when he thought I was ready to hear it, but not until then. The queerest thing is that now, although the thought of trying a case doesn't bother me, I haven't the slightest desire to practice any more!"

"That is strange. Do you still feel free of tension?"

Thorne looked surprised. For a second he stared at Ritchie without speaking. Then, "Damn it, Tom! You ought to have been a psychiatrist! I can't see how you guessed it, but I must admit I don't! This morning when I got up I found that it had returned as strong as ever. I wonder if it could have been a presentiment."

"Could be," Tom shrugged. "Maybe you ought to find another doctor. Meanwhile, would you mind telling me what you did yesterday evening after you left the doctor's office?"

"I came back to the hotel and had dinner here. I spent the rest of the time reading. About nine-thirty I went to bed and fell asleep at once. I didn't awaken once during the night."

"Well, I guess that takes you off the list of suspects all right." Ritchie turned to go but Thorne stopped him.

"Tom," the lawyer said, "If I can help you in any way I want you to call on me. I thought the world of Dr. Unger and I'd do anything to help get the man who killed him!" He was in dead earnest.

So now there were two of them! Craig wouldn't tell something that might be important and Thorne *couldn't!*

RITCHIE had small hope of getting much out of Penelope Reed. He knew little more than most people did about her. She had come to the city some twenty years before and started buying and selling real estate. In the course of those twenty years she had established herself as another Hettie Green. It was agreed that her fortune was tremendous but she never ventured into society and remained, for all her manifold activites, an almost legendary figure.

There was a high stone wall around the mansion she occupied and Tom found a surly gateman who refused him entrance until he had called the house. The butler who admitted Ritchie had an eye that was colder than Craig's.

He led Tom down a long hall to a room at the rear of the house. Then he held the door open just long enough for the detective to slip through and shut it silently behind him.

The room was as warm as the rest of the house was cold. Wide windows faced a garden that was a riot of color. The chintz drapery was gay and matched the spread that covered the bed in one corner of the huge room.

The woman who sat in the chair behind the desk near the windows was as feminine as the room itself. Her hair was an even grey that softened her features, which might otherwise have seemed a bit harsh. She wore a suit that displayed her womanly figure to advantage. When she saw Ritchie she took off the harlequin glasses she was wearing and dropped them on the abstract she had been reading.

"Oh," Tom said. "I wanted to see Miss Reed." The woman at the desk could not have been much over forty.

Her smile was appealing. "I am Miss Reed. What did you want to see me about?"

Tom found it hard to begin. He had expected someone a good deal older, certainly someone more formidable looking.

"I'm from the District Attorney's office," he said at last. He identified himself.

"I can't imagine what the District Attorney would want with me," she said.

He explained. "Someone was murdered last night and we think you may be able to give us some help."

Her eyes widened. "Murdered? Someone I know? I can't imagine who that might be."

"Dr. Unger," he told her. The smile wiped off and the sharpness was accentuated.

"Dr. Unger! Who told you I was seeing him? How did you connect me with him? I told him he mustn't tell anyone!"

The ferocity in her voice startled Tom. If she had vanished and been replaced in the chair by a tigress the change could not have been more complete.

"Why…" Tom stammered, "he didn't tell anyone! We found your name in his file this morning. That's how we knew you were his patient." His tone became conciliatory. "We don't think you murdered him but we hoped that you might be able to give us some information about him. You saw him yesterday evening?"

She nodded, her eyes remaining fixed on Tom's.

"And you left his office at seven-forty-five?"

"Seven-fifteen."

There was no explanation. She kept her eyes down, apparently studying her glasses. At last she picked them up. "I told that eye doctor these things would make me blind," she said bleakly. "Maybe that's what he wanted to do…" Without a change of expression she flung them into a corner.

"Why seven-fifteen?" Tom was ignoring the tantrum. "I thought your appointment was over at seven-forty-five."

PENELOPE REED was looking at him but not seeing him. Her eyes went through him…all the way to Unger's office perhaps…

"Why?" There was a haughty note. "Because I wanted to leave then. Do you think he told me to go?" She called Unger a filthy name. "Imagine the nerve of that—. Is that what he told you?"

Ritchie was patient. "I never saw Dr. Unger alive. We found your name in his file this morning." He got off the subject of Unger. "What time did you get home?"

"Eight o'clock," she snapped. "Now get out and don't come sneaking back here again!"

The butler was waiting in the hall. His grey face was a mask, telling nothing. Had he been outside the door, listening?

"What time did Miss Reed get home last night?" Ritchie asked.

"At the time she told you."

"And what time was that?" Tom demanded.

"At the time she told you," the butler repeated. It was like a phonograph record. Ritchie felt certain that if he asked again he would get the same reply in exactly the same tone.

The man at the gate was ready for him. As the guard turned his body toward him Ritchie caught the bulge under his coat. The man's eyes had little scars around them and his nose had been flattened. He was not tall, but very broad and Tom knew he could take care of himself.

The investigator stopped at the gate. "You on duty last night?" he asked.

The broad man studied him. "Why?" he asked. It was almost as good as a positive answer.

"I'd like to know what time Miss Reed got home," Tom said.

"I wouldn't know," the guard told him.

"You mean you wouldn't *say,*" Ritchie said gravely. The wide shoulders lifted and fell in a manner that said it didn't matter which word was used.

A horn honked outside the gate and both men looked toward the sound. The horn was attached to a low slung maroon roadster that had a lot of chromium on it.

The fellow behind the wheel was as flashy as his car. His blond hair was waved so perfectly that it looked like a wig. The moustache was parted under the perfect nose. His lips were full and sensuous and almost as red as a woman's. He wore a deep maroon sport shirt open at the throat and a yellow reefer.

The gateman didn't ask any questions this time. He just opened the gate and let the big red car slide through. The blond man nodded and smiled. He got no answering smiles.

"Friend of yours?" Ritchie asked.

The broad man's mouth turned down in a half snarl, half sneer. He started to swear and changed his mind.

"Ready to go, copper?" he asked instead.

Ritchie got into the Buick and started the motor. He took a long look at the scarred eyes and said, "So that's how it is?"

"Ahh...they're all the same," the other muttered. He shut the big iron gate behind Ritchie.

"All the same," he thought as he drove. To an extent they were all motivated by the same desires, the same passions. Ritchie had been around too long to think that anyone existed who was exempt from the common frailties. But nature had taken care to, see that a copper's life was not made too easy. People were all the same but they were all different; each had his own little individual twist that made him a separate problem by himself.

CHAPTER THREE

AS a law student of human psychology Ritchie could pass the exams in the school of experience with flying colors. A knowledge of people was the biggest part of his stock as an investigator. He had also decided long ago that he had not been sent to school to learn to read only the sport pages in the daily paper.

He knew that "Freud" did not rhyme with "food" and that Adler had not been a shortstop for the Cubs. But how much more did he know about psychiatry than that?

"Not enough, he admitted to himself." Certainly not enough to know what the connection was between banking and migraine headaches. Not enough to see the relationship between legal work and nausea.

And not enough by a hell of a long shot, he had to admit, to figure out Penelope Reed. He wondered if Dr. Unger had figured her out!

Ritchie had gone to see an old battle-ax and found a real paradox. A still young and attractive woman who had been smart enough to run a shoestring in to a fortune against the shrewdest realtors in the country, but foolish enough to keep a gigolo—and keep him in a style to which he was probably not accustomed.

She lived in a house that was as cold as a winter on the lake front, but her own room was as warm as May sunshine. And she kept an armed guard at the gate!

Part of the function of intelligence is to find the differences between things that are similar. The other part is to find the similarities between things that are different.

So far there was one thing that Unger's three patients had in common. They generated tension like a dynamo generates electricity. And where there is tension there must be fear!

Were they all afraid of the same thing, or did each have his own private fear? Did they know what they were afraid of at all? If they knew, they might not have needed Dr. Unger.

Ritchie wondered if Mrs. Amery would be afraid too. It was strange how well he knew the names and how little he knew of the people who bore them. Their names were in the papers almost daily.

Yet Tom had been unaware that there was a Mrs. Amery! It was a popular notion that Walter B. Amery had an adding machine for a head and an ice cube for a heart. His factories stretched along the river for blocks, and his interests across the continent.

He loved children, it was said, and was a contributor to several orphanages. Yet he had prosecuted and sent to jail a man who had "borrowed" a hundred dollars from the cash box so his child could have an operation! Tom was looking forward to meeting Mrs. Amery; if she were at all like her husband it was going to be an experience.

He followed the winding road that led through the grounds of the Amery estate. On either side of that road green lawns stretched into the distance until they reached the tree covered hills that formed a natural boundary between them and the next estate.

About a mile in from the public highway there was a grove and on the other side of that grove the outbuildings began. There must have been a dozen of them, ranging in size from a four-room cottage to the stables, which would have given Hercules his second biggest job.

The house itself was just a house, bigger than any Ritchie had ever seen before, but differing from them only in size. It was older than its present owner could possibly be and its red bricks were covered by ivy.

THERE was a girl on the patio. She had an easel set up and was intent on painting a herd of sheep that was grazing the grounds to the north. She was using water colors and working fast. She didn't hear Ritchie come up behind her. His shadow fell across the paper and startled her so that she dropped her brush and gave a little gasp. She turned and he could see she wasn't as young as he had thought. Her white dress was simply cut and her black hair was caught behind her neck with a clip and left to flow down to her shoulders; it gave her a look of immaturity. She was not over twenty-eight or thirty but her eyes looked a lot older than that. They were dark in her creamy smooth face.

"I'm sorry I frightened you," Tom said.

Her smile was wan. "That's quite all right; I get so engrossed in my painting that it would take an earthquake to disturb me."

Ritchie looked over her shoulder at the easel. The sheep were there, white against the green of the lawns. There was an ethereal quality in the picture, almost a transparency.

"I like that very much," Ritchie said. "You paint well."

"I really don't but it's kind of you to say so," she said.

Tom was astonished when she blushed. He changed the subject. "Are you a member of the family?" he asked. "I'm looking for Mrs. Amery."

"I'm Mrs. Amery," she said simply.

"Mrs. Walter B. Amery?" He felt a little foolish even as he asked it. Then he felt more than foolish; she'd been asked that before in exactly the same way and he could see that it embarrassed her.

"I'm Tom Ritchie, investigator from the District Attorney's office," he explained. "There has been a murder and we thought you might be able to help us."

Her eyes got very wide. "A murder?" Her mouth stayed open although she had nothing more to say.

"Dr. Unger," Tom told her. "He was found this morning." He spared her the gory details.

Mrs. Amery's reaction was the most unexpected of all. There wasn't any! Her mouth closed and she stood looking at Ritchie as though he hadn't said anything. Her eyes were utterly blank.

"I'd better put my things away," she said. "My husband will be coming home soon and I must dress." She folded the easel with the paper still on it and walked away from Tom.

"Let me carry that for you," he said.

She made no protest and he took the materials from her hand and followed her into the house.

"Put them down anywhere," she said when they were inside. She turned toward him. "What was it you said on the patio?"

Before he could repeat his words she stopped him. "Please ring for someone," she requested.

THEY were in the living room. A grand piano stood in the far corner and beyond it was a bell cord on the wall. Ritchie walked across a couple of huge oriental rugs that looked like throw rugs on the big floor and pulled the cord.

A tall man with very fine white hair appeared so suddenly that Tom was sure he had been waiting just outside the door for the ring. The white-haired man wore the conventional butler's attire. He walked past Tom as though he weren't there. When he got near Mrs. Amery he paused.

"Take those things and burn them," she said. "Immediately."

The butler bowed very slightly and said, "Yes, madam. At once." He picked up the easel and paints and walked out the way he had come.

Ritchie took up where he had left off. He was determined not to let anything surprise him. "I'll try not to take too long, Mrs. Amery. There are just a few questions I'd like to ask you."

She was paying absolutely no attention to him at all. He got red in the face.

Neither of them had heard Amery come into the room. All of a sudden he was there and Tom and Mrs. Amery knew it. Ritchie turned slowly and watched Amery come toward him. He was a big man, well fed but not soft. His hair had been blond and the grey streaks in it didn't look good. He could have been anywhere from forty-five to fifty-five.

"My dear," he nodded to his wife. He disregarded Ritchie. "I see you've been painting again," Amery pointed to a spot on her dress. His tone didn't say whether he liked it or not. Tom had to guess and he guessed that Amery didn't like it. Amery smiled, not unpleasantly.

"Won't you introduce me?" he asked. His wife just looked at him and didn't say anything so Ritchie introduced himself.

"I just want to ask your wife a few questions," he said. "It won't take long."

Amery was in no hurry. "Questions?" he asked quietly. "About what?"

"About a murder. Dr. Victor Unger was murdered last night and we found your wife's name in his file. We thought she might be able to tell us whether he seemed worried about anything or whether he might have mentioned something that would give us a lead. Also, we'd like to know what time she left his office and what she did after leaving it."

Amery thought that over. He was the kind who would give careful thought to anything. "I don't think that is asking too much," he decided.

He looked at his wife expectantly. His decisions were apparently binding for her. She might have been a child asked to recite and she did it like a child, in an entirely unemotional voice.

"I came to the doctor's office at eight o'clock. I always came at eight o'clock. We talked for an hour. At nine o'clock I left. He had suggested that I see the movie that was playing at the theatre across the street from his office. It was 'Now, Voyager', about a girl who was under a psychiatrist's care. I came just as it was beginning and I left before the end. I didn't like it. I went right home."

Ritchie had seen the movie. He recalled that it was about a girl who had been dominated by her mother all her life. He could see why Unger had recommended it.

"You came in soon after nine and left before it was over," he mused. "That means you got out between ten and ten-thirty. Is that right?"

"Ten-twenty. I looked at my watch. I went right home. My husband was angry with me."

Amery was startled. "I would hardly say angry, my dear. It was unusual for you to get home so late. I was worried."

"It's not unusual for you to get home late, is it?" she asked tonelessly. "*I'm* not to worry, am I?"

He looked very sad and Tom didn't know for which of the two he felt more sorry.

"Maybe you'd better go up to your room and lie down for a while," Amery suggested. His voice was kind, paternal. But it was still the voice of Walter B. Amery. His wife left the room and Ritchie could see her going up a curved staircase outside the double doors.

AMERY had his lower lip between his teeth and was worrying it. He shook his head. "That's terrible about Dr. Unger. He was doing wonders for my wife. Of course her illness was of a very minor nature but it has caused us some concern and I was pleased with the progress she was making. Too bad he was killed."

He made no attempt to hide the fact that he meant it was too bad for him and his wife, not Dr. Unger. It wouldn't take much practice for Tom to learn to dislike him intensely. Still, the sadness in his face as he looked at his wife had been real.

The curved stairway was high and Mrs. Amery had been walking slowly. Fortunately the stairs were thickly carpeted—fortunately, because she didn't miss one as she rolled down. There wasn't much sound, not even when she landed at the bottom.

The butler was there long before Ritchie and Amery. He seemed to have a post just outside the living room.

Amery took over. "Call a doctor," he commanded. While the butler went off somewhere he bent and lifted his wife and carried her into the living room and put her down on a wide couch. He was more than worried now; he was frantic but he kept himself under control. Tom thought that the couple looked more like a father and daughter than husband and wife.

There was no color at all in Mrs. Amery's face and when Tom reached past her husband to feel her pulse her hand was cold. The detective was worried as he looked at Emery. The blond man started to blubber.

"She's dead!" he gasped. "My God, she's dead!"

A woman in a maid's uniform came into the room carrying a bottle of smelling salts and Amery tore it out of her hand. Now that he had something to do, he stopped blubbering. He stuck the bottle under his wife's nose and held it there.

After what seemed an age she opened her eyes. Amery still had the bottle under her nose and Ritchie had to take it away from him. He couldn't keep him from talking though.

"Are you all right, darling?" Amery kept saying. His wife didn't close her eyes but she didn't answer his question either.

She had her eyes glued on Ritchie and she wouldn't take them off. He tried staring back for a while but there was something so pitiful, so hopeless there, that he got a sick feeling and turned away.

When he looked back she was crying. There was no sound; her mouth was shut tight as though to hold back any that might have escaped. The tears came slowly, filling each eye until it could hold no more and overflowed onto her cheeks.

The butler was back with another maid. He looked as scared as Amery. "The doctor will be here in ten minutes, sir. Is there anything we can do in the meantime?"

His voice brought a spark of life to Mrs. Amery's waxen features. She looked at Ritchie again and opened her mouth.

"The doctor is coming," she said faintly. She shook her head so slightly that it barely moved. "No. He won't come. He's dead. I'll never see him again. The little doctor is dead. He won't come; he's dead."

Over and over she said it. Her voice stayed low but the despair in it spread until it hung over the room like a pall. Ritchie turned away again and got out a handkerchief and took something out of his eye. He remembered the time he had to tell a little girl that her mother wouldn't be home any more. The little girl had taken it much the same way.

IT WAS a great relief when the doctor came. He was a bustling man, quick in his movements, and his first act was to send them all out of the room.

It was impossible to tell from his face when he came out ten minutes later just how serious Mrs. Amery's injuries were. He was not bustling now; instead, he wore the meditative air that some physicians effect when they leave the sickroom. The same manner presages the announcement of imminent death or quick recovery.

Amery pounced on him. "Well?" he demanded, "How is she?" "Will she be all right?"

The doctor nodded gravely. "I think so. There don't seem to be any broken bones, torn ligaments, or anything like that. She is suffering from shock, however. I gave her something that will put her to sleep for a while. You can put her to bed and see that she stays there. Call me when she wakes up and let me know how she feels."

The doctor's head bobbed up and down and he puckered his lips as though waiting to be kissed. "I'll be out in the morning to make sure she's all right," he added.

"I want you to get a nurse out here immediately," Amery told him. He was acting like himself again.

"It may be difficult to get one on such short notice," the doctor said.

Amery had been about to re-enter the living room. He stopped and turned around. He looked almost surprised at the doctor's statement. "Get one anyway," he said.

The doctor started to say "yes sir" and stopped himself. But there was no doubt he would get one.

"You'd better wait until I get down," Amery told Ritchie. "I want to have a talk with you."

Ritchie was seated in a comfortable chair, his long legs crossed, when Amery came down ten minutes later. The detective had his notebook on his right knee and was gazing intently at it. His host glanced at the notebook suspiciously.

"Got it all written down?" he asked.

Ritchie turned the notebook around and showed him what he had been looking at. It was a drawing of a key. The investigator smiled up at Amery. "Just doodling," he said.

The blond man studied him for a moment, getting his thoughts in order. At last he spoke.

"Look here," he said, "As you can see, my wife is not well. The news of her doctor's death was a great shock and has apparently aggravated her condition. I don't want her bothered anymore."

Ritchie shrugged. "Unfortunately, I have little to say about that. All I do is follow orders."

Amery nodded. "I suppose so. Well, I'll see to it that your orders are to stay away from her."

CHAPTER FOUR

THE detective was not inclined to laugh that off. There was an aura of power about Amery. It said that what he wanted done would be done or he'd know the reason why. There were never any reasons that were good enough to balk him.

Except for the few minutes when Amery had feared for his wife's life he was the most dominant person Tom had ever met. If he were a bit less dominant the detective could almost have admired him.

Still, Ritchie hardly blamed him. There was no doubt that he loved his wife deeply and even less doubt that she was in no condition for further questioning.

"Could you tell me exactly what time it was when Mrs. Amery got home last night?" Tom asked.

"It was exactly three minutes past eleven. I was so worried, especially since she was driving alone and the rain was so heavy, that my watch was not out of my hand for more than five minutes at a time. Mrs. Amery usually got home by ten o'clock, you see."

"You saw her downstairs?"

"Just a minute or two after she came in. I had gone upstairs for something but came down at once."

Ritchie pondered that. "Did she use a key or did someone open the door for her?"

"Harris, the butler, let her in."

"If you don't mind," Ritchie said, "I'll talk to Harris alone for a moment."

Amery pulled the bell cord and Harris came in. His employer told him what was wanted of him and left the room.

"You opened the door for Mrs. Amery when she came home last night?" Ritchie asked.

The white head bowed slightly. "I did, sir."

"Was there anything out of the ordinary in her appearance or manner?"

Harris hesitated and Ritchie prodded him. "Was there?" he demanded.

"Well, sir, she seemed distraught. As though something had upset her."

"I see. Anything strange about her dress?"

"Her clothes were wet and the hem of her coat and stockings were muddy."

Ritchie nodded thoughtfully. "Do you remember how Mrs. Amery was dressed, what clothes she wore?"

"Yes, sir, I do. She was wearing a beige linen suit and a light sport coat. She wore a tan straw hat with a veil that came down over her face."

The detective had given no warning of what was coming next. "Does Mr. Amery often come home late?"

Harris was shocked. "Why, no, sir. On the contrary, Mr. Amery seldom goes out in the evening. He does not like parties and does not care especially for the theatre."

"I see. He seems to be a very devoted husband."

"He is indeed. In many ways he is a very strict and stern man, but to those who obey and are loyal to him he is extremely kind."

"I don't doubt it. Well, that will be all for now, Harris."

THE butler showed him out and closed the heavy oak door behind him. Ritchie stood for several minutes looking back at the great house. The ivy gave an impression of serenity and calm that the detective now knew was false and misleading.

He saw, as though they were before him now, Mrs. Amery's eyes, and wished fervently, for her sake and his own, that it hadn't been she who killed Unger. For her sake because, for whatever reason, she had suffered enough already. For his own, because he knew that Walter Amery loved his wife and would do anything to protect her.

But Unger's head and clothing had been found in the park bushes and Mrs. Amery's coat and stockings were muddied! It had been raining last night, Ritchie reflected.

He'd have to check her story about going to see that movie. It didn't quite ring true. On the other hand neither did anyone else's story ring true. Craig had certainly lied to him; so had Penelope Reed. Thorne was the only one who was accounted for.

Ritchie drove slowly back to the city. Strangely enough, his thoughts as he drove were not long on Unger's patients. Instead he tried to figure out what the missing keys meant. It was as though he had two paths which might lead to the solution of the crime. One was the slow painful trail he was following, and he had no assurance that it was getting him anywhere; the other path was shut off by a gate. The keys that would open that gate were right before Ritchie but he didn't know how to use them!

He found Field in the office. The D. A. looked up when Ritchie entered and laid the papers he was reading aside.

"Well, Tom, how did it go? Run into any trouble?"

Ritchie gave him a complete account of his activities. Field listened intently, interrupting with a question now and then. When the detective had finished the D. A. nodded.

"So that's how it is? Well, there's only one thing to do. I'll get Craig and Miss Reed down here and we'll find out just what it is that they're holding back. It's time people found out that neither money nor position can protect them."

Ritchie was laughing and Field stared at him in bewilderment. "What's so funny about that?" he demanded.

"Those are very noble sentiments, Chief, but that's all they are. You get those big shots down here and try to push them around and you'll think every lawyer in the country has set up practice in your office. This is one case that will have to be worked up on the quiet. If and when we get something on Craig and Miss Reed there'll be plenty of time to call them in. Neither of them is going to run away."

"Well, then, what would you suggest?" Field asked. He could see the strength of Ritchie's argument.

The lanky investigator leaned forward. "For one thing, I think the tough guy who plays watchdog for Miss Reed has a record. Let's see if we can't get him to talk. Then we might try to get a line on the beautiful boy in the maroon roadster.

"As far as Craig is concerned we'll have to forget about him until we have something on him. My hunch is that the thing he was worried about has nothing to do with the murder but that when he lied about not knowing any of the other patients he was protecting someone. The only angle I can think of in connection with that is that one of them has something to do with the bank. It ought to be easy to find out who it is."

"We don't have to find out," Field told him. "I'm a depositor there and I've seen their statements. Friend Amery is chairman of the board."

"That's what I was afraid of," Ritchie said. "He knows something about Mrs. Amery and he doesn't want to talk. Amery could break him. The worst of it is that it's probably something important that he knows. Otherwise he wouldn't be worried about it."

"I've still got a good mind to call him in," Field snorted.

RITCHIE shook his head. "We wouldn't get a thing out of him. He's not a cheap hood that we can slap around. Better layoff until we've got something definite."

"And in the meantime?" Field wanted to know.

"In the meantime we can check up on the elevator operators who were on duty last night in the Arts and Professions Building. We can find out, maybe, if Mrs. Amery really went to that movie. That's routine stuff that you can get men on as soon as I leave."

"All right, Tom. But what I told you before still goes. I'll back you up on anything you do." Field looked up at him. "Have you seen the papers?"

Ritchie shook his head.

"They'd like to go to town on this," Field told him, "but they have nothing to go on. All they know is that we're working on it."

"Good," Ritchie said. "If we can keep them out of our hair for a while this might work out. Of course, if Mrs. Amery's name was mixed up in it they'd soft pedal the case."

"I doubt it," Field grunted.

"Don't be so innocent, Chief," Ritchie grinned. "They won't print anything he doesn't want them to print. That's why I don't want to make a move until I'm sure of myself."

Field got a sour look on his face and Ritchie grinned. "I know I sound cynical but that's the way things are. Don't give up hope though. I'm going out to the sanitarium now and I've got a feeling that when I get back we'll be able to start something."

He nodded to Field. "Better get the men out on the things I suggested as soon as you can."

"All right. By the way, Tom, have you eaten yet?"

Ritchie looked surprised. "Forgot all about it." He glanced at his watch. It was three o'clock. "I'll stop in on the way out there," he told Field.

The investigator found the usual crowd at the City Hall Restaurant. A reporter buttonholed him as soon as he came in.

"How about it, Tom?" he begged. "What's doing on the axe murder?"

Ritchie's eyes sparkled. "We're working on it. That's all I can tell you now."

"Ahh…" the reported snarled. "Don't give me any of that baloney. That's what Field has been telling us."

"That's all there is to tell. When there's more we'll let you know. Have I ever turned you boys down on anything?"

The reporter swore. "I know that, Tom. The trouble is that my boss doesn't. Christ, we don't even know the guy's name!"

"You will," Ritchie assured him, "Just as soon as its possible to tell you."

The reporter said "Ahh…" again in the same disgusted tone. He went back to the pinochle game he'd left when Ritchie came in.

THE detective bolted his sandwich and pie and coffee. He hated to eat at the counter because there was no place to put his legs but it took too long to get waited on at a table. He wiped his mouth with a paper napkin and got up and paid his check. The Buick was across the street in front of the city hall and his eyes were thoughtful as he slid behind the wheel. He pushed the seat back to give himself more leg room and got rolling.

Ritchie used the siren and made the sanitarium in twenty minutes. It was just outside the city limits and had once been the estate of a wealthy family. There were no signs, either over the driveway or the door, to indicate that it now served any other purpose.

The door was opened at Ritchie's ring by a white-haired man. "I'd like to see Dr. Hoelke," Tom said.

The white haired man smiled. "I am Dr. Hoelke."

Ritchie introduced himself and the doctor's face saddened. "Won't you come into my office?" he requested. The investigator followed him into a room that was more like a sitting room than an office.

The doctor pointed toward a radio that stood in a corner. "I've heard about it," he told Ritchie. "I suppose you want me to tell you whatever I can about Victor's family and friends."

The detective nodded and Dr. Hoelke shook his head. "He had neither. He was a refugee. His family was wiped out by the Germans. Most of his training was in the East and he came here only a year ago. Since that time he has lived here with me and assisted me in my work. In fact, it was at my insistence that he consented to accept any patients of his own."

Tom was startled. "You mean that you got him the patients he had? I wondered how he had managed to acquire such a wealthy clientele. I should have thought that they would have found someone better known to consult."

183

Dr. Hoelke smiled wryly. "There are so few good men in our field. Even in a city this size I could not name more than a handful, and they are so busy that they could not accept any new patients. All of Dr. Unger's patients were referred to me and I turned them over to him."

Ritchie scratched his head. "It certainly was a surprise to me when I found those names in his file. Well, that's neither here nor there. All I got out of that file was the names and a few dreams those patients had. Maybe you can tell me more about them. Did Dr. Unger talk over his cases with you?"

"Not the more intimate details. However, he kept his notes in his room upstairs here. We can go up and get them if you'd like."

Ritchie was eager. "You bet I'd like! If what you say about him having no family or friends is true, that would narrow down the list of suspects to his four patients." The detective paused. "By the way, are you sure that he didn't have more than four patients?"

"Quite sure. If he had acquired another I'm certain he would have told me."

The doctor's room upstairs was as bare as his office had been. Tom went directly to the desk which stood before the window and started pulling out drawers. Again the large bottom drawer was locked and Tom got out his keys again.

There were only about twenty sheets of paper in the locked drawer, but they were solidly covered on both sides by the doctor's neat handwriting. Each patient had about five pages devoted to his case.

Tom grunted. "Wonder why he wrote in German? The cards in his office were made out in English."

"German was his native tongue and I imagine his thoughts flowed more easily when he was writing in that language," Dr. Hoelke said. He looked at Ritchie. "Do you read German?" he asked.

"No. I don't know anyone who does, either. I'm afraid it'll be a job getting those notes deciphered."

"Not at all," Dr. Hoelke told him. "If you want me to, I'll be happy to do it for you. In fact that might be the best way. If there are any technical details of importance I can explain them to you."

"Not a bad idea," Ritchie assented. "But first I'll have to ask you a few questions. For instance, where were you last night between the hours of nine and eleven?"

Dr. Hoelke smiled. "Right here in this house. I was in my office working on a book. Most of the time I was alone but several times I was interrupted by attendants who came in to ask for instructions regarding some of the patients here."

"I guess that takes you off the list," Ritchie nodded. "Let's go downstairs and go over these papers. There doesn't seem to be anything more here that could help us."

WHEN the two were again seated in Dr. Hoelke's office the doctor checked over the notes. The fine lines about his eyes were more noticeable when he read. He could not have been less than sixty-five years old but his skin was tanned and firm and his eyes were keen and alive.

"Shall I take each case as it comes, or would you prefer that I follow a certain order?" he asked Ritchie.

"As they come," Tom replied.

"All right. I shall read them over to myself and give you a digested version. The first case is that of Miss Penelope Reed."

For almost ten minutes the doctor read silently, nodding here and there as he came to an especially interesting part. At last he laid down the papers and turned his attention to Ritchie again.

The doctor had such a queer expression that Ritchie was startled. "What is it?" he asked.

Dr. Hoelke smiled. "Something very strange indeed." He leaned forward and put his elbows on the desk. "Actually we have formed a very unusual partnership here, you and I. What I shall be doing is simply this: I shall try to tell you, from the picture I get from these case histories, whether any of these people is a potential murderer; whether any of them have indicated a desire or reason to murder Dr. Unger. If I should find that one of them had both the motive and the potential it will be up to you to discover whether that person actually committed the murder."

Tom was getting impatient. "How does that apply to this case?" he wanted to know.

"In this way. It would take a great deal of pressure to get most people to commit a crime yet others require only the vaguest motive. Often that motive is not even real; it as a hallucinatory one.

"See what I mean? To you it may appear that a person has no motive at all. I can show you that he is the type which does not need a motive, at least not one which is visible."

Ritchie's eyes narrowed. "You mean that Penelope Reed is...?"

"...is precisely that type!" Dr. Hoelke finished for him. "She is a paranoiac! That means that she has delusions of persecution which would lead her to commit murder without the slightest provocation!"

"Holy smokes!" Ritchie breathed. He recalled her remark about the doctor trying to blind her and told Dr. Hoelke about it. Hoelke nodded.

"A perfect example," he agreed. 'She is an unusual case because she developed so gradually, without any evident impairment of her, intelligence. But she has always been 'queer'.

"As a child she was moody but was exceptionally well behaved. That is always a bad sign in a child. She did well in her studies and got a job in a bank after she graduated from school. She rose to a responsible position.

"Then she stole thirty thousand dollars from the bank! But the young man to whom she was engaged was the cashier at the bank and he took the blame. He went to jail and died there."

Ritchie was bitter. "And she came here with the money and ran it into a fortune!"

"Yes. But she couldn't run it into happiness! In fact she got worse every year. She did make attempts to break out of it and developed normal relationships but all they led to was a very shabby affair with a man who was ten years younger than she.

"Her condition grew steadily worse. And here is the important thing! Dr. Unger was going to give her up! He wanted her to go to a sanitarium and she was convinced that he was trying to have her 'put away' so he could get her money!"

CHAPTER FIVE

RITCHIE said, "Oh-oh," in a very quiet voice. He told Dr. Hoelke what Miss Reed had called Dr. Unger. "So she had a strong enough motive and the potential, too."

"Yes. And she should be put away. If she didn't commit this murder she is still likely to commit a different one!"

"We'll have to see about that," Ritchie said. "Now how about the next one?" He waited while Dr. Hoelke read it. It was the case history of Oliver B. Thorne.

"This is a more complicated case," the doctor told Ritchie. "There are many ramifications but only a few facts pertinent to this inquiry.

"The most important fact is this: Oliver Thorne was a somnambulist, or sleepwalker, when he was a child. When he was fourteen years old he stopped. But the last time he walked in his sleep he set fire to the house!

"In this fire his older brother whom he hated unconsciously was burned to death! Oliver's parents never told him what he had done and he himself was of course unconscious of his crime.

"He never did find out what he had done but the unconscious knowledge and feeling of guilt are probably the factors that led to his choice of a career. You can see that by aiding people who were accused of crime he was in a manner defending himself!"

"But he always seemed so sincere!" Ritchie protested.

"He was sincere. But you may have noticed that he always put the emphasis on the social and environmental factors that led to his client's crime! In other words he did not believe that people were responsible for their crimes. So he was defending himself!"

"But at last the guilt feelings became so strong that he could not continue with his work. The feelings were of course expressed in physical symptoms. That, by the way, is very common. Most people's physical ailments have a psychological basis.

"Because his knowledge of what he had done was completely unconscious Thorne had to be hypnotized so his unconscious mind could be reached. That is how Dr. Unger found out. The proof of what I said about his physical symptoms is that after he told Dr. Unger about setting the house afire he felt much better!"

"Well, I'll be damned!" Ritchie blurted. "That's the most unbelievable thing I ever heard! But why didn't Unger tell Thorne?"

"I don't know. I would have told him if he had been my patient but there may have been other factors involved."

"Well, I hope he doesn't walk in his sleep any more, at least in my neighborhood," Ritchie commented. "Who's next?"

"James Craig. He is another whose mental difficulties took a physical form. He too had severe guilt feelings and anxiety."

"Whom did he rob or kill?" the detective grinned.

"Nobody. You don't actually have to do anything wrong to feel guilty. He had a deep feeling of inferiority and when, several months ago, he made a very unfortunate loan which cost his bank a great deal of money, he became fearful of his position. He had covered up his error but he was in constant dread that he would be found out.

"Craig had a neurosis which is quite common. It was based on the desire to be loved and the fear that he was unworthy of that love. It led to his attempt to make himself independent of others by always being top dog.

"But here he was in danger of losing his high position! So he attempted to escape from his feeling of inadequacy by having headaches which would furnish an excuse to give up that position he felt unable to fulfill."

RITCHIE was smiling and the doctor smiled back. "Seems hard to believe, doesn't it?" he asked.

The detective grunted. "I guess I'll have to take your word that it's true," he said. "But it sure does sound fantastic!"

"Not so fantastic," Dr. Hoelke assured him. "It works in practice. Lately, in Germany, we have had a variation of Craig's complex. There it took the form of a 'bicycle complex!' "

Ritchie stared at him and the doctor laughed. "That means that each person had to have someone beneath him on whose shoulders he pedaled, or kicked down. He also had to have someone above him who was pedaling on his shoulders."

"How about the person who is really on top?" Ritchie asked. "Who stands on his shoulders?"

"A very good question. When there is nobody above a certain people they will manufacture a being. Sometimes they call it 'the laws of nature'. That gives them the necessary feeling of security, the feeling that something or someone is guiding them and protecting them even though it sometimes hurts them, too."

"Seems like a pretty complicated affair," Ritchie commented. "On the other hand, I suppose people are complicated."

"They are very complicated," Dr. Hoelke told him. "That whole particular problem revolves around what we call the 'sado-masochistic' urges. The urges never work alone. Sadism makes us enjoy hurting others and masochism makes us enjoy being hurt. You can substitute 'bossing' for 'hurt'.

"Did you ever notice how some wealthy people have a group of followers about them all the time? They know that these followers are living off them but they need the followers as much as the followers need them, sometimes more!

"A person of that type will often be mean and hurtful to someone who depends on him. You would think that he is completely independent of that subordinate and the subordinate totally dependent on him. But it is not so! I have seen the threatened loss of such a subordinate cause a complete breakdown in the master! He must have that particular bicycle or he cannot live!"

Dr. Hoelke was all wound up in his subject; his eyes flashed and he waved his forefinger at Ritchie while he talked. Suddenly he stopped short and started to laugh.

"Please excuse me," he said. "I really didn't mean to give you a lecture. Have I bored you?"

The detective shook his head. "Not at all. Solving a crime is something like working a jig-saw puzzle. Sometimes you start with an outside piece and sometimes you start at the center, but the more you know about the relation between the pieces the quicker you solve it. It also helps if you have an idea of what the finished picture will look like.

"While you talked I began to see some sort of a picture and also the relationship between the various pieces. So even a little knowledge helps. But..."

"But...?" Dr. Hoelke repeated. "But I haven't got all the pieces yet," Ritchie smiled. "Better tell me about Mrs. Amery's case. That might supply some of them."

"Let us hope so. Well, Mrs. Amery's case is in many ways the most tragic of them all. Miss Reed is beyond saving; Thorne and Craig have been able to make some sort of adjustment. Mrs. Amery is the most sympathetic figure. She probably has a greater potential for happiness and creativeness than the others but it seems that life has been against her.

"TO UNDERSTAND her we'll go back to her childhood. She was the only child of a very fine artist. But he was a bad father. His wife was expected to take care of his home and child, but he himself was inconsiderate of both. He had numerous affairs with women and often stayed away from home for days. His wife dared not reproach him because he had a terrible temper and flew into a rage at any suggestion that he was in the wrong.

"As a girl Mrs. Amery showed real artistic talent but her father discouraged her. He was probably afraid of competition from her. So she never did anything with her talent.

191

"She had several suitors but couldn't bring herself to marry until Walter Amery came along. He was in many ways like her father but he was much kinder. He offered security and protection and she needed those, so she married him.

"I don't mean to say she didn't love Amery. We won't talk of love. But he loved her and was willing to do anything for her; anything, that is, except treat her as an equal!

"As their marriage progressed she became more and more submerged. But everyone must have an outlet for his aggressive drives. Some people turn them inward on themselves. Hers took a strange form.

"There are many small animals on the Amery estate. One day the gardener found her with a squirrel she had caught. It was dead. She had killed it with a kitchen knife!

"After the incident was repeated several times her husband became worried. He brought her to me for treatment but I felt that Dr. Unger had more to offer her. He had the artistic temperament himself and I felt that he could do more for her.

"So it turned out. She is an intelligent woman and once he pointed out to her how she had carried over her childhood reactions into married life, Mrs. Amery was quick to understand. Dr. Unger persuaded her to try painting again and to please him she did."

"I saw a picture she was painting," Ritchie interjected. "There was something about it that was different from any picture I've ever seen." He told the doctor what had happened to the painting and the older man shook his head sadly.

"I don't know what is going to happen to her now that Dr. Unger is dead," Dr. Hoelke told Ritchie. "She had transferred her feeling of dependency to him and he was able to direct her in the right way. Her husband, being what is called a 'practical man', thought painting a childish thing, but his wife continued with it and only a week ago one of the directors of the city art museum saw something she had done and pronounced it excellent.

"Then something not uncommon in psychoanalysis occurred. For some time she had thought that she was falling in love with Dr. Unger! It was apparently on her next to last visit that she got up the nerve to tell him she loved him.

"To an extent that was a good sign. Her ability to paint well had established her in her own mind as an individual who didn't have to depend on reflected glory! Now she was boldly asserting herself in another direction! Ordinarily a patient's love for the analyst is a sign of dependency but in this case Mrs. Amery was exceptionally vehement. Dr. Unger tried to explain the matter to her but when he had to tell her that he did not love her in return she became furious, a woman scorned!"

Dr. Hoelke put down the case history and shook his head sadly. "A pity," he said softly. "A great pity. A little longer and she might have been able to stand on her own feet. Now...who knows? I feel very sorry for her."

Ritchie nodded. "So do I. Unless..."

"Unless what?"

"Unless she killed Dr. Unger! You're so interested in her troubles that you've forgotten I have a murder to solve!"

Hoelke looked incredulous and Ritchie rushed on. "Did you forget about the squirrel she killed with a knife; that Dr. Unger was killed the same way? You yourself said she acted like a woman scorned and I can tell you from personal experience that the guy who said, 'Hell hath no fury like a woman scorned' knew what he was talking about!"

THE doctor was about to interrupt him when the phone on the desk rang. Dr. Hoelke picked it up, said, "Speaking", and then listened for a few minutes. At last the doctor said, "I'll see if I have a free hour then," and got out his appointment book. He found the page he was looking for and wrote something down.

Into the phone he said, "All right, I'll see you then," and hung up. He looked back at Ritchie. "So you think you've found the missing piece to your puzzle?"

"All but one," the detective told him. "I still can't figure out why she took his keys!"

Dr. Hoelke sighed. "I wish I could help you, my friend, but I'm afraid that is something you'll have to find out for yourself," He stood up. "Meanwhile I have my own patients to think of." The interview was over.

The doctor closed his appointment book with a snap. The sound was not loud but it brought Ritchie to his feet like a shot!

"My God!" he shouted. "What a dummy I've been! The appointment book! That's what it was! Right under my nose and I couldn't see it!"

Dr. Hoelke stared at him. "What do you mean, the book?" he asked. "What was in his appointment book?"

Ritchie looked like a lazy old bloodhound who has suddenly hit the trail he was seeking. The lanky figure was jumping with excitement. His eyes had lost their pleasant twinkle and were suddenly hard.

"That's just it," Ritchie breathed. "What do you think would be in his appointment book?"

"Why...I should think an appointment with one of his patients..." the doctor replied weakly. The sudden turn of events and Ritchie's transformation into a shouting madman had left him utterly bewildered.

"Precisely," Ritchie told him, "an appointment with one of his patients." The investigator shook his head sadly. "If I weren't so disgustingly healthy I'd have known that every doctor has an appointment book. The whole point of this is that there wasn't one in Dr. Unger's office!"

Dr. Hoelke looked as though he were going to interrupt and Ritchie waved him down. "Listen to me. I know it sounds crazy but it's the most important piece in the whole puzzle! You see, I couldn't figure out why the killer had taken Dr. Unger's keys. Somehow I had the feeling that it was in some way connected with the reason for cutting off his head and removing his clothes.

"At first I thought that the murderer took the keys in order to get something from Dr. Unger's office. But it's almost impossible to get up to the eighteenth floor of a building like that at night without being seen. After about six o'clock everyone who uses the elevator has to sign in and out.

"But if the murderer went to the office in the morning! By joining the crowd on its way to work he would pass unnoticed! So that would explain the decapitation and the missing clothes.

"After all, Dr. Unger's head and clothes had been hidden where it was certain they would be found soon. That meant that the murderer needed only a limited amount of time. Just time enough to get to the office and remove what must have been the clue to his identity! At least that's what I thought.

"But there was nothing missing! You see, I didn't realize that there should have been an appointment book. So that blew my theory about the keys and the clothes to hell. Now my theory makes sense again!"

Ritchie stared hard at Dr. Hoelke. "What time did Dr. Unger leave here yesterday afternoon?"

"Come to think of it, he left about an hour earlier than usual," the doctor replied. "It seemed strange at the time but I'd forgotten about it until just now when you asked me. Is it important?"

"Very." It was apparent that Ritchie's mind was busy but the doctor had to satisfy his curiosity.

"There is one thing more," Dr. Hoelke said. "The murderer must have known that Dr. Unger had no morning patients and that he had no nurse or secretary. Isn't that significant?"

Ritchie smiled. "You're not a bad sleuth yourself, doctor. It's a most significant clue. It certainly cuts down the number of possible murderers."

Dr. Hoelke's intent features showed that his mind was whirring at top speed and Ritchie grinned at him.

"I think you'll be able to figure it out for yourself," he told the doctor. "After all, you supplied the motive." The investigator turned to go but paused for a moment. "I've got to get back to the office now but I may need your help again."

"Call me at any time," the doctor said. His chin was still cupped thoughtfully in his hand as he watched Ritchie close the door behind himself.

CHAPTER SIX

SIMEON FIELD was pacing the floor when Tom came into the office. The D. A.'s face was dark and angry and he did not return Ritchie's greeting. The detective laughed.

"I need only one guess to know what's eating you," he said. "I should say your phone's been ringing."

"I almost told him to go to hell," Field barked. "It's a good thing I remembered your advice or I would have. Imagine the gall!"

"Don't be too harsh on him," Ritchie smiled. "People in this town are not used to having an honest District Attorney. What did he say?"

Field imitated the voice on the phone. "First he said, 'Is this Field?' His voice was as cool as a cucumber. When I told him it was he said, 'This is Walter B. Amery. One of your men was out here to see my wife. He upset her greatly. I don't want that to happen again. Do you understand?'

"'Do you understand?'" Field repeated hotly. "As though I were his office boy! I don't know how I kept my temper in control, but I did. I told him we'd try not to cause her any unnecessary inconvenience and hung up before I lost my grip."

Ritchie nodded understandingly. "I'm glad you didn't blow up, Chief. I want just a couple more hours of quiet before I'll be ready to light the fireworks."

"What fireworks?" The D. A.'s eyes were fixed on Tom. "What happened at the sanitarium?"

Ritchie gave him a complete account of his visit with Dr. Hoelke. He went over each case in great detail. When he finished telling the whole story and his interpretation of it Field's face showed a mixture of emotions.

"I get it now," he told Ritchie. "The most important clue was the appointment book and we didn't even realize that it was missing. We really flopped on that!"

"It doesn't matter now," Ritchie said. "Once we knew about it everything else just slid into place."

Field was glum. "That's what you think!" When the detective looked surprised Field held up his hand. "Oh, you've built up a wonderful case all right. There isn't a hole in it. We know why Unger was murdered and by whom. There's not a chance in the world that you're wrong. Theoretically it's perfect. But I wouldn't dare take it to court!

"You know who did it and I know who did it. But we could never get a jury to convict! We don't have a shred of concrete evidence!

"Can we produce the keys? No! The appointment book? No! The murder weapon? Again no! Why, a smart lawyer would have us laughed out of court! We don't have even a single witness!"

Ritchie's face was hard as granite when the D. A. had finished speaking. His lips were tight and his lean jaw jutted forward. When he did speak his voice was cold.

"You admit we've got the answer, don't you?" he asked.

"Beyond the shadow of a doubt," Field admitted. "I'd be willing to throw the switch on the electric chair myself."

"So we're going to let the killer walk off scot free, is that it?"

Field looked harried. "But damn it, Tom, we *don't* have any witnesses!"

"Then we'll make some!"

Field was aghast. "We couldn't do a thing like that! Why that's…"

"That's the difference between law and justice!" Ritchie cut in. "Those case histories are going to come in handy when it comes to putting on the pressure. By the way, what did the other men bring in?"

"Nothing." Field was disgusted. "I was so mad about Amery's call that I forgot to send them out."

"It's just as well. I'd rather handle this myself from here on. It'll be better if only the two of us know what's going on."

"I still don't like your idea, Tom. Where is it going to get us? I never thought you were the kind..."

"I'm a copper!" Ritchie barked. "And I don't like to see anyone get away with murder!"

"Neither do I!" Simeon Field shouted back at him. Although the D. A. was Ritchie's boss he had always treated him as an equal. Even now, in his anger, he did not use his authority.

Ritchie was contrite. "I'm sorry, Chief; I know you feel the same way I do."

"Forget it, Tom. The main reason I'm against your idea is that testimony like that never holds up in court. You know what a lawyer like Thorne could do with those witnesses."

The hardness on Ritchie's face was still there but the glint in his eye was crafty. His tone was conspiratorial and there was the hint of a lift at the corners of his mouth as he spoke.

"But I don't figure it'll get to court, Chief. Don't forget the people we're dealing with are fragile. If we squeeze hard enough something will crack. It happened once, you know. By tomorrow morning I should be ready so you better be set to have Mrs. Amery picked up for murder."

Field's mouth was hanging open as Ritchie finished. There was a look of tremendous admiration, almost awe, on the D. A.'s face as he stared at his chief investigator.

Then Field began to laugh. For a moment Ritchie stared at him in amazement and then he realized what the D. A. was laughing at. The detective permitted himself a broad smile.

"It's all right then, Chief?" he asked.

Field wiped his eyes and got his laughter under control. "Sure it's all right, Tom. Excuse me for being so thick-skulled that I couldn't follow your subtlety.

"You bet it's all right!" The D. A.'s face got as hard as Ritchie's had been. "I'm still behind you, too. All the way! Now get going!"

Ritchie paused at the door and looked back at Field. "Better wear your asbestos suit tomorrow, Chief," he said. "The heat is going to be terrific."

IT WAS six-thirty when Ritchie got to the Arts and Professions Building. For the most part the building was dark, but here and there a window showed light to indicate that someone was working late or that the cleaning women were already on the job.

Most of the occupants of the great building were doctors and few had evening hours. There was no crowd in the lobby now. Only two of the elevators were in operation and fast changing lights on the indicator showed that one of them was on its way up to the top floors.

Before the open door of the other car the operator was talking to the starter. The operator was a good-looking young fellow with red hair who wore his uniform with an air. The starter was a small man and old. His uniform was baggy and crumpled and his white shirt was several sizes too big for his scrawny neck so that the collar came together and covered the knot in his black tie.

He saw Ritchie coming toward him and recognized him as a stranger. "You'll have to sign in, sir," he called. A gnarled hand came out of his sleeve and a finger pointed to a small stand against the wall. On the stand an alarm clock ticked away beside a register.

At the top of the open page was written, Friday, May 26, and beneath it several entries. In the left hand column a few room numbers had already been filled in. On the same lines with the room numbers were the names of the people who had written them and the time they had signed in. There was a column at the right for signing out. Ritchie turned the page back to Thursday's entries.

The old man saw him and hurried over. "Looking for something?" he asked querulously.

The detective smiled. "That's right, Pop," he showed the old man his badge. "Do you know who Dr. Unger was?" The old man nodded and Ritchie told him, "He's the man who was murdered last night. The one whose head was chopped off."

The starter's jaw dropped. "No! Why me and him was just talkin' about the murder." He pointed back at the redhead. "Why the doc acted like such a nice fellow, too. Talked like a foreigner, you know, but nice."

"That's the one. He was here just two evenings a week?"

"Uh-huh. Monday and Thursday. Always had four patients, little over an hour apart. Always the same ones, too. We used to wonder what kind of a doctor he was."

"Did he always sign in?"

"Most always. We go on at five. Sometimes he'd get here earlier, like yesterday."

"Do you think you'd recognize his patients?" Ritchie asked.

"Sure." The old man pointed out the names. Thorne's was the only one easily legible. The next patient had scrawled P. Reed. The eight o'clock and nine-fifteen entries were just wavy lines.

"The first one was a short stocky fellow," the starter explained. "He always said hello. The next one was a woman. Sometimes she'd smile and sometimes she'd look so mean we were afraid to say a word to her. She's grey-haired and dresses swell.

"The next one is a woman, too. She always wears a veil so we can't see her face well. But we can see it enough so we know she's a good looker. She never says more'n hello and good-bye but her voice is sweet. Red tried to strike up a conversation a few times but it didn't get him anywhere. She dresses nice, too. Plain but you can see she's rich. Got a lot of class.

"The last guy is the worst. He's a sourpuss all the time. Hasn't said a word to us all the time he's been coming here. Looks like the kind of fellow who wouldn't give you the time of day unless there was a profit in it."

RITCHIE grinned. The description of Craig had been apt. There was no question that the old man could identify all four of Unger's patients.

"Last night was kind of funny," the starter continued. "The grey-haired woman left half an hour early. Then she came back in an hour. Said she forgot her purse so Red rode her up and waited a minute until she got it and came down again. She didn't have to sign that time but it was just about eight-thirty.

"Then the other woman stayed later than usual. She didn't sign out until almost nine-fifteen." He pointed to the entry. "See? Then, just before she signed out you can see that the last one signed in. Red took him up and about two minutes later he had to go back up to get her. She acted mad. Didn't say goodnight, just signed out and beat it."

The detective's forehead wrinkled as he widened his eyes. "So, she was mad, huh?"

"Yeah. She had both lips between her teeth and it looked like she was biting down hard. I followed her to the lobby door and watched her go across the street to the movie show.

"The door was open and I leaned against it for a while. You could tell it was gonna rain but it was warm and spring-like. Lots of people think that to old geezers like me spring don't mean anything but it does. Maybe not the way it does to young fellows like Red. But last night there wasn't much gas smell from the cars and I could catch that green spring smell and for a minute I saw a green, green island far away." He looked up at Tom. "You know?"

Tom smiled down at him. "My old man used to be like that."

"Yeah. Well, I stuck at the door and who should pull up to the curb in a big black coupe but the first patient! He got out of the car and looked at me and got right back in again and drove away."

"Are you sure it was the short stocky fellow?" Ritchie asked.

"Sure it was him. My eyes ain't bad and I recognized him. In fact I started to say something but he was gone too quick. But that ain't all. About two or three minutes after the last guy left Dr. Unger came down. Red and I watched him go out the door. The girl who went to the show was waiting for him! For a minute they stood and talked and then they walked away together. They went south."

"Well, whaddaya know about that?" Ritchie grunted. "And less than ten minutes later he was dead. It all ties in, though."

Red had just brought someone down in the elevator and was leaning against the wall watching Ritchie and the old man. The detective called him over.

"Tell you what I want," he said. "I want you and Pop to examine this page carefully so you'll remember it. Then you'll sign your names at the bottom and I'll take the book with me." They followed his instructions.

"That's all. I'll take down your addresses too, so I can get hold of you if I need you. Whatever you do, don't leave town or you'll be in a jam. Get me?" They nodded.

OLIVER THORNE still had the overnight bag in his hand when Ritchie came in. Although the desk clerk had announced the detective Thorne had a faint look of surprise on his face.

"Still working?" he asked. "There is apparently no rest for the good either."

Ritchie grinned. "Not if they happens to be coppers." He stared at the bag in Thorne's hand. "Moving?"

"Yes," the lawyer replied, "I feel as though I'm tied up in knots inside. Maybe a vacation will help, or rather a change of scene. I can't really say I've been working, hard; I don't even go out much lately."

"Maybe I can save you the expense of a vacation," Tom told him.

Thorne was startled. "How do you mean that?" He tried to catch the tall detective's eye but Ritchie refused to look squarely at him.

Tom persisted in looking over the shorter man's head. His glance flitted about the room, lingering here and there disinterestedly until the silence itself was taut to the snapping point.

"I found out what's been troubling you," he said softly. His voice was careless, nonchalant.

Thorne was caustic. "You want to sell your information? Don't try to put on an act with me, Tom. What have you got up your sleeve?"

"I told you, I found out what it was you told Dr. Unger when he hypnotized you. Aren't you curious?"

Thorne rubbed his hands nervously together. "To tell you the truth, Tom, I don't know whether I want to hear it. Dr. Unger didn't want to tell me. Maybe it would be better if I got another doctor and you gave the information to him!"

Ritchie was grim. "I'll tell it to you!" He gave Thorne the story in a few sentences, brutally, and watched the lawyer's face go pale.

But years of practice had somehow inured Thorne to shock and surprises and he recovered quickly. His training kept him from speaking until he had regained some measure of control but his voice was still unsteady when at last he spoke.

"I...I can't believe it. My brother...why, I admired him, loved him..."

Ritchie stopped him. "Don't forget your hate was unconscious. He was older than you, maybe stronger, and you were afraid not to admire him. But underneath..."

Thorne nodded heavily. "I know; I've read a good deal in psychiatry." He flared up in sudden suspicion. "But what has that to do with Dr. Unger? How does it connect up with that?"

"I didn't say there was any connection. I'm sure you had no reason to kill him. At least no conscious reason..." Ritchie let his last words hang in the air, then soak in.

"But Tom, I was asleep at ten-thirty last night! I was right here..." His voice trailed off for a moment. "Wasn't I?"

Ritchie countered with a question.

"Where do you keep your car?"

"In the hotel garage. Why?"

"You could call them and find out if you took it out last night."

CHAPTER SEVEN

THE lawyer walked slowly to the phone and lifted it. "The garage, he said shortly." When the garage answered Thorne spoke slowly and distinctly. "Do you remember what time I got my car yesterday evening?"

His eyelids dropped as he got the reply. "And what time was it when I returned? I see. Thank you." He hung up wearily and turned to Ritchie.

"Did I do it, Tom?" he asked.

The detective shrugged. "Maybe. It's plain I've got you pretty well tied up in it, isn't it?"

Thorne was shrewd. "Then why the rigmarole?"

Ritchie leaned forward. "Look. This case could be big. It involves big people. If Field got a conviction on first degree murder it might mean a lot. You could maybe beat the rap but we've got someone who couldn't. All we need is a good witness. Do you follow me?"

Thorne was breathing hard. "Yes, and you stink to high heaven! Do you think I'm a fool? Why should I be afraid? You admit that I could beat it so why should I play your filthy game?"

Ritchie spread his hands. "You *might* beat it. But on what plea?" He let the question sink in.

"On what plea? Why..." The lawyer stared at him in horror. "My God! That would be worse! I'd rather hang than—"

Tom eased up. "Listen. We don't figure it'll ever go to court. It's a thousand to one we'll get a confession if we put the screws on."

Thorne's shoulders were bowed and there was an unutterable weariness in his voice. "So, after all these years..."

"Why not look at it our way?" Ritchie asked. "We've got the murderer but we have no evidence a jury will accept. You've seen that happen many times. So we've got to get a confession.

But we can't do it in an ordinary way because we'd be hamstrung. The only way is to avoid the legal tangle for a while by getting an indictment immediately."

The lawyer was thoughtful. "I see. Put that way it makes a little sense. Of course I still wouldn't consider it if you didn't have me over a barrel. But before I go further I've got to know more. Who did it?"

"Mrs. Walter B. Amery."

Thorne whistled. "No wonder you're in a hurry. If she's indicted at once the newspapers won't be able to soft-pedal it. If an immediate trial is indicated and the odds seem against her even I would advise her to plead guilty and save her neck.

"That's what Amery's lawyers will do. If they had enough time so the case could cool off his money and power would save her. If she's weak you may get your confession without their help."

"She's weak," Ritchie said.

Thorne grinned wryly. "You haven't missed a trick, have you? Well, you'd better coach me on my testimony. I must admit I've coached many a witness but this is the first time I've been one myself."

"Okay. We'll make it short and sweet. The less you say the less they can trip you up."

For almost an hour they talked. At last both men were satisfied that Thorne's testimony would be both conclusive and unshakable. When Ritchie left he was smiling.

CRAIG was waiting for Ritchie in his study when the detective arrived. The banker had been about to leave for the theatre when Ritchie phoned and his expression was dour.

"I thought I made it clear that I know nothing more about Dr. Unger's murder than I told you this afternoon," he said sourly. "You said you wouldn't trouble me further but here you are, breaking up my evening."

"That is a shame," Ritchie replied cheerfully. The banker glared at him. Ritchie went on.

"The fact is, we've run across something that leads us to believe you *didn't* tell us all you knew. You forgot to mention that you knew Mrs. Amery was a patient of Unger's too. You saw her at his office yesterday evening but that slipped your mind. Yet I'm sure you've met the lady socially and you must have recognized her."

Craig tried to pass it off. "Very well, I did see her. It happens that her husband is a friend of mine and I could see no reason for bringing her name into the investigation."

Ritchie maintained his cheerfulness. "I always say, what good is a friend if he can't do you a favor? Isn't that true?"

Craig nodded but he had the worried look in his eyes again. He did not speak so Tom kept talking.

"Of course Amery is also the real head of the bank, isn't he? He wouldn't like it if you were the one who dragged his wife's name into it. But there's another reason you didn't want to cross him now. You see, we found Dr. Unger's case histories and he'd made note of what you told him about that loan."

Craig changed his tactics. He tried being expansive. "Well, you know how those things are! Everyone makes a mistake now and then. Since it was beyond recall I could see no reason to make it public. That wouldn't do the bank or me any good."

Ritchie grinned. "Especially you!" Craig essayed an answering smile but wiped it off at the sudden change in Ritchie's manner. The lanky detective looked as though he were going to attack the gray haired man.

"You could tell that to Dr. Unger but you can't tell it to me! You didn't want to lie to the doctor but you couldn't tell him the truth either. It would be impossible to keep a big loan a secret from everyone else at the bank unless the loan was to yourself!"

Craig's ashen features told plainly how true the accusation was. He started to say something but his lips were dry and he had to wet them first. "I...I... Well, everyone does it," he gulped lamely.

"Do they? That must be why a lot of people keep their money under the mattress. But there must be more to it than that. If you don't talk you'll go to jail. If you do talk you'll still have time to straighten it out with the bank before Amery gets around to tossing you out on your ear. Better play it smart!"

Craig nodded. "All right, there *was* more to it than just seeing Mrs. Amery in the office." He was talking fast now, eager to spill everything. "I came a few minutes early and went right up. It had happened several times before and there had never been anyone there. This time I could hear loud voices in the inner office. One of them was a woman's voice.

"At the time I didn't know who the woman was. I didn't know that Mrs. Amery was a patient of the doctor's. I didn't want to eavesdrop so I started to go into the hall, intending to wait until the patient left.

"But I heard something that stopped me. The woman was screaming with anger. I could hear every word. 'I'll kill you and I'll kill myself,' she screamed. 'I'll take this knife and I'll kill us both!' "

Craig mopped his brow. His recital had brought back some of the emotions he had felt at the time. "Dr. Unger was a small man and I was really afraid he might be injured if the woman were violent. I started back toward the door of his inner office but before I had taken two steps it opened and the woman ran past me, looking straight ahead and not even seeing me as I dodged out of her way. Of course I recognized her but did not say anything. Dr. Unger looked worried and I could see that he wasn't paying any attention to me during the hour I was there."

"I figured it must be something like that," Ritchie said. "Are you positive she said *'this knife?'* "

"I couldn't be mistaken. Her words were as clear as though she were in the room with me."

"Well, that's just lovely. Everything is going to be all right. You can expect a call from us tomorrow morning. You remember to tell your story right, the way you told it to me just now, and you won't have to worry about a thing."

Craig nodded. "I don't see how I can do otherwise." He looked like the man who took the frying pan instead of the fire and was waiting for it to start sizzling.

RITCHIE took the street behind Penelope Reed's house and saw that the room he had been in that morning had lights in it. He turned left at the corner, drove to the end of the block and turned left again. The Buick slid to the curb a few feet before the beginning of the tall fence.

He popped a cigarette into his mouth and lit it with the dashboard lighter. Ritchie smoked with short rapid puffs, using the movements to drain off physical energy that conflicted with his thoughts.

There was plenty to think about. Once Craig had a chance to think it over he would realize that he could make a deal with Amery. If he did there wasn't a thing Ritchie could do about it. Amery could hold up any investigation of the bank's books until they had been straightened out. That wouldn't take long. Maybe Craig would stay worried until morning and maybe he wouldn't.

If he didn't, Ritchie would need Penelope Reed. He hated to take a chance on her. She was likely to blow up at any time and blow up his case right along with her.

It was six of one or a half dozen of the other, Ritchie reflected. He made up his mind while he watched the butt he had thrown from the car window arc its glowing way through the dusk.

He left the car where it was and walked down to the gate. The dark husky man watched him come. Ritchie grinned at him.

"Still playing watch dog, eh? Well, you call your mistress and tell her Lieutenant Ritchie of the D. A.'s office waits without— without patience. I want to see her right away."

"She ain't in," the husky man said. He turned his head to loose a stream of tobacco juice at a freshly seeded flower bed.

"She just came down the chimney," Ritchie told him. He had stopped grinning and his voice was brittle. "Tell her I want to see her about that sanitarium deal. Right now."

A minute later the gate swung open. The detective went up the walk feeling the husky man's eyes on his back all the way. Inside the house, the butler led him along the hall to the room in back. Miss Reed stood in front of the desk. She had changed her suit for a black dress with a white print. It was cut low and square across the neckline.

"What is this about a sanitarium deal?" she demanded. Her voice was cool, level. It was a period of normalcy for her.

"The one Dr. Unger mentioned to you," Ritchie said. He watched the tight waist of the dress suck inward.

"I also want to talk about thirty thousand bucks and a guy who died in jail. Of course we could talk about something different if you'd rather."

For a moment she was silent. Then, "I'd rather. What else would you be interested in?" She dropped her eyes and checked the front of the dress. The bodice needed straightening. It was an offer and Ritchie was almost shocked.

"Not that," he told Miss Reed. "Let's try something else; for instance anything you might have heard when you went back to Dr. Unger's office for your purse last night."

She hadn't expected that. There was surprise and more than a little relief in her eyes. "Oh," she said, "was there anything I should have heard?"

"I imagine."

"That's odd. I can't seem to recall anything. Perhaps you could refresh my memory."

GOD, she was smart, Ritchie thought. He suddenly felt a vast respect for the mind behind the lovely hazel eyes. She was sharper by far than Craig or Amery or even Thorne. But sooner or later her emotions would cut that mind off from reality and she would spin beautifully logical arguments that were based on fantastic premises.

How many were there who walked the streets unsuspected, Ritchie wondered, whose thoughts had foundations as unreal? Where was the dividing line between reality and delusion?

He couldn't answer that one; thank Heaven he would never be forced to answer it! For the while it sufficed that Penelope Reed would remember anything he wanted her to remember.

"It was about eight-thirty when you went back to the office," Ritchie said. She nodded.

"I remember that. I knocked on the door and Dr. Unger opened it. He was expecting me because he had the purse in his hand. I could see past him and there was a woman in the room. What was it they were saying just before I interrupted them?"

Ritchie told her. The words were probably not exact but they would be the words that could have been used, that filled the gap and made sense.

"Oh, yes. I remember she looked excited. She was pretty too. She wore a beige suit and a hat with a veil. Is that all?"

"That's all. Think you'll remember, it tomorrow morning?"

"I'm sure I shall."

"I'll be going then. Are you going out tonight?"

She smiled shyly and straightened her bodice again. "Yes, I have a date."

Ritchie felt a sudden wrench at his heart but didn't let it show. Time was running short for her and she must have sensed it.

"Have a good time," he said. "Have lots of fun." He didn't look back as he walked down the hall and out of the door. The short walk to the gate seemed much too long. The gate-man was waiting for him and had the gate open.

"Get what you came for, copper?" he asked. There was a leer in his voice.

Ritchie's bony fist caught him on the side of the neck and smashed him to the ground. He lay retching.

"I can't stand a wise guy!" the detective said bitterly. The Buick looked like a hearse as he walked toward it.

CHAPTER EIGHT

MAYOR DALL'S little pig eyes were bitter as he glared at Simeon Field. If the mayor had a neck it was impossible to see it under the series of chins that hung to his collar. His ordinarily good-humored face was red and creased into folds of reproach.

"Damn it, Field," he groaned, "how could you put me in a spot like this? You might at least have told me what you were up to!"

"I didn't think you'd be interested in a police case," Field told him.

"Hogwash! You even kept your investigation secret from the police! The first they knew about it was when they saw the headlines in this morning's papers. You knew what you were doing all right!"

Field expostulated with him. "What would you have me do, cover up a murder?"

Dall shook with fury. "Don't pull that moralistic malarkey on me! I run this city as clean as any city of its size in the world!" His righteous air was laughable and he knew it. He quieted down.

"It's not only myself I'm thinking of. You're a young man, Field, and you could have a brilliant future!" Dall leaned across the desk and his voice got confidential. "Just this morning I had Washington on the wire. The national chairman told me there's a Federal judgeship open. He's been asked for a recommendation. It could be you!"

Ritchie had been sitting quietly until now. He perked up. "Say, that's a good offer!"

Dall turned on him. "You better keep your trap shut! When this blows over you're going to be walking a beat in the sticks— if I can't have you thrown off the force altogether!"

"I'm in civil service and my pension comes up soon," Ritchie reminded him. "I've got nothing to worry about."

The mayor looked ready to cry. "Sure, you've got nothing to worry about! Let me do it all! Do you know what Washington told me? They were thinking of pushing through a Federal appropriation for a subway for us! Do you know what that would mean to this city?"

"Yes," Field said drily, "it would mean you'd have your hand in the nation's pocket."

The ringing of Field's phone saved the mayor from a stroke. The D. A. listened intently for several minutes and then said simply, "No, I wouldn't be interested. Thank you." He hung up and looked at the mayor. "You were right about that judgeship. I just turned it down."

"You're a fool!"

"Only if I lose! The grand jury is sitting now and I'll have an indictment by tomorrow. Then we'll see. What if I win?"

"If you win," the mayor said slowly, "I'll be the first to congratulate you. You'll be a hero and we'll all rush to get on the bandwagon. But there'll be a new mayor next election. It's the money that runs politics and don't you forget it. A man who can't deliver won't be elected."

He stared at Field and Ritchie bleakly. "You're ruining me and my machine. For that I hate your guts. But I wish I had them."

He shrugged. "Well, I'd better beat it. I'll just step out this door here. If I go through the outer office I'm sure to run into someone and right now all I want is a little peace and quiet."

DALL almost made it. But as he turned the knob the outer door burst open and Walter Amery stormed in. Behind him was his attorney, a huge man with a flowing mane of dark hair.

"Dall!" Amery barked. The mayor turned around and came back. He had a sheepish air. Amery let him stand and turned a white face toward Field.

"You're going to remember this day for the rest of your life!" he said. "You'll find out that no cheap publicity hound can cross me and get away with it!"

Field kept his temper in check. "I wish you wouldn't take it that way. I am simply doing my duty."

"Is this what you call duty?" "To drag a sick woman from her bed and haul her off to jail like a common criminal?" Amery was about to say more but his lawyer stopped him.

"Please, Walter. I understand how you feel but the only way to help your wife is to get the facts." His voice rolled out of his deep chest as from a cavern.

"I am Thomas Eaves," the big man told Field. The D. A. nodded. "I am familiar with your name and that of your firm," he said to Eaves.

"Good. Then let us get down to cases. I understand you have arrested Mrs. Amery on a charge of murder. Mr. Amery's doctor informs me that she is still suffering from shock. You will be held responsible for any aggravation of her condition."

Amery broke out again. "You bet he'll be held responsible. I'll make it my life work to ruin him."

Field was calm. "Your wife is being carefully watched by a competent physician. We want to keep her in good health until the trial I assure you."

"There won't be any trial and you know it!" Amery roared. "You know she didn't kill Dr. Unger! This is just a cheap attempt to get your name in the newspapers and you're low enough to try to frame an innocent woman to do it!"

"On the contrary," Field told him, "she will be given every chance to prove she is not guilty."

Eaves' voice boomed out again. "If that is so then why are you in such a hurry to get an indictment? After all, the wife of a man of Mr. Amery's position need not be treated so brutally."

"I know exactly what Mr. Amery's position is," Field retorted. "In the few hours I have been offered several genteel bribes and been threatened with every conceivable disaster. Mr. Amery is using every bit of his power to get his wife out of this. He doesn't care if she is guilty or not!

"That is why we are rushing the indictment. Given enough time he could get rid of me and my assistant and save her. We can prove she is guilty and we shall prove it!"

"There isn't a shred of evidence against her!" Amery snapped.

"More than enough to send her to the electric chair," Field assured him. "We have no intention of holding it secret from you as we might do if we had a weak case. Our witnesses are unimpeachable."

"Then why don't you produce them?"

"All right, I will!" The D. A. looked at Ritchie. "Ask them to come in."

Ritchie went through the door that Dall had been about to use and returned in a few minutes.

CRAIG looked at Amery and turned his eyes quickly away. Amery was staring at him in astonishment. Behind the banker Penelope Reed and Oliver Thorne followed. Ritchie brought up the rear.

Eaves looked worried when he saw Thorne. He had been trying to reach him all morning and now the realization that the famed criminal lawyer might be in the opposition dismayed him. He nodded curtly to Thorne.

"Do you know these people?" Field asked Amery.

"Just Craig." Amery's eyes were filled with unveiled threat as he glared at the banker. Craig looked miserable.

Field told Amery the names of the other two. "You can understand that when people like Mr. Craig, Mr. Thorne, and Miss Reed offer testimony I cannot regard it lightly. Nor will a court! That is why I am so sure of myself."

"I don't care who your witnesses are. I still maintain my wife's innocence!"

"Very well. Then you shall hear what they have to say. Is that fair enough?" Field looked at Eaves. The lawyer said one word, "Quite."

Penelope Reed told her story first. Her voice was cold and unemotional and rang of truth. "I could not be mistaken," she finished. "Mrs. Amery plainly said, 'If you spurn me I'll do something desperate! I might even kill you!'"

Craig spoke swiftly, keeping his gaze fixed on the floor. It took but a moment for him to say what he had to. When he was through he sat down.

Thorne was completely at ease as he talked. He was used to speaking before an audience and there was no sign of nervousness, as there had been with Craig.

"I was driving along Clark Street, going north toward Van Buren, when I saw Dr. Unger and Mrs. Amery standing at the mouth of the alley where his body was found yesterday morning," Thorne said.

"It was evident that they were engaged in a heated argument. I was driving slowly and got a good look at them. As I drove past them they turned and walked into the alley. I thought that Mrs. Amery's car might be parked there and continued on my way. I never gave it another thought until I heard of Dr. Unger's death."

Eaves had been watching Thorne closely as he talked. "Just one thing, counselor," he boomed. "It is apparent that Mr. Craig and Miss Reed were patients of Dr. Unger. You must have known him well to have been able to identify him so easily. Were you too a patient of his?"

Thorne nodded. "I was."

Eaves said, "Hmmmm."

Thorne laughed. "I would advise you not to try to question my sanity. It would be difficult to convince a jury that men like myself and Mr. Craig are mentally incompetent. After all, he is the president of a bank controlled by Mr. Amery.

"As for my identification of Dr. Unger, it was easy. He was a short man and also slender. He always wore his hair cut very short, crew style. He had little interest in clothes and wore the same suit all the time. It was a light gray with a half belt in back. I would have recognized it at an even greater distance.

"Although I have never met Mrs. Amery I have seen her many times at public functions with her husband. She is not an ordinary woman by any means. If you wish I can describe the clothes she wore that evening."

"That won't be necessary," Eaves told him. "I'm convinced you are an acute observer!"

"Then I should like to go," Thorne turned to Field. "I've signed a statement which covers my testimony. I shall be staying at my home up north for the summer and you can reach me there if you want me." He gave the D. A. the address and telephone number.

"You two can go now," Field said to Craig and Miss Reed. "We'll let you know when we want you again." He waited until they were gone and then gave his attention to Eaves and Walter Amery. Eaves looked far from confident; Amery almost broken.

The D. A. smiled grimly. "Well, I see we have raised doubts in your minds. We have other witnesses whose testimony will reinforce that of the three you have heard.

"Mrs. Amery will be fortunate indeed if she escapes the death penalty. If I were her lawyer I would advise her to plead guilty and take a life sentence. In either case, Mr. Amery, I am afraid you are going to lose your wife."

Amery was silent. The fire was gone from his eyes and he looked old and tame, like a lion whose teeth have been pulled. He turned on his heel and walked out the way he had come, Eaves trotting behind him like a huge shaggy dog.

EARLIER in the night the moon had been full and bright. Now it was completely obscured by heavy clouds which the fresh moist wind had carried in from the lake.

There had been no suggestion of rain and the window of Thorne's bedroom was half open. The fresh white curtains were alternately being blown in and out of the window with a rustling, starched sound.

217

The sound seemed not to trouble Thorne's sleep nor did the choppy crash of the surf on the beach behind the house. Leaves on the trees that separated the house from the highway and neighboring homes were still too soft to make more than a swishing sound.

If it were dark outside the house, it was Stygian in the bedroom and the figure outside the window waited vainly for a chance to make out objects in the room.

At last a glow from a flashlight showed. It lasted but a second, just long enough to show the bed on the far side of the room and to disclose that there was nothing near the window which might be knocked over.

Satisfied that all was well the intruder raised a leg and slid it over the low sill. There was a moment of tense hesitation before the other leg followed. The curtains were pushed carefully aside and then a light thud as feet hit the floor beneath the window.

The man in the bed stirred slightly and the intruder froze until the normal breathing was resumed. Then the flashlight showed again, covered by a handkerchief that diffused the light.

The glow moved slowly across the floor, inching toward the sleeping figure. A sudden gust of wind rattled the window and Thorne turned again in his sleep and exposed his shoulders as the thin summer blanket slipped down a little. A faint intake of breath that was almost a sigh came from the man behind the flashlight and his free hand dipped into a pocket and reappeared holding a knife. There was an upward movement of the knife.

A voice shouted, "Drop it!"

The man with the knife whirled and was caught and transfixed by a white beam that blinded him.

Ritchie came slowly from the closet in which he had been waiting. He kept the light in the other's eyes.

"I said drop it!" he commanded again.

Walter Amery closed his eyes to shut out the blinding beam. "Ritchie!" he gasped. His breath was coming in harsh gulps, like sobs. "I was afraid it was a trap but I had to come. I couldn't help myself. I had to come."

As he spoke Amery moved forward toward Ritchie. "One more step and I'll let you have it!" the detective warned.

Amery kept coming. Ritchie lowered his light and tried to duck aside but the other followed him.

There was nothing else for Ritchie to do. The gun in his right hand roared once and a heavy slug ripped into Amery's thigh. The millionaire dropped screaming to the floor like a wounded animal. In sightless rage he flung the knife at Ritchie. It missed by feet.

CHAPTER NINE

THERE were only the four of them left in the D. A.'s office now: Field, Ritchie, Dr. Hoelke and Mrs. Amery. The reporters and photographers had gone, and with them Mayor Dall who had insisted on being photographed congratulating Simeon Field and Ritchie. He had also made statements informing the world at large that in his city no man, however powerful, was immune from punishment for his crimes.

Dr. Hoelke was shaking his head. "I hope you will not think me dull," he said to Ritchie, "but I still cannot guess how you knew that Mr. Amery was the guilty man."

"You told me yourself," Tom grinned.

"I? How? After you left me yesterday I spent hours puzzling the matter over and at the end I was more confused than when I started!"

"That's because you're a psychiatrist. While you were teaching me psychiatric theory I was learning about hidden motives for murder."

The white-haired man looked more baffled than ever so Ritchie went on with his explanation.

"You explained to me the cause of Craig's trouble, didn't you?" Tom asked. The doctor nodded.

"But you were so wound up in your explanation that you didn't see it would be an equally good description of someone else's mind! Amery had all the symptoms Dr. Unger found in Craig and to an even greater degree!"

Dr. Hoelke's face lit up with sudden understanding. "So that was it! It was a case of my not seeing the forest for a tree!"

"That puts it very neatly," Ritchie smiled. "But the clincher was the appointment book." He paused.

"Go on, please," the doctor urged. "I must confess that I could not for the life of me see the significance of that.

Especially since the book was missing! How could you know what was written there?"

"There's only one thing that would be there—appointments! That's why I immediately ruled out his patients as possible suspects."

"This is getting worse!" Dr. Hoelke protested. "I can't see the basis for that last deduction at all."

The D. A. interrupted. "Start at the beginning, Tom. I think Dr. Hoelke is entitled to hear the whole story since he supplied the most vital clues."

"An excellent idea," the doctor assented. "Begin at the beginning with the keys."

"I'll do better than that," Ritchie said, "I'll start with the murder itself. Mutilation of the victim is a gangster trick but it was obviously not a gang murder. They would have brought their own cleaver.

"That meant the killer had been prepared to use his knife for the purpose. In that case he must have been a coldblooded individual; it was plainly a premeditated murder.

"But why were the clothes missing too? And why run the risk of taking the time to remove them only to leave them where they were sure to be found soon?

"There could be only one purpose: to prevent identification for a short time. The keys told why. The killer had to get to the office ahead of the police and remove something that would point directly to him.

"When I found out that it was the appointment book I knew the killer's name must have been in it. But it could not be one of the regular patients. Why?

"Because there were only four patients and their names were all on file in Dr. Unger's desk! It would have been ridiculous to take only the appointment book and leave the card behind!

"There was only one person who had a motive and who was not a patient—Walter B. Amery. He was losing his wife because of Dr. Unger. As you explained to me, a person like Amery cannot stand losing his dependent.

"He tried ridiculing Mrs. Amery's painting but that did not stop her. Then her work was praised by an authority and it gave her even greater confidence in herself. If she continued her analysis she was certain to become completely independent of Amery. She would refuse to stand for his bullying any longer and since he could not give that up either it would be the end of their marriage.

"So, he made an appointment with Dr. Unger, and he tried to get him to give up the analysis. I suppose he tried to buy him off. That's the way his mind worked. He thought he could get anything for money.

"This time he was wrong! He became desperate and decided to kill Unger. He knew what time the doctor would leave his office and he waited for him.

"It must have been a shock when he saw his wife waiting at the door of the building. But she left the doctor at the corner and then Amery followed him to the alley.

"The funny thing is that Amery knew Thorne was lying about having seen Mrs. Amery in front of the alley! But he didn't know that we suspected him. He thought we were really out to frame Mrs. Amery and it looked like we might make it stick! That put him right where he was before he murdered Dr. Unger: *He was still going to lose his wife!*

"Thorne was the main witness and if Amery killed him it would serve two purposes: it would ruin our case and it would prove Mrs. Amery innocent because she was in custody at the time. So he walked into the trap."

DR. HOELKE smiled. "You make it sound very simple," he said. "Actually you arranged the trap so cleverly that his own drives gave him no alternative but to enter it."

Simeon Field nodded. "Now we've taken care of Amery. But how about the others involved? Thorne and Craig can find other analysts and will eventually get over their troubles. What are Miss Reed and Mrs. Amery going to do?"

"I have spoken to Miss Reed," the doctor told him, "and she has consented to go to a sanitarium run by a friend of mine. She will be well cared for."

Dr. Hoelke paused for a moment and looked at Mrs. Amery. "As for Mrs. Amery, she will stay at my place for a while, at least until things have become more quiet. I feel confident that after a short time, if she resumes her painting, she will be able to face the world as a strong independent woman."

For the first time Mrs. Amery spoke. Her voice was so soft as to be barely audible. "I hope so," she said. "I hope I'll be able to forget I was ever married to...him."

She stared at Dr. Hoelke for a while without speaking. At last she murmured. "May we go now?"

Field nodded. "Of course. I'm sorry we were forced to use you for bait."

Her smile was sad. "It turned out for the best. I can't say I'm sorry."

She rose and Dr. Hoelke got up with her. The white-haired man offered her his arm gallantly and the D. A. and Ritchie watched them go out together. For a long time the two men did not speak.

Ritchie heaved a sigh. "I sure hope the trial doesn't drag on too long. The sooner it's over the sooner everyone will forget all about it and the easier it will be for her."

"I'm afraid she won't be allowed to forget it," Field told him. "Amery is going to put up a fight and I don't see how she can escape being pulled into it."

Before Ritchie could say anything in reply the phone rang. Field was disgusted. "Probably the newspapers again," he said. Ritchie picked up the phone. Field had been wrong. It was the County Jail.

"Who is it?" the voice at the other end asked. Ritchie told him.

"Well, listen," the voice said. "We don't know what to do with this Amery. It looks like he's breaking down completely and we're afraid that he might even commit suicide if we don't put him in solitary and take away his tie and belt. What do you think we ought to do?"

Ritchie did not answer at once. He was staring at the door and still seeing in his mind's eye a white-haired man and a lovely young woman who leaned on his arm. There was hope for the young woman if she were allowed to forget.

Tom spoke slowly, "Don't worry about it," he said. "Leave him where he is and don't take anything away from him."

THE END

Made in the USA
Columbia, SC
02 September 2024

41455379R00136